25.95 B7

26.00

GAYLORD R

INTO THE FOREST

INTO THE FOREST

A NOVEL

BY JEAN HEGLAND

CALYX BOOKS —— CORVALLIS OREGON

The publication of this book was supported in part with grants from the Oregon Arts Commission and Oregon Literary Arts.

Cover art by Kristina Kennedy Daniels
Cover and book design by Cheryl McLean

CALYX Books are distributed to the trade through **Consortium Book Sales and Distribution, Inc., St. Paul, MN, 1-800-283-3572**.

CALYX Books are also available through major library distributors, jobbers, and most small press distributors including: Airlift, Baker & Taylor, Banyan Tree, Bookpeople, Ingram, Pacific Pipeline, and Small Press Distribution. For personal orders or other information write: CALYX Books, PO Box B, Corvallis, OR 97339, (541) 753-9384, FAX (541) 753-0515.

∞ The paper in this book meets the guidelines for permanence and durability of the Committee on Production Guidelines for Book Longevity of the Council on Library Resources and the minimum requirements of the American National Standard for the Permanence of Paper for Printed Library Materials Z38.48-1984.

Library of Congress Cataloging-in-Publication Data

Hegland, Jean.
    Into the forest / Jean Hegland.
        p. cm.
    ISBN 0-934971-50-1 (cloth : alk. paper) : $25.95 —ISBN 0-934971-49-8 (pbk. : alk. paper) : $13.95
    I. Wilderness survival—California, Northern—Fiction. 2. Teenage girls—California, Northern—Fiction. 3. Sisters—California, Northern—Fiction. I. Title.
        PS3558.E419158   1996
        813'.54—dc20
                                     96-33919
                                     CIP

Printed in the U.S.A.
    9 8 7 6 5 4 3 2 1

The author is donating a portion of her royalties from *Into the Forest* to World Stewardship Institute (Santa Rosa, CA) for reforestation efforts.

ACKNOWLEDGMENTS

INTO THE FOREST is a work of fiction. Sally Bell's story is the only material quoted directly from another source ("Sinkyone Notes" by Gladys Nomland, *University of California Publications in American Archeology and Ethnology*, Vol. 36 (2), 1935).

I would like to acknowledge the following sources for background information: *The Way We Lived: California Indian Reminiscences, Stories, and Songs*, edited by Malcolm Margolin (Berkeley: Heyday Books, 1981), in which I first discovered the Sally Bell material, and *Original Accounts of the Lone Woman of San Nicholas Island*, edited by Robert F. Heizer and Albert B. Elasser (Ramona, CA: Ballena Press, 1973).

It's strange, writing these first words, like leaning down into the musty stillness of a well and seeing my face peer up from the water—so small and from such an unfamiliar angle I'm startled to realize the reflection is my own. After all this time a pen feels stiff and awkward in my hand. And I have to admit that this notebook, with its wilderness of blank pages, seems almost more threat than gift—for what can I write here that it will not hurt to remember?

You could write about now, Eva said, *about this time.* This morning I was so certain I would use this notebook for studying that I had to work to keep from scoffing at her suggestion. But now I see she may be right. Every subject I think of—from economics to meteorology, from anatomy to geography to history—seems to circle around on itself, to lead me unavoidably back to now, to here, today.

Today is Christmas Day. I can't avoid that. We've crossed the days off the calendar much too conscientiously to be wrong about the date, however much we might wish we were. Today is Christmas Day, and Christmas Day is one more day to live through, one more day to be endured so that someday soon this time will be behind us.

By next Christmas this will all be over, and my sister and I will have regained the lives we are meant to live. The electricity will be back, the phones will work. Planes will fly above our clearing once again. In town there will be food in the stores and gas at the service stations. Long before next Christmas we will have indulged in everything we now lack and crave—soap and shampoo, toilet paper and milk, fresh fruit and meat. My computer will be running, Eva's CD player will be working. We'll be listening to the radio, watching videos, reading the newspaper. Banks and schools and libraries will have reopened, and Eva and I will have left this house where we now live like shipwrecked orphans. She will be dancing with the corps of the San Francisco Ballet, I'll have finished my first semester at Harvard, and this wet, dark day the calendar has insisted we call Christmas will be long, long over.

"Merry semi-pagan, slightly literary, and very commercial Christmas," our father would always announce on Christmas morning, when, long before the midwinter dawn, Eva and I would team up in the hall outside our parents' bedroom. Jittery with excitement, we would plead with them to get up, to come downstairs, to hurry, while they yawned, insisted on donning bathrobes, on washing their faces and brushing their teeth, even—if our father was being particularly infuriating—on making coffee.

After the clutter and laughter of present-opening came the midday dinner we used to take for granted, phone calls from distant relatives, Handel's *Messiah* issuing triumphantly from the CD player. At some point during the afternoon the four of us would take a walk down the dirt road that ends at our clearing. The brisk air and green winter forest would clear our senses and our palates, and by the time we reached the bridge and were ready to turn back, our father would have inevitably announced, "This is the real Christmas present, by god—peace and quiet and clean air. No neighbors for four miles, and no town for thirty-two. Thank Buddha, Shiva, Jehovah, and the California Department of Forestry we live at the end of the road!"

Later, after night had fallen and the house was dark except for the glow of bulbs on the Christmas tree, Mother would light the candles of the nativity carousel, and we would spend a quiet moment standing together before it, watching the shepherds, wise men, and angels circle around the little holy family.

"Yep," our father would say, before we all wandered off to nibble at the turkey carcass and cut slivers off the cold plum pudding, "that's the story. Could be better, could be worse. But at least there's a baby at the center of it."

This Christmas there's none of that.

This Christmas there are no strings of lights, no Christmas cards. There are no piles of presents, no long-distance phone calls from great-aunts and second cousins, no Christmas carols. There is no turkey, no plum pudding, no stroll to the bridge with our parents, no *Messiah*. This year Christmas is nothing but another white square on a calendar that is almost out of dates, an extra cup of tea, a few moments of candlelight, and, for each of us, a single gift.

Why do we bother?

Three years ago—when I was fourteen and Eva fifteen—I asked that same question one rainy night a week before Christmas. Father was grumbling over the number of cards he still had to write, and Mother was hidden in her workroom with her growling sewing machine, emerging periodically to take another batch of cookies from the oven and prod me into washing the mixing bowls.

"Nell, I need those dishes done so I can start the pudding before I go to bed," she said as she closed the oven door on the final sheet of cookies.

"Okay," I muttered, turning the next page of the book in which I was immersed.

"Tonight, Nell," she said.

"Why are we doing this?" I demanded, looking up from my book in irritation.

"Because they're dirty," she answered, pausing to hand me a warm gingersnap before she swept back to the mysteries of her sewing.

"Not the dishes," I grumbled.

"Then what, Pumpkin?" asked my father as he licked another envelope and emphatically crossed another name off his list.

"Christmas. All this mess and fuss and we aren't even really Christians."

"Goddamn right we aren't," said our father, laying down his pen, bounding up from the table by the front window, already warming to the energy of his own talk.

"We're not Christians, we're capitalists," he said. "Everybody in this whangdanged country is a capitalist, whether he likes it or not. Everyone in this country is one of the world's most voracious consumers, using resources at a rate twenty times greater than that of anyone else on this poor earth. And Christmas is our golden opportunity to pick up the pace."

When he saw I was turning back to my book, he added, "Why are we doing Christmas? Beats me. Tell you what—let's quit. Throw in the towel. I'll drive into town tomorrow and return the gifts. We'll give the cookies to the chickens and write all our friends and relations and explain we've given up Christmas for Lent. It's a shame to waste my vacation, though," he continued in mock sadness.

"I know." He snapped his fingers and ducked as though an idea had just struck him on the back of the head. "We'll replace the beams under the utility room. Forget those dishes, Nell, and find me the jack."

I glared at him, hating him for half a second for the effortless way he deflected my barbs and bad temper. I huffed into the kitchen, grabbed a handful of cookies, and wandered upstairs to hide in my bedroom with my book.

Later I could hear him in the kitchen, washing the dishes I had ignored and singing at the top of his voice,

We three kings of Orient tar,
tried to smoke a rubber cigar.

It was loaded, and it exploded,
higher than yonder star.

The next year even I wouldn't have dared to question Christmas. Mother was sick, and we all clung to everything that was bright and sweet and warm, as though we thought if we ignored the shadows, they would vanish into the brilliance of hope. But the following spring the cancer took her anyway, and last Christmas Eva and I did our best to bake and wrap and sing in a frantic effort to convince our father—and ourselves—that we could be happy without her.

I thought we were miserable last Christmas. I thought we were miserable because our mother was dead and our father had grown distant and silent. But there were lights on the tree and a turkey in the oven. Eva was Clara in the Redwood Ballet's performance of *The Nutcracker*, and I had just received the results of my Scholastic Aptitude Tests, which were good enough—if I did okay on the College Board Achievement Tests—to justify the letter I was composing to the Harvard Admissions Committee.

But this year all that is either gone or in abeyance. This year Eva and I celebrate only because it's less painful to admit that today is Christmas than to pretend it isn't.

It's hard to come up with a present for someone when there is no store in which to buy it, when there is little privacy in which to make it, when everything you own, every bean and grain of rice, each spoon and pen and paper clip, is also owned by the person to whom you want to give a gift.

I gave Eva a pair of her own toe shoes. Two weeks ago I snuck the least battered pair from the closet in her studio and renovated them as best I could, working on them in secret while she was practicing. With the last drops of our mother's spot remover, I cleaned the tattered satin. I restitched the leather soles with monofilament from our father's tackle box. I soaked the mashed toe boxes in a mixture of water and wood glue, did my best to reshape them, hid them behind the stove to dry, and then soaked and shaped and dried them again and again. Then I darned the worn satin at the tips of the toes so that she could get a few more hours of use from them by first dancing on the web of stitches I had sewn.

She gasped when she opened the box and saw them.

"I don't know if they're any good," I said. "They're probably way too soft. I had no idea what I was doing."

But while I was still protesting, she flung her arms around me. We clung together for a long second and then we both leapt back. These days our bodies carry our sorrows as though they were bowls brimming with water. We must always be careful; the slightest jolt or unexpected shift and the water will spill and spill and spill.

Eva's gift to me was this notebook.

"It's not a computer," she said, as I lifted it from its wrinkled wrapping paper, recycled from some birthday long ago and not yet sacrificed as fire-starter. "But it's all blank, every page."

"Blank paper!" I marveled. "Where on earth did you get it?"

"I found it behind my dresser. It must have fallen back there years ago. I thought you could use it to write about this time. For our grandchildren or something."

Right now, grandchildren seem less likely than aliens from Mars, and when I first lifted the stained cardboard cover and flipped through these pages, slightly musty and blank except for their scaffolding of lines, I have to admit I was thinking more about studying for the Achievement Tests than about chronicling this time. And yet it feels good to write. I miss the quick click of my computer keys and the glow of the screen, but tonight this pen feels like Plaza wine in my hand, and already the lines that lead these words down the page seem more like the warp of our mother's loom and less like the bars I had first imagined them to be. Already I see how much there is to say.

What I really wanted to give Eva was gasoline. Just a little gas—enough to run the generator so she could play even a single CD, could let its music soak back into her bones; just a gallon or two of gasoline to give her a rest from having to dance to the thud and squeak of her shoes, the creak and pop of her joints, and the harsh tick of the metronome.

But there is no more gas. When we got back from town that last time, the implacable needle on the truck's gas gauge had sunk far below empty.

"We drove those last three miles on fumes, girls," our father said. "Looks like we'll be staying put for a while. But don't worry—we've got more than enough food, and when things get going again, I'll take the gas can and hike to town."

Now our father is buried in the forest, the empty can rusts somewhere in his cluttered workshop, and Eva will have to dance to the weakening strains of her memory for a while longer.

Here she comes from her studio, her ragged leotard dark with sweat, her ribs still heaving as she bends to open the woodstove door. The light from that boxed fire streams out, makes new shadows in the darkening room, and I pause from my writing to watch my sister stoke the fire.

I'm no good at fires. Eva says mine choke and smoulder or fall apart be-cause I'm always thinking—but never about what my hands are doing. She says I'm too impatient. Yet she can build a fire twice as fast as I can. She works with fire as though it were a living thing, coddling flame from dusty coals, coaxing it from damp sticks, knowing instinctively how to bank the embers so they will last till morning. Now that our father is dead, Eva is always the fire-tender.

She adds another length of wood to the coals, then sits on the floor in front of the stove to untie her shoes.

"How'd it go?" I ask.

"It hurt," she answers cheerfully, as she examines her bleeding feet by firelight. And I know that after our awful autumn, she is finally dancing again, just as I am finally studying.

"How do they work?" I ask, pointing to the recycled shoes.

She looks at me, grins. "Fine," she says. "I wouldn't have stopped, but it got so dark in there I couldn't see a thing. How's the notebook?"

"Fine, too," I say.

She lifts her arms above her head in third position and rises from the floor without touching the ground, as effortlessly as a cresting wave. "Time to light the carousel?" she asks.

"It's dark enough," I answer. "But do you really think we should? I keep wondering if we shouldn't save those candles for an emergency."

She gives a little shrug. "It's Christmas, isn't it?"

Carved of pine and painted with bright enamel, the carousel is a round, three-tiered nativity set, the glowing centerpiece of my earliest and most enduring Christmas memories. It was made in China, and our father took a yearly delight in the fact that the shepherds all wear the dark suits of Chinese peasants, the angels have their black hair cut in the blunt-banged style of Chinese women, and everyone, baby Jesus included, has elegant Asian eyes.

"I hope we're sending them blond Buddhas in return," he'd say with ironic delight. "Nothing more likely to break down religious chauvinism than a good, free-market, world-wide economy."

"Ready?" Eva asks, gesturing towards the table where the carousel waits.

I nod, trying to keep from calculating how many minutes of candlelight are left in those six candle stumps, trying not to imagine the time when we might need them more desperately than we need them tonight.

She pokes a piece of kindling among the coals, and when it ignites, she lifts it from the fire and bears it to the carousel. One by one, she touches her little brand to the candle stubs that ring the bottom tier. One by one, the fire leaps from wood to wick until there are six flames undulating in the still air.

It takes my breath away. We haven't seen this much light at night since the kerosene lamp finally sputtered out last spring. It changes our voices, makes our words sound round and soft and full, a little awed. The flames flicker, pure and smokeless, swaying and leaping like dancers around their stiff black wicks, and everything in the room seems warm and tender. My eyes fill with tears, and still I stare at those bright tongues, those petals of fire blossoming from their charred stems.

The wax softens, glistens, and as the heat of the candle flames rises, the wooden blades above the angels catch the warm updraft, and the whole carousel begins to move. Silently, sedately, the angels and shepherds and sheep, the wise men and their camel, all revolve around the stationary Mary and Joseph and infant Jesus.

We watch in silence, while all our Christmases come flooding over us in a feeling so sharp it's awful to admit, impossible to refuse.

I ask Eva, "Do you remember when you asked if Jesus were a he or a she?" It's an old family joke, one that used to be brought out every Christmas like the plum pudding recipe.

She smiles, playing along. "Mom said Jesus was a he, but that it was just an accident. She said, 'He might just as well have been a she.'"

"And then Dad asked her if the Virgin Mary could just as well have been a he."

Each of us nods, smiles. Each of us attempts the complicated business of remembering the pleasure of the past without allowing it any significance in the present.

One of the candles falters. The flame sputters, leaping up for oxygen and then collapsing into itself. The carousel slows. We watch in silence, mesmerized by the spinning shadows on the ceiling, by the pulse of the five remaining flames, by the slow burn and turn of memory.

"I think she was wrong," says Eva after the second flame dims and finally disappears.

"What?"

"Jesus couldn't have been a girl."

"Why not?"

"Things would have turned out differently, a long time ago."

"How?" I ask, eager to talk with my sister about an idea.

She shrugs, a little indifferent, a little impatient, the toss of her shoulders and the movement of her body her only eloquence. "I don't know, but it just wouldn't have been the same if Jesus had been a girl."

I give up on analysis. "Jesetta? Jesusphina?" I quip. But it sounds so much like one of our father's jokes that it falls flat.

Another candle dies and the carousel stops. In the weakening light of the three remaining flames, the shepherds kneel patiently among their sheep. The wise men hold their gifts stiffly in their wooden arms, as far away as ever from their goal. Mary and Joseph stand rigidly on either side of the wooden infant. The candles dim and glare. The last wick topples. The final flame vanishes. Christmas is over.

Darkness reclaims us once again.

————

Another rainy day. Except for a dash outside this morning to get wood and open the chicken coop so Bathsheba, Lilith, and Pinkie can scratch in the sodden yard, we've spent the day indoors. Christmas was only yesterday, but if it weren't for this notebook and the fact that Eva disappeared into her studio at dawn, no one would ever know it.

"You'll wear those shoes out again in a day," I said to her, when she came out at noon.

"I know."

She tugged her sweat-soaked tee shirt away from her chest, took another deep drink of the water that collects, one drop at a time, in the kitchen sink. Then she lunged back into her studio without another word.

Even now Eva can use things up. I want to save everything, to dribble it out forever. I can make a dozen raisins or half an inch of a stale candy cane last an evening, eking out the pleasure as though it were a geriatric patient going for a ride in her wheelchair in the winter sun. But Eva can still gobble.

"Might as well enjoy it while we've got it," she says, and she dances her shoes to tatters, swallows her share of the raisins in a single mouthful, lights candles and lets them burn, and never frets about the lost light. "Why not?" she asks with a toss of her head, a deft flip of her wrist. "Nothing lasts forever. And besides, it's not like we'll never see another raisin."

Last week I read in the encyclopedia about an indigenous tribe in Baja for whom meat was such a rare delicacy that they would tie a string to a scrap of animal flesh so they could chew it, swallow it, and then haul it back up, to have the pleasure of chewing and swallowing again. I was embarrassed when I read that, because it reminded me of myself, unable to let go of anything more, unable to face even the smallest loss.

Eva's not like that. "We have enough food," she scoffs when she sees me agonizing over a handful of stale peanuts or the last few drops of soy sauce. "We won't starve."

She's right. The pantry shelves are still crowded with the supplies we bought on our last trip to town and with the quarts of tomatoes, beets, green beans, applesauce, apricots, peaches, plums, and pears we helped our father can last summer. We still have rice, flour, cornmeal, pinto beans, and lentils. We still have macaroni, tuna fish, and canned soup. We still have a little sugar, a little salt, a sprinkle of baking powder. We still have dried milk and powdered cheese. We still have half a can of shortening, a motley variety of spices, and an odd jumble of other edibles—the unlabeled cans we bought at Fastco, a box of orange Jell-O that must be at least six years old, a jar of stuffed olives.

We have more than enough to see us through. But even so I have to fight my urge to hang on to everything we have left, as though to lose another drop or scrap could cast us adrift for good. When I think of how we used to live, the casual way we used things, I'm both appalled and filled with longing. I remember emptying wastebaskets that would seem like fortunes now—baskets filled with the cardboard cores of toilet paper rolls, with used tissues, broken pencils, twisted paper clips, sheets of crumpled notebook paper, and empty plastic bags.

I remember throwing away clothes because they were ripped or stained or no longer in style. I remember tossing out food—scraping heaps of food from our dinner plates into the compost bucket—simply because it had sat untouched on someone's plate for the course of a meal. How I long for those brimming wastebaskets, those leftovers. I long to gulp down whole boxes of raisins, to burn a dozen candles at once. I long to consume, to forget, to ignore. I want to live with abandon, with the careless grace of a consumer, instead of hanging on like an old peasant woman, fretting over bits and scraps.

In the encyclopedia the other day I read: *Amnesia, a condition of memory loss caused by brain injury, shock, fatigue, or illness. When amnesia continues for an extended period of time, the amnesiac occasionally begins a new life entirely unrelated to his previous condition. This response is called a "fugue state."*

I lifted my head from the page, looked out the window at the chickens scratching in the empty yard, and thought, *This is our fugue state—the lost time between the two halves of our real lives.*

Last winter when the electricity first began going off, it was so occasional and brief we didn't pay much attention. "They're probably working on the lines," we'd say, or "The rains must have brought a tree down. They'll have the power back soon." And soon enough, the lights would blink on, the washing machine would resume its hum and churn in the utility room, the vacuum cleaner would roar back to life, and a second later we would be taking electricity for granted once again.

Looking back on it now, I'm sure the three of us were in shock. We were numb, still stunned by Mother's death less than nine months earlier, so maybe we didn't realize as soon as we might have that after decades of warnings and predictions things were actually starting to fail. Besides, living as far out as we do, we were used to having the electricity go off occasionally, to having to wait until the power in the more populated areas was restored before we got our power back. Perhaps it took longer than it should have for us to suspect that something different was happening. But even in town, I think the changes began so slowly—or were so much a part of the familiar fabric of trouble and inconvenience—that nobody really recognized them until later that spring.

For a long time the power quit only for a few minutes every day or so, just enough to be an irritation, a nuisance. The microwave would stop dead, the clothes would flop wetly to the bottom of the dryer, dinner would cool half-cooked in the oven. If one of us were taking a shower, the water would dribble to a gravity-fed trickle without the electric pump to give it pressure. If I were working at my computer, the screen would go blank and the machine would moan as it crashed, taking with it all the work I hadn't saved. If Eva were practicing at home, the CD she had been dancing to would stop as suddenly as if it had been cut, and she would stumble out of her studio, looking as though she had just been slapped awake.

If it were night and our father were home from work, the sudden lack of light would sometimes propel him out of the grief in which he had lost himself, and he would entertain us by inventing absurd curses while he stomped and fussed in the darkness. "God whack a doughnut," he'd yell, or "Turds grow roses," as he bumped into the corners of tables and knocked things off counters, looking for the flashlight, the candles, matches. After ten or fifteen minutes when the lights would flick back on, Eva and I would be almost disappointed because we knew that all too soon his manic energy would drain away and he would once again slump back into despair.

For a long time it was a rare day when the power didn't go off at least once. Finally it was a rare day when the power came on. At some point we realized we had lost the habit of groping for the light switch whenever we entered a room. We no longer automatically reached for the knob on the stove when we wanted to cook something or flung the refrigerator door open when we were hungry. We took the electric blankets off our beds, put the electric coffee maker away, rolled up the carpets we could no longer vacuum. Our father taught us how to trim, fill, and light the kerosene lamps he had once refused to let our mother throw out, and for a time we lit those when darkness fell.

As winter faded and spring blossomed, we became accustomed to the unreliability of electricity, and we developed a routine to take advantage of it whenever it appeared. We left certain lights switched on all the time, and when they blinked into being, Eva would rush out to the utility room to start a load of laundry and then race into her studio, load a CD, and, skipping her barre work, begin to dance, while I flushed the murky toilet and turned on the faucets to fill the tub and the kitchen sink while the electric pump was operating. Then I would run to the computer, where I worked furiously until it all came crashing down again.

Father had long ago bought a gas generator to power the water pump in case there was a fire and our electricity failed, and sometimes Eva or I would turn it on to run our computer and CD player, though as time passed and gas grew scarcer, Father convinced us to save it for emergencies.

At first when the power went off while we were fixing a meal, we would get out the Coleman stove and finish cooking over its hissing burners, until one day we didn't bother putting the Coleman away. When we had used the last of the white gas and the hardware store had no more to sell, we dismantled it again and figured out how to bake potatoes among the coals in the woodstove in the living room, learned to fry pancakes and boil beans and steam rice on its top.

We had long since used up the food in the freezer. Finally we had to give up on the refrigerator, too. Our father dug a hole in the creek, lined it with rocks and black plastic garbage sacks, covered it with a Yield sign he had once scavenged from the dump, and proudly called it a refrigerator. Eva and I complained about having to wrap everything so that the water wouldn't soak it, about having to hike down to the creek every time we wanted milk or lettuce or margarine, until there was nothing left to keep cool.

The telephone faded in the same way the electricity did. For a while after the power had ceased to be reliable, we could still make a call if we were persistent enough. It might take all morning, dialing the number until those seven digits jeered in our brains, only to hear the electronically polite voice of the phone company say, "We're sorry. All lines are busy now. Please hang up and try your call again later." But sooner or later we could get through, could still talk to friends or report to the power company's answering machine that the electricity was out again.

One evening in early May, Father came home with a hunting rifle, and a little later a day came when he didn't go to work at all.

"Looks like summer vacation's early this year," he had said the night before, as he fried eggs on the woodstove for our dinner. "That damn strep is keeping attendance down by half, and nobody can seem to find an antibiotic to touch it. Now there's a rumor of meningitis. The board seems to think they'll save everybody a lot of money if they close school a month early."

He sighed and added, "Normally I'd fight that, but this year I guess I'm ready for a break. Besides, I've got to get the roof reshingled and replace those rotten supports under the utility room before things start up again next fall."

During this time the mail delivery was becoming sporadic, and banks and businesses were closed more often. For a few months state employees were paid with promissory notes, until the banks refused to honor the government IOU's, and then they went unpaid altogether.

It's amazing how quickly everyone adapted to those changes. I suppose it's like the way people beyond our forest had already gotten used to having to drink bottled water, drive on overcrowded freeways, and deal with the automated voices that answered almost every telephone. Then, too, they cursed and complained, and soon adjusted, almost forgetting their lives had ever been any other way.

Maybe it's true that the people who live through the times that become history's pivotal points are those least likely to understand them. I wonder if Abraham Lincoln himself could have answered the inevitable test questions about the causes of the Civil War. Once the daily newspapers ceased to appear every morning and radio broadcasts grew more and more sporadic, what news we did get was so fragmentary and conflicting as to tell us almost nothing about what was really happening.

Of course, there was a war going on. We had moved our mother's radio from her workroom into the kitchen, and before the batteries died last spring we used to coax it into muttering its litany of disaster while we were fixing dinner. Sometimes the news of the war would make Father stomp and swear, and sometimes it would send him upstairs to his bedroom long before our meal was cooked.

The fighting was taking place half a world away, taking place to protect freedoms, to defend a way of life, the politicians promised. It was a distant war, but it seemed to cling to our days, to permeate our awareness like a far-off, nasty smoke. It didn't directly affect what we ate, how we worked and played, yet we couldn't shake it—it wouldn't go away. Some people said it was that war that caused the breakdown.

But I think there were other causes, too. Sometime in January we heard that a paramilitary group had bombed the Golden Gate Bridge, and less than a month later we read that the overseas currency market had failed. In March an earthquake caused one of California's nuclear reactors to melt down, and the Mississippi River flooded more violently than had ever been imagined possible. All last winter the newspapers—when we could get them—were choked with news of ruin, and I wonder if the convergence of all those disasters brought us to this standstill.

Then, too, there were all the usual problems. The government's deficit had been snowballing for over a quarter of a century. The economy had been floundering for decades. We had been in an oil crisis for at least two generations. There were holes in the ozone, our forests were vanishing, our farmlands were demanding more and more fertilizers and pesticides to yield increasingly less—and more poisonous—food. There was an appalling unemployment rate, an overloaded welfare system, and people in the inner cities were seething with frustration, rage, and despair. Schoolchildren were shooting each other at recess. Teenagers were gunning down motorists on the freeways. Grown-ups were opening fire on strangers in fast-food restaurants.

But all those things had been happening for so long they seemed almost normal, and as things got darker and more uncertain, people began to grasp at new explanations for what was going wrong. All last spring, every time the three of us went to town we were met by more and wilder versions of what was happening in the world beyond Redwood.

Once the papers were no longer being printed and the radio stations shut down, the only news left was the ragged bits of gossip and rumor we gleaned in town on Saturday nights, news as reliable as the garbled nonsense we used to giggle at as children when we passed a whispered message around a circle of friends.

We heard the United States had a new president, that she was arranging for a loan from the Commonwealth to bail us out. We heard the White House was burning and the National Guard was fighting the Secret Service in the streets of D.C. We heard there was no water left in Los Angeles, that hordes of people were trying to walk north through the drought-ridden Central Valley. We heard that the county to the east of us still had electricity and that the Third World was rallying to send us support. And then we heard that China and Russia were at war and the U.S. had been forgotten.

Although the Fundamentalists' predictions of Armageddon grew more intense, and everyone else complained with increasing bitterness about everything from the lack of chewing gum to the closure of Redwood General Hospital, still, among most people there was an odd sense of buoyancy, a sort of surreptitious relief, the same feeling Eva and I used to have every few years when the river that flows through Redwood flooded and Father had to cancel school. We knew a flood was inconvenient and destructive. At the same time we couldn't help but feel a peculiar sort of delight that something beyond us was large enough to destroy the inexorability of our routines.

Along with all the worry and confusion there came a feeling of energy, of liberation. The old rules had been temporarily suspended, and it was exciting to imagine the changes that would inevitably grow out of all the upheaval, to contemplate what would have been learned—and corrected—when things began again. Even as everyone's lives grew more unstable, most people seemed to experience a new optimism, to share the sense that we were weathering the worst of it, and that soon—when things got straightened out—the problems that had caused this mess would have been purged from the system, and America and the future would be in better shape than ever.

People looked to the past for reassurance and inspiration. At the library, the supermarket, the gas station, and even on the Plaza, we listened to talk about the sacrifices and hardships of the pilgrims and the pioneers. Echoing the vanished newspaper columnists and talk show hosts, people reminisced about the Depression and World Wars, talked about how those hard times had built character and brought families and communities together, how they had strengthened our country and given it new energy and direction. This time, too, they claimed, a little patience and endurance was all that was required to further the causes of freedom and democracy. We each just needed to do our part and pull together and wait it out.

Of course Father scoffed at those platitudes, though even his contempt was half-hearted. If Mother had still been alive, I'm sure the patriotic rhetoric we culled along with the other tidings from town would have inspired some grand tirades on his part about humanity's gullibility and politicians' banality. As it was, he was mostly too sad to care.

Even so, he sent a voluntary donation along with his income tax payment that spring, and he, too, predicted that by fall the worst of our hardships would be over. In fact, the one conviction that all but the most wild-eyed extremists shared was that this situation is only temporary, that the world we belong to will soon begin again, and we will be able to look back on the way we are living now as a momentary interruption, a good story to tell the grandkids.

Once Father quit going to work, we were so isolated from even Redwood that it was sometimes hard to remember anything unusual was happening in the world beyond our forest. Our isolation felt like a protection. Last June when the moon shone red from the fires of Oakland, it seemed like a warning to stay close to home, and the news we got on Saturday nights reinforced its message. So we settled in to wait for fall. As Father kept reminding me whenever I chafed for town, at least out here we have a well-stocked pantry, a garden and orchard, fresh water, a forest full of firewood, and a house. At least here we have a buffer from the obsessions, greeds, and germs of other people. At least here some recognizable shape remains—even now—to our interrupted lives.

The B's begin with fighter planes—*B-17, B-24, B-29, B-52*. Next is *B Cassiopeia*. Then comes *Ba, the human-headed falcon believed by the ancient Egyptians to symbolize the immortality and divinity of the soul after death.*

Fighter planes and supernovas and the falcon-like divinity of the soul: death and flight, Heaven and the heavens. Even though it's only an alphabetical accident, there is a serendipitous rightness to that juxtaposition, and for a moment I wish my father were here so I could prove him wrong.

My father always scorned encyclopedias.

"There's no poetry in them, no mystery, no magic. Studying the encyclopedia is like eating carob powder and calling it chocolate mousse," he used to complain after an afternoon spent trying to convince the fifth-grade teacher to let her students learn about scientific research by raising tadpoles and growing molds instead of copying articles from the encyclopedia.

"Education is about connections, about the relationships that exist between everything in the universe, about how every kid in Redwood Elementary has a few of Shakespeare's atoms in his body."

"Along with Hitler's," my mother added wryly, but my father ignored her, intent on his own idea.

"The encyclopedia takes any subject in the world and dissects it, sucks the blood out of it, rips it from its matrix. What does that teach little Tommy? That research is dry and boring, that it's much more fun to watch TV, steal candy, and destroy private property. And if your sole introduction to research has been an encyclopedia, it's a fairly bright conclusion."

"Now, Robert," my mother would answer as she set the table for dinner, "encyclopedias have their place. Maybe Janice is just showing those kids how to use them before she turns them loose on their own projects."

"She's not. *She* thinks research is dry and boring, too. And Janice'll never turn them loose on anything—they might come up with questions she can't answer."

"Dinner's ready."

"First let's burn all the encyclopedias!"

But our set had come to him as a gift from his faculty the year he walked with them up and down in front of the school with a picket sign, so it was never in much risk of being burnt, and sometimes one of us actually did heave out a volume to look up something.

Still, they probably hadn't been used more than a dozen times until I got them out a few weeks ago. When the public library in Redwood closed last spring, the librarian let me take an extra armload of books. "You go ahead, honey," she said, because my mother was dead, because my father was on the Board of Directors of the library, because I had been checking out books from her since before I could talk, because I had gone to her for the address of the Office of Admissions at Harvard.

"No one else will be reading these this summer if you don't take them," she said, stamping the books with a date three months in the future. "This should be enough to keep you busy until we open up again in the fall."

But I had worked my way through that stack by July, we buried our father in September, and it was the end of November by the time Eva and I were finally recovered enough for her to return to her dancing and me to my studies. Then for a full day I sat at the table, my letter from the Harvard Office of Admissions lying beside the *Official Register of Harvard University* while I looked back and forth between them, staring at the same few phrases over and over again.

Although we do not accept students more than a year before they are due to matriculate, we have reviewed your file and are very favorably impressed with both your outline of study and your intellectual and verbal abilities, as evidenced by your Scholastic Aptitude Test scores, said the letter. *If your College Board Achievement Tests scores are similarly high, we would encourage you to make a formal application to Harvard at the appropriate time next winter.*

But in the *Register* I read, *Although College Board Achievement Tests taken through the January series will satisfy our requirements, we urge you to complete your testing by December, since by applying early, you will ensure that the Committee has time to give your application the most thorough consideration.*

It was like a calculus derivative I was unable to solve, a passage from Saint-Exupéry I couldn't translate. "What will I do?" I finally wailed to Eva when she emerged from her studio that afternoon.

"About what?" she asked, casually grabbing her extended leg and pulling it up so that it was almost vertical against her torso.

"I'm supposed to have taken my Achievement Tests by now."

"Well, you aren't the only one who hasn't. I'm sure even Harvard is going to have to bend their rules this year."

"But what if things have already started up again back there?"

"We'd know about it."

"How?"

"There'd be a plane or something. Something."

"Even if the lights come on tomorrow, I won't be ready to take the tests."

She set her leg down and rose into an unwavering arabesque. "Why not?"

"I can't use my computer or my language tapes; the batteries are dead in my calculator. I don't even have any paper left."

"Then read. Books don't need batteries."

"I've already read everything in the house. Twice."

"Have you read the encyclopedias?" she asked, sweeping down from her arabesque into a deep curtsey.

I wish I had started sooner. I can't believe how much I'm learning. It's all there—every date, every place, every artist and philosopher and scientist, every statesman and king, every star and mineral and species, every fact and theory, every bit of human knowledge. It's all in one place, everything that matters, everything I'll ever need, and all I have to do is turn the page. It may be a little dry, but it's no drier than my calculus text or my French tapes. It's no drier than what Eva does hour after hour alone in her studio.

Our parents never structured our studies. "Let 'em learn what they like," my father used to say. "A child will eat a well-balanced diet if she's given a choice of wholesome foods and left alone. If a kid's body knows what it needs to grow and stay healthy, why wouldn't its mind, too?"

To his friends he explained, "My girls have free run of the forest and the public library. They have a mother who is around to fix them lunch and define any words they don't know. School would only get in the way of that. Besides, if they went to school, they'd spend over two hours a day in the car. Lord knows I could use company on those drives, but it's better for my kids to stay in the woods."

So while other children were reciting their times tables and asking permission to get drinks of water, Eva and I were free to roam and learn as we pleased. Together we painted murals and made up plays, built forts, raised butterflies, and designed computer games. We made paper, concocted new recipes for cookies, edited newspapers, and caught minnows. We grew gourds and nursed fledglings and played with prisms, and our parents told the state that what we did was school.

For years I studied what I wanted to, when and how I wanted to study it. One book led to another in a random pattern, meandering from interest to interest like a good conversation, and the only thing that connected them was their accidental juxtaposition on the crowded bookshelves in Mother's workroom.

Because our father sometimes brought home tests for us to take, by the time I was twelve I knew I was at least four or five grades ahead of the school kids my age. I also knew that if you went to school, you had to sit in rows, do long assignments in dreary workbooks, and ask to be allowed to go to the bathroom. But there came a time when I didn't care, when I yearned for the life contained in those swaying yellow school buses, longed to be part of the jostle of other kids with their armloads of slick-paged books, their careful hair and easy laughter, and I began a campaign to demand that my parents send me to school.

It was not long after Eva had discovered ballet, when I was still smarting from the hole her dancing had carved in my life, and I think I tried to convince my parents to let me go to school as a way of easing my loneliness.

"If I don't have Eva, I need someone," I said. "It's too boring here all day by myself."

"I'm around," my mother answered.

"But you're always busy with your tapestries."

"You could help me. I think you'd like working with the dyes. And I could use another set of hands to help me warp my loom."

When I rolled my eyes and slumped in my chair, she answered briskly, "I know you can figure out what to do with yourself, Nell. We didn't keep you out of school for all these years just to let you start now. Junior high school's one of the most toxic experiences I can imagine."

The battle continued and every skirmish ended in hot indignation and resentment on my part and in pained bafflement on the part of my parents, who claimed they wanted me to be happy but who wanted me to be happy in the way they chose.

I sulked and balked, but finally I stumbled across an article about another family of homeschoolers who lived even further out than we and whose children had all attended Harvard. I decided that if those kids could do it, so could I. If Eva wouldn't stop dancing, then I would go to Harvard; if I couldn't attend public school in Redwood, then it would serve everybody right when I matriculated at the best college in the country.

I asked for a new computer for my thirteenth birthday and started pestering my father to bring home history and science textbooks, French tapes, math workbooks. He always complied with my requests—though he usually managed to slip a few mystery novels into the stack. But whenever I mentioned Harvard, his response was noncommittal. "Don't know if that particular institution's all you've cracked it up to be, Pumpkin, though I have to admit I'd be proud if you got there under your own steam. But remember, that was quite awhile ago when those other homeschoolers got in."

"Harvard likes students from unusual backgrounds," I said.

"Back then it did. Who knows what the admissions policy looks like now. Anyway, what makes Harvard so special? What're you going to study there?"

It had seemed to me that getting into Harvard was goal enough, so his question took me by surprise. Since I had just finished reading a biography of Sir Alexander Fleming, I answered the first thing that came to mind, "Medicine."

"You want to be a doctor?"

"Maybe," I answered, "or a researcher."

"Well, more power to you, Pumpkin. I know you'll be a whiz at whatever you decide to do. I just don't want to see you limit yourself before you get a taste of what's out there in the wide, wide world."

As time passed I worked even harder, studying everything I thought Harvard would expect me to know, and last spring, when I received my reply from the Admissions Office, I thought I had learned a lot. Now, volume by volume, article after article, page by page, the encyclopedia is revealing all I didn't know. I could be almost grateful for this fugue state for giving me one last chance to prepare for Harvard.

I'm trying to be disciplined about my reading and not skip articles that don't interest me or don't seem pertinent to my education. I want to study the encyclopedia from beginning to end. But today is New Year's Day, so I had to jump ahead to the C's to make sure the calendar I'm making is accurate.

The problem with calendars is that nothing fits precisely. The rotations and revolutions of the Earth and sun and moon don't coincide, and everything ends in unwieldy decimal points: there are 365.2422 days in a solar year, 29.53059 days in a lunar month, and weeks exist nowhere but in our superstitious human heads.

The encyclopedia gave me an algebraic formula for telling on which day of the week a particular date will fall, so I figured out when the next leap year will be and then sacrificed a whole sheet of notebook paper to make a calendar. As I drew those twelve grids, numbered their squares, and labeled the holidays and birthdays they represented, I couldn't help but wonder which one of those yet unlived days would turn out to be the biggest festival of all—the lucky day on which the world will return to us and make my homemade calendar obsolete.

We wake each morning to the flat light that seeps through the January rain. We rise from our mattresses, trade the tee shirts in which we sleep for sweaters and jeans. Eva feeds the fire and I go outside to open the chicken coop and bring in more wood. For breakfast we eat milkless oatmeal or leftover rice, sweetened with the smallest possible dusting of cinnamon.

After breakfast we do our chores—chopping wood, cleaning, or adding to the inventory we are making of what we own. Eva dances all afternoon while I study and write. When the threat of darkness stops us, we coax the hens back inside, eat our dinner of beans or lentils or one of the unlabeled cans from Fastco, and take turns indulging in the day's greatest satisfaction.

The only soap we have left is the tiny sliver we're saving for our victorious hike to town when we can fill our empty gas can and start our lives anew. Even so, a bath is one of the few pleasures in which I can completely revel, for not only is it not a weaker version of what I remember a bath to be, it is also renewable. As long as the spring continues to fill the water tank and the water tank can send its trickle through the pipes into the house, as long as the fire can heat another kettle, there can always be a bath at the end of the day, a bath to try to soak the nightmares out, to leave me so limp I almost have to crawl through the darkness to my mattress opposite Eva's by the stove.

But even the hottest, deepest, longest bath won't work forever, and there comes a time in almost every night when my dreams chase me from my sleep, so that I burst through to wakefulness still saturated with their horror.

I dreamed about worms again last night. Not the little, rosy things we find in the pantry these days, but the maggots that in my dreams fill my father's grave. Paralyzed and voiceless, I am lying next to him in that clammy hole, and our two bodies—his dead and mine living—are writhing with maggots. His body cannot comfort me. It is an inert thing, infecting me with its decay. And I am unable to help myself, as I lie there, eaten alive by death.

I woke to blackness and the sound of my sister's voice, the solid feel of her hands.

"It's okay," she promised. "You were dreaming."

Even as she said it, and my conscious self was nodding in reply, I think we both knew that dreams come from somewhere real, that any dream can only echo what's already been lived.

"Want a cup of tea?" she asked.

"I've already had yesterday's," I fretted, "and I don't want to waste today's now."

"I'll give you my today's cup."

"But that wouldn't be fair to you."

"It's okay."

When I didn't answer, she rose to open the stove door, and, working in that red half-light, she filled a mug with hot water from the kettle on the back of the stove and added the smallest possible pinch of tea.

"Thanks," I said when she handed me the steaming mug.

"What else are sisters for?" she answered wryly.

I know she meant it. But she spoke so lightly, I couldn't respond as my heart wanted, couldn't bury myself forever in her arms.

———

Ballet is a form of dance that developed out of the court spectacles of the Renaissance. Its characteristic movements emphasize a stylized and ethereal grace. In order to achieve this effect, the aspiring dancer must begin at a very early age to train his body to perform in ways that are not within the natural range of movements for the human body.

Sometimes when my head feels so thick I know I can't retain another word, I'll abandon the encyclopedia, leave my place at the table by the front window, and migrate down the hall to Eva's studio. The door is always open, though she hardly seems to notice when I slip inside, seat myself against the wall, and watch her at her work.

Usually she'll be at the barre, working her way through the endless chain of exercises that began with her first wavering, stiff-armed *plié* and won't end until she quits dancing: Watching her there, lowering and rising with the *pliés* she'll never finish, reminds me of a story about a Bolshoi ballerina during that period of Russian martial law in the early nineties who said: "Revolutions will come and go, but we will still be here doing our *battements tendus.*"

That dance continues—*pliés, relevés, battements tendus, ronds de jambes, développés*, first at the barre and then in the center, that same little alphabet, over and over and over again to the relentless tick of the metronome, until now, a million repetitions later, each move is pliant, fluent, perfect. Even something as simple as her leg stretching in *tendu* or her arm opening out to second position speaks to some longing or delight or knowledge far beyond words.

Sometimes while I'm sitting there, she'll abandon her exercises and dance for me. Today she began with Clara's first solo from *The Nutcracker*. It's a pretty little *divertissement*, quick and pert, and I remember how it delighted the Christmas crowds the year she danced it.

But just before she reached the point where Fritz is supposed to snatch the nutcracker from her hands, her steps changed, and she was dancing something I had never seen, a haunting, jarring dance that began with a series of slow, pensive arabesques from which she collapsed into a knock-kneed, flat-footed second position. Then, with her feet still spread in second, she rose *en pointe*, her open legs making her look unsettlingly strong and tall. From there she flung herself into a run of quick, tight, classical turns, ending again with her heels out, her ankle cocked, her elbows up. Then again she rose into another faultless arabesque.

So compelling was her dancing that at some point as I was watching her, I found myself believing I could hear the music she was dancing to, a discordant and disturbing music, a music of contrasts and quick reversals. There was a sense of suspension, suppression, a feeling of waiting to it. Yet for all its tight control, there was also the disconcerting feeling of something wild rising, as though some untamed thing were being unleashed by those cocked ankles and crooked elbows, by those clean turns and perfect leaps, as if some wilderness in Eva that I had never known was struggling to surface.

It was embarrassing to see her dance that way, so unlike my composed and graceful sister, and I was thinking of leaving, of returning to the B's, when suddenly she stopped, her hands on her hips, her left foot pointed out in second, her head turned to the right. She held that pose for a beat, and then she shifted her weight to her left foot, her right foot shot out, and her head snapped in the opposite direction, as though she could sense something approaching behind her which she wasn't yet ready to turn and face. Then she dropped her hands, rolled her head, and broke the moment by gasping, "What do you think?"

"I'm not sure," I answered. "It's good, I guess. Anyhow, it's different. Interesting. Why don't you keep going?"

She gave an ironic half-laugh and said, between deep breaths, "That's when my partner's supposed to make his entrance. Then comes the *pas de deux.*"

"What was it?" I asked.

"The opening of *Tzigane.* Katherine Lee was understudying it, and I used to watch her work on it till my bus came. So I picked up a little of it myself."

"Did you ever dance it with a partner?"

"No." We were both silent for a moment, and then she said, "But that's okay. I always liked leaps better than lifts, anyway. Stupid partners, sweating on you and heaving you around like a hunk of meat."

She gave a *glissade* and a *plié* and flung herself into a *grand jeté* so high and wide that she seemed suspended in both air and time. When she finally consented to return to earth, she came down in a *plié* so easy that only the thump of her shoes on the floor gave any clue effort was involved in her leap. Then she broke into one of the peasant dances from *Giselle,* a sprightly little thing, with quick steps, a tossed head, and arms lithe and teasing. It was a wonderfully deceptive dance, a dance so apparently simple it was hard to remember that every movement was unnatural, part of an aesthetics that defies both physics and anatomy.

"Bravo!" I cried when she finished, though my voice sounded too small to fill the void her dancing had left. She gave me a wry little country curtsey, and I left her to stretch out her legs, mop the sweat from her face, remove the shreds of her renovated shoes, and come out to fix dinner with me in the last of the day's dim light.

The spring Eva was twelve, when our family made its semi-yearly trek to San Francisco to the ballet, she rode home as silent and distant as our mother, staring out the car window beyond the faint reflection of her face to the moving, light-spangled darkness. While our mother's moodiness evaporated in a day or so, Eva's remained. And intensified. She began to talk about ballet lessons.

"No, sweet," our mother said, "I won't let you ruin your life like that. Ballet's horrible for you. It'll make you neurotic and anorexic and narcissistic and arthritic and illiterate. It's unnatural. Look at what it did to me."

Our father looked up from his paper to ask, "*What* did it do to you?" and Eva said, "Please—"

"It's too far. To find decent classes, we'd have to drive at least to San Francisco. I won't have your feet ruined by some wannabe teacher in Redwood who can't wait to get you *en pointe*."

"I could ride into Redwood with Father and then take the bus from there."

"You're too young."

"Why don't you give me lessons?" Eva asked. "You used to give lessons—that's how you paid for your classes."

"I hated teaching. I hated putting up with all the little girls who just wanted to wear pink tutus, and I hated having to tyrannize the few girls who were any good. It's brutally hard work.

"And besides," she added, playing what she considered was her trump card, "you're too old to start dancing. Any dancer with any chance at all began when she was five or six—eight at the very latest. There'll be no more dancers in this family, and that's final."

But a day or two later she was calling down to her friends in the city, trying to get recommendations for a ballet school. She swore—and our father laughed—when she learned that the best teacher north of the city had her studio in Redwood.

"Well," she sighed, "Eva's her own person."

"And she's certainly your daughter, Gloria," added our father.

The following week, Eva attended her first lesson, all gangling knees and elbows in a class of sway-backed, pot-bellied six-year-olds. It was our mother's hope that Eva was attracted to the lights and sequins and not to the dance itself. She wanted to believe that the pain and tedium of practice would make Eva lose interest. But Eva loved that mix of work and sweat. She loved the freedom and demand of dance, and she loved dancing—both for herself and for an audience. She loved to share her passion with us earthbound, wordbound mortals.

From the beginning she lived to practice, and in six months she was outdancing the girls her age who had been taking lessons since they were preschoolers. Six months later she had the lead in the school's recital, and six months after that she began to take the bus down to the city two days a week for classes with the San Francisco Ballet School. Her Redwood teacher was thrilled, her teacher in San Francisco said she had promise, and even our mother had to admit Eva had a good extension and a strong turnout.

But when she refused all food but yogurt and apples, when her periods became inconsistent and she danced until her blisters bled, our mother showed her own twisted feet to Eva and begged her to give up ballet. "It's no life," she said. "Please don't be a dancer, sweet. There's too much of you to give it all to one thing. And what will you do when you're thirty-five, and your career's over, when all you know is ballet, and you can't even walk?"

When Eva first announced that she wanted lessons, I hardly noticed, although, as always, I was automatically on her side. After all, Eva was my sister. She was my playmate, my best friend, my should-have-been-twin, and whatever she wanted, I wanted unquestioningly for her. But after she had been dancing for a while, my enthusiasm began to pale even as hers grew. The hours she used to spend with me—playing in the forest, working in the house on one of our many projects, or spinning out never-ending games of pretend in the clearing—were now the hours she devoted to lessons and practice. At first I felt puzzled and a little hurt, and I, too, kept waiting for Eva to give up ballet and return to me.

Later, when it was clear that no matter how I pleaded or what I promised, Eva would not quit dancing, I cut the ribbons off her first pair of toe shoes. She was furious when she discovered what I had done to the slippers she had coveted for so long.

"Nell's ruined my life," she shrieked, racing into the workroom where Mother was bent over her loom and I was hanging around in a state of restless boredom.

"Well, Eva's ruined mine!" I flared.

My mother took one look at the severed ribbons, sighed, and set down the butterfly of silk she had been using for weft. "No one can ruin anyone else's life," she said. "Settle down, Eva. Penelope, bring me the sewing basket."

While she sewed the ribbons back into place, and Eva sulked in her bedroom, Mother talked to me.

"Why the sabotage, Nellie?" she asked, threading a needle with pink thread.

"Eva won't play with me. She's always practicing. And anyway, it's no good for her."

Mother sighed again. "Well, it's not what I'd have chosen for her either. But if she's decided to be a dancer, then surely we want her to be the best dancer she can possibly be."

"But she never plays with me anymore."

"You can't *make* her play with you. Nell, I know there's a gap in your life right now. But it's up to you to figure out how to fill it."

"But—"

"She's her own person, sweetheart. And, like it or not, so are you."

She raised Eva's shoe to her lips and bit the thread that anchored the reattached ribbon. "Here," she said, handing me the mended shoes with a smile so warm it might have melted rock, "go give these to your sister."

So despite Mother's misgivings and my loneliness, Eva kept dancing. For her fourteenth birthday, Father laid mylar over the hardwood floor in the back room. He hung a barre along one wall, covered the opposite wall with mirrors, and there Eva stayed until someone managed to coax or bribe or command her out.

By that time we were all in a well-established routine. Every morning Eva rode into town with Father, while I studied and chafed in the still house, and Mother worked on her tapestries. Three days a week Eva took morning and afternoon classes with Miss Markova in Redwood. Tuesdays and Fridays she caught the bus to San Francisco to take classes with the company, and on the weekends she danced at home, trying to give herself a harder workout on her own than either of her teachers would have. *Another year*, everyone was saying—*certainly by next spring—and she'll be ready to audition with the company. Another year and there will be no stopping her.*

But that summer—the summer Eva turned sixteen—was the summer we first realized that Mother was sick. She died the following spring, and less than a year after that the busses had quit running into the city and there was no longer gas enough to drive to town three times a week for classes. At first, Eva talked of moving down to the city, or at least into Redwood where she could live with Miss Markova and keep up with her classes. But our father was so distraught at the thought of her leaving and everyone seemed so certain that things would be back to normal by fall, that nothing ever came of her plans.

Of everything Eva suffered when the power was fading and the gas was disappearing, I think the hardest part for her wasn't having to give up classes or postpone her audition or even do without partners or new toe shoes, but was having to dance without music. Every time the power went off, her music died, so that one minute she would be practicing *grands jetés* to the stately joy of *Water Music*, and the next she would be plummeting on musicless, as though she had just stumbled off a cliff.

She got in the habit of making herself dance whenever the lights flickered on. Even if it were midnight, even if she had just eaten or were taking a bath, when the electricity returned, she would jump up, race to her studio, start the music, and dance. But the power came on less and less often and stayed on for shorter and shorter periods, until, despite all her discipline, she despaired.

One day I heard her crying behind the closed door of her studio, sobbing quietly like a child crying itself to sleep when it has given up hope of any other comfort, and in an odd way it seemed as self-sufficient as everything else about Eva. I stood at the closed door for a long time, afraid to enter and unable to leave, until finally the crying stopped and I crept away, feeling both guilty and unendurably lonely.

A few days later she burst into the living room where Father and I were each bent silently over our books.

"I'm losing everything," she railed. "A dancer's body starts to lose its condition after seventy-two hours, and I haven't had a good workout in five days. How will I ever be ready for my audition?"

Just as I was ready to make Eva's drama my own, our father spoke. "So, dance," he said in the practical tone that always infuriated me when it was addressed to me.

"How?" she moaned.

"You know—" he lifted his arms over his head in third position and flailed a wobbling, work-booted foot in the air— "like this."

She didn't laugh. "I have to have music," she said.

"What do you need music for?"

"Without music, it's not dancing—it's exercise. I need the feel, the emotion."

"I'd think a good dancer'd have those things inside her."

"But you need music to let them come out."

"There were ballerinas long before there was electricity. What did they do?"

"They had accompanists," she answered grandly.

"Well, we don't have a piano or even a harpsichord, but I might be able to make a workable drum. I think I saw a coffee can and an old innertube floating around here somewhere."

"Father," said Eva with a quiet intensity, "this is my life."

"I know, Eva. I know." He sighed. "I'm just trying to help, is all. Seems like a dancer good as you could keep the emotion in her head."

"How about the rhythm?" she said triumphantly. "How can I keep the beat in my head?"

Father was silent for a moment and then he said, "I think I've got something for you out in my shop. Don't go away—I'll be right back."

"I don't want a goddamn drum," Eva yelled after him, but the door was already closed.

It was almost dark by the time he returned, but he came in grinning like his old self. He bowed to Eva and handed her a metronome. "This was in the last load I rescued from the dump. It's a little beat up, I'm afraid. But it still keeps a beat."

So she taught herself to dance without music, to dance to the dead, ungiving rhythm of the metronome. She learned to bring her own music to her dance, and I think it has made her dancing finer than ever, although no one but me has yet seen it.

Despite her way with fire, Eva always makes me think of water. She's quick and slender and sparkling as the stream beyond our clearing, and like that stream she seems content to live a part of her life underground, seems certain—even now—that she is headed somewhere.

For a long time Mother worried that Eva would become like other ballerinas with their gaping ambitions, tittering obsessions, and flat minds, but even before our mother died I think it was clear that Eva would remain Eva—no matter how far she went with her ballet.

Eva is always unalterably herself. Even when she faces herself in the wall of mirrors in her studio, she studies her reflection with neither a dancer's vanity nor a dancer's compulsive criticisms. She meets her own eyes with the same candor with which she meets anyone else's, whereas if I scrutinize my reflection, I plead with it, get coy. I suck at my cheeks to make their bones more prominent. I wish my nose were narrower and my chin less round. I admire the indigo of my eyes and practice smiling so my teeth don't show. I try to imagine that I am someone else seeing me.

The question I bring to my reflection, time and time again, is, *Who are you?* But it would never cross Eva's mind to wonder who she is. She knows herself in every bone and cell, and her beauty is not an ornament, it is the element in which she lives.

When she dances, you can see it. When she dances she is so certain, so alive, it enlivens whoever watches her. When she's not dancing, she's quiet, calm-tempered, a little dreamy, as if dancing were living for her, and as long as she can suffer and exalt in her dance, she has no need of suffering and exaltation when she is simply passing through her days.

I'm the one with the sour moods, the angry questions. I'm the one who doesn't fit inside my skin, who can't read my own face. I'm the one who can't trust what will happen next, who has to force, demand, control, who has to face herself—night after night—when Eva's already asleep.

———

Today I read *When Beethoven composed his Ninth Symphony, which many believe to be his masterwork, he was almost totally deaf,* and I thought of Eva, dancing alone to the music in her head.

———

This morning we worked upstairs in the cool dimness of our parents' bedroom, sorting their clothes and trinkets, inventorying all we now own.

Our mother used to claim that, whereas other families had one junk drawer—in which nails, lock washers, spark plugs, broken earrings, chewed-up pencils, safety pins, sea shells, keys, ancient grocery receipts, and other unsortable objects collected—our family had one drawer that wasn't a junk drawer, and then only because it was in such an awkward place that no one could get to it.

"It makes everything seem so temporary," she would complain.

Our father would answer her gleefully, "Oh no, my darling Gloria. All this junk will last forever—and some of it may even come in handy sometime before then."

Whether he is right on either count remains to be seen, I suppose, though each new drawer we open yields something else we might possibly need or use before the stores reopen, and I'm glad we're finally taking stock of what we've got.

We started only a few weeks before Christmas. All fall we sat on the deck, stunned by the accident that was our father's death. Down in the orchard the last of the fruit fell to the ground unnoticed, and in the garden the final bounty of the crops our father had planted and hoed and watered with our vague help went to seed, to weed, and then rotted, shriveled, collapsed into itself. All fall we sat stricken, unable to think of either the past or the future while the few maple trees scattered among the evergreens that ring our clearing turned gold, sang against the constant green of the rest of the forest, and then lost their leaves.

I didn't study. I didn't even read. Eva danced only one desultory hour a day. In the morning we gave the hens their increasingly meager ration of cracked corn, checked their nest boxes for their increasingly infrequent eggs, and let them out into the yard to scratch. We played endless games of Backgammon on a board that opened like a suitcase. Round and round we circled with our markers, traveling, getting safely nowhere, while we waited for the phone to ring or the power to come back on, waited for night to fall so we could cross another blank day off the calendar in the kitchen, waited to be rescued from the mistaken detour our lives had taken.

The weather grew colder, and we moved from the deck to the dim front room, abandoned Backgammon for the thousand-piece puzzles our father had once loved. The rains came, and we lit the woodstove and pieced our puzzles while in the pantry the sacks of beans and rice and flour began to slump, the rows of home-canned vegetables and fruits grew shorter. But hour after hour, we thought only of the bits of colored cardboard spread out on the table between us. As long as there was yet another convoluted scrap to fit into place, as long as the whole puzzle could be dismantled and begun again, we could remain suspended, waiting, safe.

But one morning we woke up and the fire was out. Our breaths plumed whitely into the chill air, and when we went outdoors for armloads of stovewood, the world was etched with a rare frost. We chattered back inside, dropped our wood beside the cold stove. I filled the teakettle with the water that had collected in the sink overnight, replaced it on top of the stove, and bent again over the tidy sea of puzzle pieces while Eva knelt to start the fire. She chopped a batch of kindling, crumpled a quarter of a page from an old catalog, reached for the box of kitchen matches, and gasped.

I thought she had been stung, so sudden and shocked was the sound she made, and before I could even ask, "What's wrong?" the image of a scorpion came to me. I saw it arching out of the opened matchbox, and everything I had heard and feared about scorpion stings dashed through my mind. Then I saw that instead of having flung the matchbox from her, she had clasped it to her chest, and in answer to my question, she held it out to me, too stunned to speak.

I took the box gingerly, but instead of the ugly, naked brown of a scorpion, I saw only four red-tipped matches—in a box that had once held hundreds.

"What happened?" I asked.

Eva answered, "We must have used them."

No one else could have, so it must have been us. But we had used them so slowly—a match every few mornings to start the fire if the banked coals didn't keep until we woke—that Eva had never noticed when we were down to half a box, a third of a box, a handful.

"Aren't there any more?" I whispered.

"I don't know."

We looked at each other. Eva stood up, straight as a dancer once again. "We'll have to look," she said.

And so our search began. At first it was a frantic rush through the house, fumbling under sofa cushions and mattresses, tearing through closets and pockets and drawers. By the time we had assembled an old Bic lighter still sloshing with butane, a half-dozen ragged books of matches, and the magnifying glass from Father's *Compact Edition of the Oxford English Dictionary*, our immediate concern was relieved, but our real fears were intensified. We had left that numb place we'd inhabited since our father died. We had seen—and could no longer ignore—that not only were our matches numbered, but also that the supplies in the pantry weren't limitless, the woodpile was diminishing, there were only a few aspirin at the bottom of the plastic bottle, a handful of tampons in the blue box in the bathroom, that even our clothes and shoes might wear out before all this is finally over.

We became systematic then, going through the house room by room, first the kitchen, pantry, utility room, and bathroom, and now our parents' bedroom—sorting, organizing, evaluating our legacy—planning how we might use or barter every old bottle of cough medicine, each roll of duct tape, every torn sheet and screwdriver and pair of sneakers, every bit of the stuff that filled our house.

The other day while I was studying bats I skipped ahead to the F's so I could read about frosted bats, and there the entry above caught my eye:

Frostbite, an injury that occurs when heat loss allows ice crystals to form in living tissue. Frostbitten tissue becomes bloodless, hard, and numb. In order to prevent complications, such as infection and tissue death, it is important to warm the affected areas as quickly and gently as possible; however, the pain during thawing may be severe.

That's what it felt like, as we began to work our way through those rooms, examining the artifacts of our childhood, the possessions of the parents who were lost to us. Slowly the tissue softened, warmed, slowly the blood returned, but at times the pain of that thawing was so intense I longed to remain ice. Still, a kind of life burnt its way—cell by screaming cell—back through my frozen self.

At first it seemed as though the whole house were filled with what we no longer had. Each drawer was a Pandora's box of loss and despair. Here were our father's worn bookbag, his splayed toothbrush, his battered coffee mug. Here was our mother's loom, on which her final tapestry waits, the warp shed open for the next pass of the abandoned weft. Here were her canning jars and crystal glasses, and—since our father could get rid of nothing that had been hers—her perfume bottles and slips.

Even something as anonymous as a mixing bowl seemed to fill with a childhood's worth of cake batters when we lifted it off the shelf, examined it, trying to imagine its current and future uses, to assess its value, trying not to dwell on the last sweet lick we had tasted from its depths.

Each time we opened a new closet or another drawer we braced ourselves, ready to flinch and run as memory struck, rattles buzzing, fangs bared and sinking into our flesh. But in a funny way, even when they bit, those memories weren't venomous enough. This afternoon what saddened me was how little remains after a person's gone. A few photographs, a silk scarf, a checkbook—and where are they, the people who once owned those things? In which barrette or workshirt do our mother and father reside?

I kept thinking we would run across something that would reveal them to us. I steeled myself for the discovery of a packet of letters or a book of pornography or a newspaper clipping that would give us some new understanding of our parents. But there were no surprises. Everything we found seems almost anonymous in its familiarity. Here are our mother's bras, worn to the shape of her vanished breasts. Here are our father's socks with their candid, threadbare heels.

Trying to understand my parents is like trying to see my own eyeballs or taste my own tongue. It's like trying to step outside the air. I know they were eccentric. But even when I wished they would move to town, drive new cars, and wear crisp slacks and sweaters, I could never really imagine any other parents for my own.

My mother was beautiful, there's no doubt of that. I always thought she looked like a dancer, straight and slender, with startling grey eyes and a halo of pale gold hair that sprang from her head like an aura, surrounding her face with its own source of light. She moved like a ballerina until the very end. She never lost her turnout, and her gestures were both larger and more precise than they needed to be, as though each movement, each moment meant something. Even when she was just doing chores—sorting laundry or turning the compost pile—she moved with a full, efficient grace, as though there were an art or a secret pleasure to folding sheets or forking yard clippings.

But for all her ethereal beauty, my mother had an earthy side. She had a dancer's earthy feet, with twisted toes and bunions that ached for days when the weather changed, and she was always unswervingly frank with us about what Father called "The Interesting Stinks": elimination, menstruation, sex, and—until it was she who was dying—death.

She had joined the San Francisco Ballet Company when she was eighteen, and she danced for three seasons before she shattered her ankle during a dress rehearsal for *The Sleeping Beauty*, a production in which she was to have her first solo role—as Little Red Riding Hood. She met our father in the emergency room, where he was waiting with a second-grader who had shown up at school that morning with a black eye and a broken arm.

It was Father's first year of teaching, and he had chosen the toughest school San Francisco could offer. But by the time he saw my mother limp into the ER waiting room in her Red Riding Hood costume, white-faced and clinging to the properties manager, he was more than ready to spend his evenings contemplating something other than the demise of the school's hot breakfast program and the increase of preteen pregnancies.

Later, after a year of grueling physical therapy, when my mother was told she would have to stay off her ankle for at least another season, and even then might never be able to dance professionally again, she abandoned ballet entirely, married Father, and moved with him to the property he had found outside of Redwood, eighty acres of second-growth forest whose isolation he felt was guaranteed by the fact that it was tucked up against an expanse of state-owned forest. That summer she helped him add indoor plumbing and a utility room to the loose-jointed, two-story summer cabin that sat at the center of their land, and by the next spring she was pregnant.

Before she defected to my father, Mother had been considered one of the most promising young ballerinas in the company, and no one—from her friends in the corps to her own parents—could understand why she had forsaken that life so completely. She claimed she didn't regret her choice, but twice a year, every spring and fall, the four of us dressed in our best clothes, piled into whatever old car our father had running at the time, and drove the three hours to San Francisco to see the ballet.

After the performance we would go backstage, where we stood, clumsy and heavy in our thick street clothes, while women in tutus and tights swirled around our mother, stretching their long necks towards her to kiss the air beside her cheeks. It seemed like only yesterday, they said, when she was dancing with them, and now look—they were nearing the end of their careers and Mother had two lovely daughters. They made dramatic and very general comments about how wonderful families were, how much they envied our mother, how they wished they, too, would get married and have babies.

The drives home were always quiet. Eva and I would fall asleep in the backseat and wake to feel our father lifting us from the car. "The Buick stops here," he would say, even more heartily than usual. "All ashore that's going ashore," and as he carried us across the deck and into the house, we could glimpse over his shoulder our mother standing in the black yard, her shoulders square, her head held high, facing away from the house, facing the darkness, facing the stars.

For a day or two after those trips, she was even more silent than usual. The laundry piled up, and our dinners came from boxes and cans. But inevitably we would wake one morning to Bach or Handel or Vivaldi pouring from the radio in her workroom, and when we came downstairs, there would be pans of cinnamon rolls rising on the freshly scrubbed kitchen counter and a cup of tea cooling on the table beside her as she designed the cartoons or wound the silk for her next tapestry.

I don't suppose Mother was ever meant to be a country woman. She loved the isolation of our house and the view of the trees from the picture window she insisted our father install in the front room. But she never really cared about country life or the forest. She didn't like the work of gardening, and she was allergic to all the pets Eva and I proposed. She never lost her fear of rattlesnakes, ticks, and wild pigs, and whenever she ventured beyond the clearing she managed to come home with a rash of poison oak. Even so she seemed content enough with the work and silence and family that filled her life.

Since she'd quit dancing, she'd pursued several other arts or occupations with what seemed like equal passion. When we were little, she had a potter's wheel and kiln in her workroom, and I can remember making pinch pots and lumpy animals on the floor beside her while her wheel spun to the rhythmic kick of her foot.

But at some point her injured ankle started to bother her, and rather than get an electric wheel or learn to keep the kick-wheel turning with her other foot, she traded her potter's wheel and kiln for a loom, a warping board, and a bobbin winder, and she learned to weave. Her allergies kept her from working with wool, so she used silk yarns and wove tapestries of intricate flowers that she modeled after the millefleurs tapestries of Gothic Europe and sold through one of the most exclusive galleries in the city.

She dyed the silks herself, and it used to be a magic no chemical formula could ever explain away, how the dull-colored and bitter-smelling powders she added to her kettles could produce the indigos and amethysts, emeralds and crimsons, carnelians and ochers and umbers with which she filled her tapestries.

In the kitchen were a whole set of pots and bowls and spoons we knew not to use for food because of the toxic dyes and mordants they held or stirred. But after her cancer was diagnosed, Mother became interested in using natural dyes, in using benign alum and gentle vinegar as mordants, and just before she grew too sick to think of working, she was talking of learning how to get her colors from the plants in the forest.

I know she loved us, though she left us mainly alone. She wasn't a talker like my father, and her love came in the form of quick hugs and cookies and a sort of distant interest, an indulgent neglect. She lived deeply in the center of her life, and she expected Eva and me to do the same. I think she saw little need to act as companion or playmate to us. *You're your own person,* she would say whenever either of us came to her lonely or bored in the middle of the day, *You'll figure it out.* And she would give us a warm, firm smile and turn back to her loom.

You're your own person. When one of us came running to her with a complaint about the other—*Eva won't be the prince, Nell is cutting her doll's hair, Eva won't clean her room*—she would answer half-sternly, half-proudly, *Your sister is her own person. And so are you. You'll figure it out.* Then she'd ruffle our hair, her long fingers massaging our scalps for a brief, sweet instant before she took up her shuttle again.

We spent the morning in our father's workshop, in an attempt to organize and inventory the chaos there. I used to hate his shop with its untamed clutter and dank smell of molds and chemicals, but now every wire and hose and bolt, each tool and gadget and machine may have a use, and it seems both a solace and a reproach to sit among his things, attending to them, sorting and cleaning, giving them the care he never had time to devote to them.

Father kept everything and sorted nothing. Our mother used to complain he was like those housewives approaching senility who hoard grocery bags, margarine tubs, and styrofoam meat trays. He saved it all—broken appliances, used toilet seats, rusted chicken wire. I have to admit he did make use of some of it. He always had a board or a screw that would work, although—as our mother liked to point out—it might take him half an afternoon to find the right one.

It's ironic to think that all his junk may now be our greatest treasure. Beyond our clearing there is nothing but forest, a useless waste of trees and weeds, wild pigs and worms. But our father's workshop is crammed with things that may finally have some value.

There was nothing much unusual about my father's background, although he always seemed an even greater eccentric than my mother. He grew up the middle son in a midwestern farm family. "I'm a middle man," he used to claim, "middle income, middle class, middle aged, but I've still got my middle finger, and by God, I still know how to use it."

It occurs to me now that it must have been a bitter childhood, although for all his talk he never mentioned it. It seemed his father's farm was under constant threat of foreclosure. His older brother drowned in a swimming accident the summer he was seven and his mother never recovered from that loss. But the only thing my father seemed to retain from all those hardships was a dislike of powdered milk and a genius for maintaining old trucks and cars.

He even remembered midwestern weather fondly. He had grown up where winter meant a long siege of snow and sub-zero weather, and he always showed his disdain for what Californians called winter by refusing to even own a coat. "Out here, there's summer and there's sweater weather," he would scoff. "Winter—ha! No season deserves the name unless you can count on being snowed in for at least a week. Here you can't even assume there'll be frost."

My father wasn't a big man. He was only inches taller than my mother—scrawny, almost, but strong—with hair that was always a little too long, unless it had just been cut, in which case it exposed a rim of untanned skin across his forehead and behind his ears and along the back of his neck. My father had the world's bluest eyes and the deep crow's-feet at their corners only made them sweeter. He had nimble hands, a smile like a gift, and a quick, almost manic energy. He was always bristling with jokes and projects and ideas. He was always doing something, always tinkering or fiddling or fixing, adding another room to the makeshift ramble of our house, rebuilding an engine, digging a new leach line for the septic field, repairing the water tank.

He was always working and he always called it play.

"Think I'll go play on the roof for a while," he would call to Mother as he went out to patch the most recent leak.

"Time to play in the garden," he would say on a Saturday afternoon, or "I'm going to play around with that carburetor today." And on Monday morning he would stuff his great, sloppy notebooks into his canvas bookbag, toss a rumpled corduroy sports jacket over his shoulder, and announce, "I'm off to play principal."

Our mother used to say that Father had an infinite capacity for entertainment, though now I wonder if it weren't just an infinite capacity for loving her, because after she was gone that all changed. When she died, his kinetic joy and energy evaporated. When she died, his life seemed to collapse like a black hole, creating the density the encyclopedia calls singularity, a force from which nothing can escape, a negativity that devours even light.

———

Life these mid-January days is a tired round of the same small business—studying, eating, trying to sleep. The roof has started leaking over Eva's old bedroom, but other than that there's nothing current to chronicle but meals and dreams and more wet weather. Eva dances and I read, and the only news comes from the encyclopedia. Even so, it's uncanny how frequently the alphabet's strict order haunts my life.

Today I read: *Bulb, a structure of fleshy leaves that constitutes the resting stage of some plants. The bulb's food reserves allow it to lie dormant during inclement weather and to resume growing when conducive conditions return.*

Our mother died before the telephones quit working. She died when electricity still seemed as natural as breathing, when there were still new songs on the radio. She died in a hospital—that's how long ago it was—died slowly of some complicated cancer, instead of the quick viruses or accidents or flus that kill people now.

The final winter she was alive, she drove to town one Sunday when the sky was sodden and the earth inert, and she came back with shopping bags bulging with tulip bulbs.

"I bought every red one in town," she announced triumphantly.

"They look brown to me," said our father, peering into one of the bags and then taking out a bulb, holding it up to the light as though he were checking its color. "What are they, deer food?"

"The gardening book says deer won't eat tulips," she said.

"Hope the deer read the same book," he answered. To his delight, she sighed with elaborate patience, rolled her eyes, and asked him how deep he thought she should plant them. Then she carried her bags outside and spent the next week setting out bulbs. She was already bone-thin from the cancer, but I remember how she seemed to draw a vitality from the fresh dirt, the still bulbs, and the keen air. I remember her hands red and chapped from the cold, and the clean and earthy smell of her when she came indoors to warm herself at the stove where I sat with my book and cup of cocoa.

"Don't you girls want to help?" she would ask, joyful, playful, enlivened by earth and work and the promise contained in each homely knob, teasing me by sneaking her icy fingers down my back or pressing her cheeks against my neck, pausing by the open door to Eva's studio to ask again, "Don't you want to help me?"

We would mumble *later, after this chapter—in a little while, when I finish these pliés,* and I would go back to the private, chocolate warmth of my cocoa mug and the closed world of my book, and Eva would finish her *pliés* and begin work on her *frappés.*

I wonder now if she asked us to help her so she could talk to us about her dying. She, who had always been so candid with our questions about injured birds and sick grandmothers, never spoke with us about what was happening to her, and I wonder if she weren't trying to create a way for us to talk about her impending death. Perhaps outside, kneeling on the earth, while we worked together to bury the bulbs that would outlive her, she would have been able to ask us how we felt, would have been able to tell us what she thought her dying meant, what it was she wanted us to remember when she was gone.

But all I knew back then was that I didn't want to leave the house. It was too cold outside, and I was comfortable by the fire, doing what I knew how to do. I didn't want to risk having to meet her eyes, having to hear those words—*cancer* and *dying*—from my mother, who had cancer, who might be dying.

I think unconsciously I was afraid that if she asked me how I felt, my unleashed grief and rage would kill us all. In some unadmitted corner of myself I was already weeping and screaming and begging her not to leave me, not to go. If I started crying for real, only her comfort could make me stop, and if she died before she had finished comforting me, then I would be left to cry forever. Besides, I had read somewhere that cancer patients' attitudes could cause or cure their disease, and I think I was afraid that if we admitted she might be dying, then that alone would kill her.

So she planted her tulips alone, buried every one herself, and when they were all beneath the earth, she returned to the flowers on her loom and never worked outdoors again. By the time the rains had stopped and the first tulip leaves speared up through the damp earth, there was no escaping the fact that she was dying, but by then she was too feeble and we were too frightened to mention it.

That spring the clearing was ringed with fire, a circle of red tulips broken only where the road intersected it. The resident deer must have nibbled at an early shoot or two and then decided that tulips weren't to their taste, because soon through every window we saw a line of scarlet tulips, their bright color and elementary shape making them seem like the flowers in a child's drawing or the thousand flowers of all her tapestries.

They made a band of red that separated the spring green of our lawn from the wild green of the forest. Each day Mother would sit on the bed our father had arranged on the deck for her, wrapped in blankets, propped on pillows, her bald head shrouded in a turban, her eyes hidden behind dark glasses, watching her tulips until the warm insistence of the sun sent her back into the doze that seemed more and more to be the place where she resided.

"They'll come up every year," she whispered once. She died a month later, just as the wisteria at the south end of the house had begun to bloom. By then her tulips were withered stalks, the green grown out of them as they sagged at the edge of the clearing.

They buried her in the cemetery in town, on an April day of bright light and hard breezes, a day when our eyes smarted not only from grief, but also from unfiltered sunlight and wind-blown grit. Some part of her is there still, I suppose, rotting into the satin and plywood of the coffin the mortician sold our father. But I think she buried herself in that ring of dormant bulbs, and now I wish I had helped her with her work.

———

We never even liked tea before all this happened. I used to drink cocoa and Eva avoided caffeine, but now our mother's stale teabags are one of the few treats we use to ease us through these days. Even Eva is willing to ration tea. Out of a Fastco box that once held four hundred bags, there are only nine left. But if you take the staple from the top of the bag and sift the tea out into a bowl, you'll see that it really only takes a pinch of tea, just a few dusty crumbs, to transform boiled water to a liquid with a hint of bulk and flavor, a kind of alchemy that civilizes water, that brings to life the ghost—at least—of tea.

We can make a single teabag last for a week that way, and maybe counting teabags tells us more than any calendar about how this time is passing.

———

I'm racing through the encyclopedia. I finished *D* last week, and this afternoon I read from *Eden* to *Electricity*. While I was reading about charges and currents and conductors and fields by the dull light of the rain-drenched sun, the odd thought came to me that perhaps our electricity was already back. It was entirely possible the bulb we left on six months ago could have burnt out without our ever knowing it.

The more I sat at the table and looked out at the wet yard, the more I was convinced that all I had to do was get up and switch on the light for our fugue state to be over. I felt a surge of thrill, and the caution I felt after it was not so much a warning that I might be wrong as a way of prolonging the delicious instant of discovery—in a moment I was going to rise from my chair, cross the dim room, and turn on a light. I could already feel the tiny resistance as the switch snapped into place. I could already see the light burning from the filament. I could already hear the joy in my voice when I cried, "Eva, Eva, come see!"

I waited as long as I could, and then slowly I crossed the room, put my finger on the switch, took a deep breath, and pushed it up. There was a barely audible click.

And that was all.

I felt a brutal disappointment, and then I thought, *Maybe it's just that this bulb's burnt out.*

I rushed into the bathroom and tried that light. It seemed that if only I wanted it enough, if only I could focus my whole self on making electricity flow through those miles of colored wires to this little switch, then there would be light. It seemed as though it were up to me, as though I could do it, if only I tried hard enough. I closed my eyes, held my breath, and flipped the switch.

For a moment I was certain I could see light through my shut lids, but when I opened them, the bathroom was dark. My hand dropped from the switch. I felt my whole self slump into a defeat so vast there seemed no escape.

Then an even stupider hope buoyed me. If the electricity weren't back yet, the phone might be, but until someone thought to call us, we would never know it. I leapt to the kitchen to pick up the phone the way I used to race for it when it rang. I snatched the receiver off the cradle, slammed it to my ear. But instead of the hum that had once made it seem like a living thing, there was silence. Flat blank silence.

Beyond that silence I heard the relentless tick of Eva's metronome, the rhythmless noise of the rain.

Though the rain that falls so steadily on the ragged yard and patient trees might well be the same rain that fell a week ago, the calendar claims today's the first of February. We're down to eight and one-fourth teabags, and I'm more than halfway through the F's.

Today I reached *Forest, an extensive and complex ecological community dominated by trees and having the potential for self-perpetuation.* But before I could memorize the five major types of forest, along with their typical tree densities, climates, and soils, I was interrupted by yet another memory, and I raised my gaze from the page to look out the window at the forest.

As soon as Eva and I were able to toddle, our father took us on long, slow rambles down the dirt road that led from our clearing through the woods. We looked at wildflowers, listened to birds, and splashed in the clear trickle of the creek. We picked up leaves and poked at centipedes and waterstriders while he towered above us, patient and benevolent as a tree.

When we got a little older, Mother occasionally gave us permission to journey by ourselves down the quarter-mile of road to the bridge so we could meet Father on his way home from work. *Don't cross the bridge,* Mother would warn, until the bridge seemed such a natural boundary it never occurred to us to cross it.

What we really wanted to do was play in the forest. Every flower and bird and mysterious crashing beckoned for us to leave the road, to clamber up through the trees and ferns, but our mother insisted that we keep to the road.

"You're too young," she said when, at six and seven, we begged to go exploring. "You'll get lost. It's not safe."

"Please," we sang.

"What do you want to do there, anyway?"

"We just want to explore," we pleaded, "go for walks, maybe build a fort. We'll be careful."

"You can build a fort in the clearing," she offered.

"It's not the same if it's not in the forest."

"But there're ticks and rattlesnakes and poison oak in the forest."

That stopped us for a moment, until Eva reasoned, "There's ticks and rattlesnakes and poison oak in the clearing, too. Remember when Daddy found a rattlesnake in the woodpile?"

"Well, what about pigs?" our mother asked.

Mother hated wild pigs. They lived in the forest like ghostly rototillers, seldom seen, but leaving deep gashes in the earth where they rooted for grubs and bulbs, and dirty muck holes where they wallowed in the streams. Although no one we knew had ever been hurt by one, they seemed to embody all our mother's fears about the forest.

"They can weigh two hundred pounds. Their tusks are sharp as razors. Even rattlesnakes can't bite through their hides. They eat dirt and carrion," she said. "They could kill you. What are you girls going to do when you meet one of them in the woods?"

I was ready to stay forever in the safety of the clearing when suddenly our father broke in. "It's okay, Gloria. It'll be all right. Like it or not, these two are bound to play in the forest sooner or later. Besides, pigs are shy. Eva and Nell'll make enough racket to scare off every wild pig in Northern California. Hell, if there were any bears left, they'd run them off, too. I say let the girls go."

Mother glared at him, but in the end she backed down. She gave us each police whistles to blow if we got into trouble, and she bundled us in rules: we couldn't wander out of whistle-range of home, we had to stay together, we couldn't put our hands or feet anywhere we hadn't first checked for rattlesnakes, we had to submit to a tick search before we came back inside, and we couldn't eat anything but the snacks she packed for us.

"Don't you girls ever eat anything wild," she reminded us each time we left the clearing. "Do you understand? Wild plants can kill you."

Okay, Mother. Yes, Mother, we promise, we said as, thrilled and scared, we edged towards the woods.

Ours is a mixed forest, predominantly fir and second-growth redwood but with a smattering of oak and madrone and maple. Father said that our land had once been covered with redwoods a thousand years old, but all that remained of that mythic place were a few fallen trunks the length and girth of beached whales and several charred stumps the size of small sheds.

When we were nine and ten, Eva and I discovered one of those hulks and claimed it for our own. About a mile above our house, we found a redwood stump that rose out of the forest floor like the broken hull of an ancient ship. It was hollow, and the space inside was large enough to serve as fort, castle, teepee, and cottage. There we spent every minute we could steal or wheedle for the next two years.

A tributary of the creek that borders our clearing ran near the stump and provided us with water for wading, washing, and mudpie making. We kept a chipped tea set up there along with blankets, dressup clothes, and broken pans, and there we passed our days, playing Pretend.

"Pretend," one of us would say, as soon as we reached the stump, while we were still panting from the exertion of our climb, "we're Indians." *Or goddesses. Or orphans. Or witches.* "And pretend," the other of us would answer with the hushed intensity the game required, "that we're lost." *That we're stalking deer. That we're going to dance with the fairies. That a bear's coming to get us and we have to hide.*

Back then, it seemed the forest had everything we needed. Every mushroom or flower or fern or stone was a gift. Every noise was an adventure to be investigated. Frequently we glimpsed deer or rabbits or heard the call of wild turkeys. Occasionally we saw a grey fox or a skunk. Once we caught a glimpse of a bobcat when we were hurrying home to supper much later than we should have been. Twice we ran across rattlesnakes basking in the summer sun, but each time we were able to back away without disturbing them. Later we came across a pack of wild pigs, dark and blunt and thick-chested, snuffling their way contentedly through the autumn mast. Immobilized with terror, we watched as they poked and grunted beneath the oaks and finally drifted into the forest without a backward glance.

We never told our mother about the snakes or the pigs, and she began to call us "wood nymphs," laugh at our tangled hair and scratched arms, and forget to check us for ticks before she let us come inside. It was all idyllic, and at the end of a day in the forest we would abandon our imaginary lives and hurry back to the clearing and our parents and the cozy realities of hot food and steaming baths and goodnight kisses.

But then Eva started dancing and all that changed. In the beginning I tried to beg or bribe her to come with me into the forest. "Not now," she would say. "I've got to work on my *fouettés*. Maybe later." On those few occasions when I was able to convince her to pack a lunch and venture into the woods, our games felt forced and childish and we always seemed to return to the house sun-burnt, tick-bitten, and bad-tempered. I tried going up to the stump alone, but my time there always seemed to drag; the distant crashings of pigs or deer made me jump, fallen branches began to startle me with their resemblance to dozing snakes, and finally the forest came to mean nothing more than the interminable distance between home and town.

It rains and rains and rains and rains and rains and rains. The rain falls and falls, great silver needles stitching the dull sky to the sodden earth. Downstairs, the house is dark and warm, though all our mother's dye pots have been put into service upstairs, catching the rainwater that leaks through the roof our father never had a chance to repair.

When I open the front door to let in a little more light to read by, I can hear the stream hissing with rain. Eva stays in her studio, and above the drumming of the rain I can hear the ticking of her metronome, her hummed snatches of *Water Music,* and the brush and thud of her feet across the mylar floor.

For the last few days I've been craving hot dogs. Hot dogs—a bland sausage on a white bun, a ribbon of yellow mustard scribbled down it. When you bite, there's the pillowy give of the bun, the mild sting of the mustard, the tiny resistance as your teeth break through the hot dog's skin, sink through the grainless meat, and then the lovely gooey chew of bread and mustard and beef.

I can't remember the last hot dog I've eaten, though it must have been at the Uptown Café, with Eva and Eli and the rest of the Plaza-folk. Usually we all claimed those hot dogs were disgusting, made of things you wouldn't want to think about, cow's lips, we used to scoff, and who knows what other organs and parts. But occasionally one of us would order one, and then someone else would, and then everyone but Eva would be sharing ravenous, bloated bites. Now I want one so urgently I think I would give even this notebook to be back at the Uptown with a hot dog in my fist.

Even when Mother finally had to move to the hospital we all kept acting as though she would soon be coming home. Looking back, I truly cannot say whether we were driven by fear or hope, whether we were too cowardly to admit she was dying, or whether we were heroically clinging to the final crumbs of faith in her recovery. I don't know if we were being complicit or ignorant or innocent when we promised each other that she would be back home before her wisteria faded.

She seemed to be at her best late at night, so after work Father would pick up Eva at Miss Markova's studio, and they would drive home for me in the old Dodge pickup that had become the only vehicle Father had time to keep running. The three of us would drive back into Redwood as the sun was setting. There, he would drop Eva and me off at the Uptown Café, where Eva sipped a diet soda and I devoured a basket of fries while he went on ahead to the hospital, helped his wife through whatever procedures she had to endure, urged her to swallow a little broth or Jell-O, another sip of water.

When she was sitting up and the sheer strength of his love had forced a wisp of color into her wan face, he would leave her, drive back through the streetlit town to the café where I sat licking the catsup from my fingers, and Eva sucked the last drops of soda through her hiccupping straw.

Silently we rode through the quiet neighborhoods of Redwood to the little hospital where our mother lay. Eva and I sat side by side, staring out at the cones of light the streetlights cast, gazing with a dull hunger at the windows of the passing houses, through whose opened curtains we imagined we were catching glimpses of normal lives.

We were composing ourselves as we rode, making the transition from one world to another, and Father was lost in his own thoughts. At the time, the truck seemed filled with an unspeakable sadness, and yet now I remember those drives with longing. Despite all the worries and fears that traveled with us, our father was driving, Eva and I were still children in the warm cab, the streets were still blazing with lights, and our mother was still waiting for us with a smile that would illuminate her whole face.

———

This morning we discovered the bathtub hadn't refilled during the night, and for several minutes I was in despair, certain the spring had dried up, certain we would have to haul water from the creek, certain I would never have another bath.

"Why would the spring dry up in the winter?" Eva asked, checking the faucet handles to make sure they hadn't been turned off.

As usual, her question calmed me, and together we examined the water tank, and then climbed up behind the house to the little grotto where the spring seeps from the hillside. Kneeling on the earth beside the wooden cover, I could hear the murmur of water beneath, could smell its mineral scent. I shifted the cover off the concrete basin, and we could see that the drain at the bottom was clogged with silt. Instead of running down the pipe that leads to the tank in the clearing, our bath water was soaking back into the earth.

It took much of the day to clean it out, though most of that time was devoted to fetching tools, figuring out strategies, and forestalling problems. Our father had built our water system before we were born, and as with everything he made, it was both simple and temperamental—a perfect example of his idiosyncratic logic.

There were moments, as the springwater rilled over our cold hands and we labored to repair his work, that I felt a deep connection to him. But mostly I felt exasperated by the way he had always either done things for us or left us to figure them out for ourselves.

Finally we had the pool drained and cleaned and rinsed, the screen replaced, and all the pipes reconnected, and although the water that fills our tub this evening is a little murky, at least tomorrow night we will be able to have our baths.

———

After Mother died, our evening trips to town continued. It was almost as though the three of us were all so hungry for routine that even a routine linked to her dying added a sort of structure to our lives. Then, too, a trip to town was an escape from the house to which we could no longer pretend she would return, from the unwieldy burden of our individual griefs. It appeared our sorrow could not be shared, even among ourselves. On the surface Eva's suffering looked too much like my own, and our father's anguish threatened to subsume us all.

Besides, in the midst of the nightmare of my mother's death there were instants that shocked me even more than the vastness of my woe, milliseconds when I felt relief that she was gone, when I recognized there was a sort of freedom in being released from a mother, in being able to live on without her. And there were other times when I felt a surge of such searing joy at being alive at all that I appalled myself. Even wracked with misery, there were moments when the thrill of living was so keen it made my mother's death seem not too large a price to pay for such sensation.

I was aghast by the betrayal those thoughts represented, by the callous creature they proved me to be. If Father and Eva knew similar moments they never spoke of them, and I could imagine no way to tell them of mine without disappointing or disgusting them. So we each grieved alone, and looked forward, in our separate ways, to those nights when we could escape to town.

Every Saturday night, and, before gas got too scarce, often on weeknights, too, the three of us would pile into the truck after a hasty dinner and drive into Redwood. Once in town, there were always errands to run. We would stock up on groceries, stop at the hardware or drugstore, go to the library.

Finally, our business completed, Father would drop us at the Uptown Café, where we had been timid regulars since the days our mother was in the hospital. There we would begin the evening with an icy Coke and the throb of the jukebox, while Father drove across town to a quiet bar where he could sit alone at a little table, reading library books and taking measured sips of a single beer.

For a long time we were outsiders at the Uptown. Eva and I were country kids, homeschoolers, a breed apart from the quick town kids who seemed to own those vinyl-covered booths and chrome-rimmed counters. No matter how carefully I tried to dress for those evenings it seemed that my clothes were always just slightly wrong, and I could never get my hair to look like the other girls'. When we first began going to the Uptown, only the waitresses noticed and welcomed us.

The other kids all seemed so sure of themselves as they called for burgers and fries, punched their requests into the jukebox, and swirled from one booth to the next in what seemed like a sophisticated version of musical chairs. They bantered and joked. They pinched and pushed and hugged each other. They rolled their eyes. They leaned together to whisper and then exploded into laughter, and I yearned to abandon the morass of myself and become one of them.

I'm not sure how we finally crossed that boundary, but one night a few months after our mother died, when the midsummer sun didn't set till after nine and the air outside the Uptown was tender and fragrant in the long twilight, we found that the group in the café had swollen to include us as naturally as a stream accepts another few drops of water.

Maybe they were attracted by what had so terrified me. In the midst of my grief and shock I knew a kind of frantic joy. Against all odds Eva and I were alive, and maybe the irrepressible knowledge of our vitality gave us a sheen that more than made up for our homeschoolers' awkwardness. We had the passion of survivors, and survivors' lack of caution. We were immortal that summer, immortal in an ephemeral world, and the group at the Uptown must have sensed it and opened to let us in.

From that night on, every evening we spent in town began when we pushed against the glass door of the Uptown and entered to hear our own names ringing in our ears—"Nell! Eva! Over here! Come here!" We would hang around the café, gabbing with those who were there before us, flinging ourselves from booth to booth, sharing drinks and jokes, yelling out opinions about what songs should be played next, and calling out greetings to the new arrivals. Finally, when we had drunk all the soda we could hold or afford, and our group was overflowing the booths, a new restlessness would strike us. Then, in twos and threes and fours, we would spill out into the balmy evening, wander across the street to the grass-scented Plaza.

The Plaza was a city block at the heart of Redwood, a wide square of grass ringed by an unlikely mix of palm and redwood trees, crisscrossed by a concrete path, and dotted with wooden benches and mercury vapor streetlights. At one end was a gazebo where local quartets and jazz bands used to perform on Sunday afternoons, and at the very center was a splashy fountain into which Eva and I had once tossed the pennies our mother gave us for wishing. There we would congregate, along with the rest of the town's young people, our faces illuminated by the buzzing, orange-tinged streetlights as we grouped and regrouped, flitting like moths from one light to the next.

I don't know whether it was the uncertainty of the times that added a sense of urgency and significance to those evenings, or whether to all people there comes a moment when they feel as though they are the chosen ones, blazing brighter, hotter, fiercer than anyone else ever has or will. But now it seems as though, on some unconscious, pheromonal level we could already sense the changes that were to come. Now, when I look back on those evenings from the cloistered stillness of this clearing, it seems that the very air was charged with an intense thrill, and I remember feeling a sort of pity for everyone who was not us.

At eleven o'clock, our father would pull the pickup along the south side of the Plaza, and we would hurry to meet him, calling our good-byes over our shoulders, running like Cinderellas across the dark grass, crossing the vast divide between the keen immediacy of Saturday night and the sad and interminable rest of the week.

Despite the fact that, at the Plaza, I was surrounded by people whom I called friends, I still felt achingly alone. My days were spent studying, isolated with my books, tapes, and dreams of Harvard. I longed to be with someone as I had once been with my sister, back in those days before she had begun dancing, when she and I had lived like twin streams, chattering and laughing through the forest.

At first I tried to find a best friend among the other girls who congregated at the Plaza. But I was a newcomer and it seemed they had all known each other forever. They were friendly with me, but with each other they shared an entire universe of jokes and memories and a knowledge of TV shows, algebra teachers, and school lunches I soon realized I couldn't hope to replicate.

So I abandoned my wooing of the girls and began to consider the possibility that a boy might put an end to my loneliness. Of course I had observed other relationships between the boys and girls of our group, had seen them flare and die, and had even added my observations and speculations to the web of gossip that surrounded each pair. I studied those couples with a sort of confused longing as they talked together for hours, or gazed silently into each other's eyes. I saw them vanish into the darkness of the trees and watched them emerge much later, their faces soft and puffy, their clothes rumpled and mis-buttoned as they stood blinking beneath the streetlights. And I thought that perhaps my sorrows would ease, if only I, too, had a boyfriend.

But I had no idea how to get one. Under those streetlights my knowledge of *Anna Karenina, Wuthering Heights,* and *Romeo and Juliet* seemed to be of little help. I couldn't imagine what to do or where to begin. Once I tried to discuss it with Eva. "Don't you ever want a boyfriend?" I asked. But she only answered "What for?" with such astonishment in her voice that I could think of nothing to answer.

I always thought Eva was the prettiest girl at the Plaza, with her blond hair, her dark eyes and dancer's legs, and yet she never seemed to notice any of the boys who, in elaborate displays of nonchalance, drifted her way during those long summer evenings. She was nice to all of them and yet so self-contained that not one of them ever made her giggle or startle or blush. She never kept surreptitious track of any of them as they made their rounds from streetlight to streetlight. They saw that and sought out other girls. And only I ever seemed to notice what she had lost.

One autumn night, as a group of us stood on the dark grass beyond the reach of the streetlights, someone passed me a bottle. I could feel the slosh of the liquid it contained and I knew a moment of scare and thrill before I raised it to my lips. I leaned back into a long, bare-throated swallow and handed the bottle on as the shock of the alcohol ripped through me. I bit my tongue to keep from sputtering and was thankful for the darkness that hid my tears. But when the bottle circled back, I took another drink and found the next swallow was easier. It was almost like going down the high slide in the park for the second time—the slide was just as steep, but there was a line of other kids waiting impatiently behind me, and besides, I had survived one plunge, had learned the surge and tingle were worth the fear.

For one thing, after that first drink, I began to feel a warm, new comradeship with the people whose mouths had also touched the bottle's lip. It seemed my loneliness eased a little. Nobody said anything different, but somehow the usual talk meant more than it had before, as if our words were a kind of code that only hinted at all that resided beneath them.

After that night, I was always there when the bottle appeared, and I drank whatever it contained, usually beer or wine, occasionally rum, or gin, or brandy. It became the sweetest moment of the week, to stand with that ring of friends in the dark, drinking from a bottle that traveled from hand to hand. It was a ritual that sometimes struck me as religious and at other times seemed like a children's circle game, but always it helped to soothe my gaping loneliness.

———

Sometimes I wonder if someone will ever come for me, if there will ever be a boy—a man—for me to open to. I wonder if I will always be like this, alone, always forced to content myself with myself, my own hand tucked between my legs so that my body makes a kind of circle, a zero, enclosing the clean emptiness of nothingness, a mobius strip or an ouroboros, a serpent swallowing its own tail. I am a closed system, and I yearn, I ache, I hanker for someone to claim what I long to give.

And still the only face I have for my desire is Eli's.

———

All last winter the Uptown Café seemed to grow darker, Saturday by Saturday. Sometime after Christmas the neon sign in the window was turned off, then one by one the fluorescent tubes overhead burnt out and weren't replaced. Slowly the Cokes seemed to get weaker and weaker, the fries more rancid, and the burgers shrank until they almost disappeared. The juke box broke and was never fixed. Paper napkins and straws vanished. And more and more often, long before 9:00 closing time, the fat proprietor would come huffing around to each booth saying, "Okay, kids. Café's closing. You gotta go now. Come back soon, okay?"

We would grumble, order sodas to go—as long as there were still paper cups left to put them in—and reluctantly bundle ourselves to leave the café for the damp chill of the winter night.

By late January the power outages were becoming more frequent than the winter storms could account for, and by the end of February, the city of Redwood could no longer afford to keep the streetlights on in the Plaza. Of course we all made sour jokes about third-world countries in which the peasants' power went off whenever the castle lights were turned on, but in a way we almost welcomed the lack of the streetlights' glow and buzz. The night grew larger and closer and more stirring, and it didn't take more than an hour or two of milling in the darkness for us to discover fire.

It became another ritual, building that bonfire. Someone figured out we could use the concrete trough of the empty fountain for a firepit, and gradually everyone got in the habit of bringing something burnable to the Plaza— a splintered two by four, a branch, a piece of twisted plywood, an armful of pinecones.

When enough wood and trash had accumulated in the fountain basin, someone would strike a match, would touch it to the scraps of paper and dried grass at the bottom of our communal pyre. We all watched quietly as the fire snaked up through the tangle of twigs and boards and the first sparks rose to the stars. For that long moment we were all aware of the new darkness that pressed in against our backs, but then our solemnity would collapse and we turned our attention again to each other, to the web the group of us wove each Saturday night.

Week by week, as the weather began to grow a little warmer, the rumors grew wilder and more threatening. We heard that a new kind of hemorrhagic fever was sweeping the country, as well as more virulent strains of TB and AIDS. We heard that the rioting was increasing, that smoke from the fires of Los Angeles had grown so thick the airports had to be shut down, and freeways were clogged with cars that had been abandoned when their drivers could no longer see to steer them.

Even with the power gone entirely, it's funny how little those rumors meant to us at the Plaza on Saturday night. They were part of our entertainment, something to speculate about, a fuel for our conversations, but little more. The world beyond the Plaza was crazy and out of our control, but that was nothing new—hadn't the grown-up world always been like that? What mattered to us were the events inside the circle our bonfire cast, for it seemed that nothing as compelling could possibly be taking place elsewhere.

Sometime in March, there came a bottle of whiskey that burned like lighter fluid when I swallowed it. Again and again, I took my turn at it, until finally the bottle came round no more. Suddenly the night was more aromatic, keener and sweeter than it had ever been, and I felt a deep regret that I had never before been open to all its beauty.

Regret seemed a familiar emotion. My mind groped around itself, as though the light had been turned off in a familiar room, until I stumbled over the pain of my mother's death. Mournfully I reminded myself she had been gone for almost a year. But somehow even that pain was not as acute as my sorrow over the loveliness of the night.

"It's a beautiful, beautiful, beautiful night," I said to Eva. My mouth felt as though I had just come from the dentist's, but my eyes were sharp with tears.

My sister looked at me strangely.

"It's like music," I said, mournfully. "Beautiful music. *Water Music*. Beautiful night water music."

Then I was dancing.

I shrugged off my jacket, kicked off my shoes, tugged my socks loose, and I was dancing across the grass, leaping and turning and running, dancing to the music of the night. I was dancing to the stars, dancing instinctively what it had taken Eva years of training to learn. All of those people, those kids in their thick, dark clothes, I pitied them. They didn't understand what I knew in all my bones. They didn't know their own sweet muscles, the fullness of their own fine lungs. Gravity and I had come to some new agreement. My body was a moment's conjunction of flesh and fire and a music only I could hear, and I understood I could make it do whatever I bid.

As I danced I decided that I, too, would become a ballerina. I, too, would ignore my mother's wishes and follow in her footsteps. I knew in my newly discovered muscles that I could be as fine a dancer as Eva—maybe finer. We would train together, dance together. We could share her studio as we had once shared the forest. I would never be lonely again. Together, my sister and I would devote our lives to dancing.

I was turning back to find Eva, to call to her through that marvelous darkness, *Now I know. I understand. Watch me! Look at me!* when a final, glorious *tour jeté* catapulted me onto the sidewalk at the Plaza's center, and I *glissaded* my bare foot across the concrete, scraping my big toe over it as though it were chalk instead of flesh.

I was a heap on the sidewalk, stunned and gasping. The stars were wheeling overhead, and I was saying, "It's okay. It's okay. I'm okay," to the circle of faces that stared down at me. "I just tripped," I explained. "I fell."

I felt little at the time, although for days afterwards the agony of that drunken leap throbbed all the way to my thigh. But that night I was only aware of a new sensation in my foot, not pain, but simply change.

Eva nursed me home. She bandaged my foot in a bandanna someone had produced, and when our father came to pick us up, she told him, "Nell stubbed her toe." I think she said it more to protect him from the pain of having to know I was drunk than to protect me from his disappointment or anger, and at the time I was aware of feeling both grateful to her discretion and sorry that he wouldn't know the truth, for maybe that would have roused him from his indifference.

But Eva slid in next to him on the pickup seat, let me loll and doze against the door while she kept him company, and when we got home, she helped me into the house, helped me up to bed, while our father said vaguely, "Goodnight, girls. Hope your toe's better in the morning, Pumpkin."

In the morning I was hung over, so hung over that—despite my embarrassment—I couldn't attempt to hide my pain. But by the time I eased myself out of bed, Father had already left to cut wood, so there was only Eva to face. She was sitting at the table, primly sectioning a grapefruit, when I hobbled downstairs. My whole body felt misshapen. My skin crawled across my hollow bones and my brain clawed at itself. My toe was a minor annoyance beside the agony in my head.

"Hi," I said miserably, sheepishly, desperate for sympathy.

"Hi," she answered, giving nothing.

"Sorry about that."

"It's okay."

"Thanks for helping me."

She shrugged. "What else are sisters for?" she asked. She rose and disappeared into her studio, leaving me throbbing with pain and isolation.

Eva and I spent this morning in the pantry, sifting worms and bits of web from the flour and cornmeal, killing the powdery-winged moths that fluttered up out of the noodles and beans.

The first time I found worms in our food was last summer. Just as I was starting to pour a cupful of oatmeal into the pan of water boiling on top of the woodstove, I glanced down and saw a worm writhing its way up through the oats.

"Ugh," I said involuntarily, and flung the cup away from me, broadcasting oats across the floor and the hot stovetop.

My father was sitting at the table, slumped silently over a book whose pages he never turned, and he looked up at me in surprise.

"What is it?" he asked.

"A worm," I said, feeling sick and foolish. The oats on the stove began smoking and shriveling, and their smell added to my queasiness.

"Where'd it come from?" he asked.

"The oats. It was in the oats."

He closed the book heavily and pushed himself from the table. "Let's go see," he said.

I followed him to the pantry, where we opened the sack of oatmeal to see a couple of dusty moths flutter into the air. Clinging to the torn paper were clots of floury web. A few slender worms writhed through the flakes of meal.

My skin began to creep.

"We'll have to throw it out," I said.

"We can't," he said.

"We can't eat it."

"So what are we going to do, Pumpkin? Hop in the truck and drive to Fastco for more? We can't throw out food now just because it's got a few bugs in it."

"But we can't eat worms."

"Then we'll have to get rid of them. We'll sift them out, just like the pioneers used to."

"But even if we sift them, there'll still be the webs or eggs or something. There'll still be the idea."

He shrugged wearily, "Ideas won't kill you—and neither will eggs or webs, especially if you're hungry enough."

It was a hot, hard day, sorting beans and macaroni and rice, sifting flour and cornmeal through Mother's old sifter until I thought my hand would be permanently cramped. Together the three of us moved every can and sack and box. We washed the shelves and all the canning jars with boiling water and the last of the bleach and dried them and filled them with sifted flour and sorted grain. The whole time we worked, it was all I could do to keep from crying, to think of all our food infested with worms, to think of worms in my mother's pantry.

This morning it was a chore like any other, and I was immune to both memory and queasiness until, after an hour or so of killing moths and sifting out their larvae, I happened to look up and catch sight of the shelf our father used to call the "wine cellar." Suddenly, I was remembering again, was possessed by memory, awash in it, and though the memory triggered by those last two dusty bottles was of an unimportant event, I relived it with such anguish that for a moment I couldn't breathe.

It was sometime early in September, only days before Father died. We were just sitting down to our dinner of corn and tomatoes and boiled potatoes, when suddenly he jumped up and vanished into the pantry.

"The best occasion is no occasion," he said, returning a moment later with a bottle of red wine and three of our mother's crystal wine glasses. He uncorked the bottle, touched its lip to the rim of a glass, and poured it full.

With a bow he handed it to Eva and poured glasses for me and for himself. Then he lifted his glass to us. "Here's looking at you, kids," he said so heartily I cringed, torn between my relief that he seemed to be trying to return to his old self after more than a year and my resentment that it had taken him so long.

He twirled the glass, sniffed its contents, sipped, and nodded to himself appreciatively. "Well, girls, drink up and tell me what you think—is alcohol all we grown-ups've cracked it up to be?"

Eva shot me a look of cold irony, and I knew that she, too, was remembering my Saturday nights at the Plaza. But she said nothing. She took a single sip and left the rest untouched. I drank mine slowly, trying not to think of Eli, and it did seem to have an unfamiliar taste—drunk indoors, out of a glass, and with my father. Father emptied his glass, then Eva's, and then the bottle, straining as he did so to keep up a patter of jokes and talk, as though he were trying to conjure happiness out of air.

It was painful to watch him try to force an animation he didn't feel, but every flat joke and half-failed conversation only added to the tally of offenses I was, almost reluctantly, continuing to keep against him. I sat woodenly, unwilling or unable to respond until finally, the bottle finished, we each went up to bed.

After that, all the alcohol that remained in the house were an almost-empty bottle of sherry and a bottle of Grand Marnier so covered with kitchen grime and dust you could no longer see how much liqueur it contained.

"We'll hang on to those two," Father had said that night, "for medicinal purposes—snake bite, frost bite, or childbirth. Which means," he continued, "there won't be a whole lot of drinking going on around here any time soon, unless the polar ice caps start to shift or one of us gets lucky and gets attacked by an obliging rattler."

We do hang on, I thought as I sifted the wormy flour—*and on*—*and all that attacks is memory, all I suffer is regret.*

———

I quit reading today at *Hershey, Milton Snavely.* Why is it that of all I've lost, sometimes it's food I miss the most?

Although I didn't know it at the time, somewhere among those figures bending over me while the night sky reeled and my toe bled, was Eli—Eli with his mane of tawny hair, Eli with his slow hazel eyes, the stud of an emerald jabbed in his right ear lobe, and a harmonica cupped to his mouth, Eli the loner, Eli who came up to me the Saturday after my fall and said, "I saw you dance." Not, *How's your toe?* Or, *What did your Father say?* Or even, *Were you hung over?* but, *I saw you dance.*

He never asked about my toe, although I was still hobbling and hopping. Instead he said, "I saw you dance," and I knew he had seen both my leaps and my fall. I felt naked—proud and embarrassed at the same time. His words took my breath away. They put nipples on my breasts, put an arch and twist in my waist, and the hint of want in that newly discovered place between my legs.

Those were the first words he had ever spoken directly to me, though of course I knew him, had catalogued him along with all the other Plaza-goers, and had even tried to evaluate his potential as the boyfriend who would relieve my loneliness. But although I appreciated his sly humor and the hunger of the music he played, he seemed to be surrounded by a shield of self-possession I had no idea how to penetrate.

Eli had a sort of remoteness I found both exciting and oddly familiar. A loner, an observer, he always seemed to be hovering at the edge of things, and in that reticence I liked to think I recognized myself. I liked to think it was my own sophistication that kept me, too, from belonging entirely to the group, and I imagined Eli and I were two of a kind, grown-ups condescending to be kids while the rest of the group were kids playing at being grown-up.

I saw you dance, he said, and from that moment it seemed we were paired. The rest of the evening we stood facing the bonfire side by side, and I basked in the warmth of my proximity to him, in the sound of his voice in the darkness above my head. True, he played his harmonica almost as though I weren't there, but standing beside him I felt alive in a way I had never felt before, each pore open, every cell awake, and it seemed impossible that I could be so intensely aware of his presence if he weren't equally aware of mine.

He didn't speak much, but it seemed that everything he said—about the job he had lost when the lumberyard closed down, about the motorcycle helmet he wanted to trade for another harmonica, about the outrageous price of gasoline, and where we might find more wine—contained an underlayer of meaning intended for me alone.

I returned the next Saturday ready to marry him, ready to dump my whole sad life at his feet, to give up my plans for Harvard and live with him forever in Redwood. I had borrowed Eva's Navajo blouse with its row of silver buttons and its wide velvet sleeves, and after the sun went down, I almost froze rather than cover it with my jacket. But although I spent the entire evening in a froth of anticipation, Eli never came.

All that week I fretted, vacillating between my fear that he didn't like me and my certainty that he had died. But the Saturday after that he was back at the bonfire again, and I spent the evening by his side, giddy and glowing, listening fervently when he spoke, and saying little myself. Late in the evening he played a long piece on his harmonica, something halfway between an elegy and a lullaby, sweet and hard and sad. It was a music that both flayed and cradled me and I was convinced he was playing it for me, to me, about me. I was convinced his music was telling me, *I understand, I know, and everything's okay.*

I was convinced we were linked by a wordless awareness of each other's presence, and when, just minutes before my father arrived to drive us home, Eli put his hand on my waist, I swear I could hardly breathe because of the connection between us. Oh, I will always remember that moment when, even with the universe spackled above us, bright with an infinity of stars and dark with infinite space, it was impossible for me to believe that Ptolemy wasn't right, that our own Earth, our little tribe, and Eli's hand on my waist were not the center of everything there was.

The next Saturday he was absent again, and I spent all that week studying with a morose and ferocious single-mindedness. By the following Saturday, I had persuaded myself I had imagined the whole thing. But that night Eli was waiting by the trees at the edge of the Plaza when we arrived, watching as I called good-bye to my father and swung the truck door shut behind me.

It was the end of April, the first warm evening of the season. The air was smooth as breathable water, the lingering sunset bathed everything in orchid light, and there was Eli, standing on the sidewalk in front of us.

"Hello," he said. Eva answered, "Hello," and *chassé* past him towards the freshly kindled fire.

But I stopped, stood facing him, equally wary and rapturous.

"Hello," he said again, quietly this time, as though that single word were too private a thing for him to want anyone else to overhear.

I longed to ask him *Where were you last week? What do you do when you're not here? Do you like my hair like this?* I wanted to tell him about my mother's funeral, my father's silences, my latest breakthrough with integral calculus, what I had eaten for dinner. Instead I said, "Hello."

"Here," he answered, flourishing something in my direction.

I took it and saw it was a deep crimson rose, its outer petals already loose and soft, its inner petals still curved tightly around each other.

He must have misinterpreted my silent delight because he asked hurriedly, "Don't you want it?"

"Yes," I answered, tucking it into my hair, where it stayed all evening while I tried to ignore its awkward weight against my ear and the poking of its stem and thorns.

At home the next morning, in the private daylight of my bedroom, I ate one of its petals, tucked another in my bra, and set the rest of the rose in a vase, where I studied it like an icon for the next few days, trying to extract love from those shreds of crimson protoplasm.

So it continued, Saturday by Saturday through May and into June. Some nights Eli would not come, and sometimes when he came he hardly noticed me. Even when he did, I always felt stiff and tongue-tied in his presence, my jokes too elaborate, my conversations too serious, my silences too long. Still there were moments when it seemed that all the electricity Redwood had lost was arcing between us.

During the long weeks between Saturday nights, I studied calculus and memorized irregular French verbs and planned weddings and named babies. I outlined European history and read the *Illiad* and learned the Krebs cycle and practiced writing Eli's name. I held my breath for luck, wished on falling stars and four-leaf clovers. Even here it's all so embarrassing to admit.

My father was so immersed in his own sorrows he never noticed what I was doing, but Eva finally did.

"What's the deal with that guy?" she asked one Sunday morning in early June when Father was in the garden and she and I were back in the utility room, washing our laundry in the galvanized sink that was so heavy its weight was warping the rotten floor.

"What guy?" I said cautiously as I grabbed a pair of water-laden jeans and began scrubbing the unwieldy denim against itself.

"Eli."

"What about him?" I asked, thrilled to hear his name spoken in my home.

"What about him?" she echoed.

"I like him," I answered courageously, vigorously dunking the jeans.

"Why?"

"Because," I began. And stopped.

Eva had quit scrubbing to watch me. "Because what?"

"Because." I said it indignantly this time, as though it were more than answer enough to such a stupid question.

"He must be at least twenty."

"So?"

"When's he going to college?"

"I don't know. We haven't talked about it," I said, trying to make it sound as though we had been too busy talking about other things.

"Has he ever read a book in his life?"

"Well, sure."

"What one?"

"What difference does it make what one? You don't read, either."

"Yes, but you do."

"So?"

She looked at me curiously. "If I had a boyfriend, he'd have to know ballet."

At the time I told myself she was jealous, and after that I wrote out long lists of reasons why I liked Eli, why he was right for me, so that the next time she asked, I wouldn't have to falter for an answer. But she never asked again.

Sometime at the end of June, when the garden was beginning to burgeon and the summer heat lingered long into the darkness, there came a Saturday night when on the way home from town our father said, "Girls, I hate to disappoint you, but I'm afraid that was our last trip to town for a little while. This is the second week there's been no gas. We've got about three gallons left in the truck, but I think we'd better save that for emergencies until we know for sure when we can get more."

I was sitting in silent agony on the stiff seat between him and Eva, and his words wrenched me out of my private misery, took my breath away.

"But we've got to go back next week," I gasped.

He was gazing into the beam of light the truck thrust ahead of itself and when he spoke, he sounded distracted. "Why?" he asked.

"Because," I answered desperately, unable to say more.

Because I had to see Eli.

I had gone into town that evening with a scheme as desperate and definite as though I were going to rob a bank. I had decided I was finally going to break through the barriers of reserve that kept us apart. All week I had imagined my plan, going over and over it as though it were a movie script, lovingly changing a word here, a gesture there, until I was as certain of its outcome as if I had already lived it.

I had decided that my need for a tangible connection with Eli was greater than either my pride or my fear, and I planned to wait until we had had our share of whatever bottle was circling, and then to take his hand and lead him from the group.

Night after night I had watched other couples return from their forays into the trees, soft and loose and cozy in each other's company, and it seemed that if only Eli and I could find our own nook in the darkness, away from that oppressive ring of firelight and friends, then together we would surely find a way to express the force that was building between us. I thought with our bodies we could forge a path for our words to cross, and I was convinced that if only I could feel comfortable in Eli's company, I could slough off all my sorrows.

I had spent all afternoon getting ready, heating water for my bath, brushing my hair dry in the sun, dressing as carefully as I could. By the time our father dropped us off at the Plaza, I was thrilled, terrified, and numb, and I felt like both a hunter and a deer as I waited for Eli to arrive.

But he came late that night. For three long hours I suffered, watching surreptitiously as each newcomer joined us at the bonfire, each time feeling a new twist of agony when I realized it wasn't he. Of course I was too proud and shy to ask anyone where he was, and when, every now and then, someone asked me, "Where's Eli?" I had to shrug, and answer as carelessly as I could, "Who knows?"

The bottle appeared, and circled, and was emptied, and still he hadn't arrived. Other couples had long since drifted off into the darkness and were already beginning to straggle back to the fire. The fire itself was sinking to embers. I saw my plan twist and snarl like a tangled warp, and my mind raced back and forth through that now-familiar maze of worry and indignation.

Finally, half an hour before our father was due to pick us up, Eli appeared. I had given up on him and was standing by the waning bonfire, tense and seething, when some instinct made me turn to look behind me. He was strolling up the moonlit walk as though he had no reason to hurry. When he saw me watching him, he lifted his arm and pointed his forefinger at me as though he were shooting a gun or choosing a prize. It was an intimate gesture, both ironic and proprietorial, and usually it would have delighted me. But before he reached me, he stopped to talk to a group of people standing back from the ebbing fire.

"Hey, Eli," I heard them say. I heard his voice answering, heard the first low notes rise from his harmonica, and I turned back to face what fire was left with tears burning in my eyes like acid. As my blurred vision melted the flames, I suddenly realized I had no right to feel hurt or angry, no right to complain or be indignant. Our relationship was that undefined. We couldn't even fight. We had never even admitted the bond that would make a fight possible. In some way we were more remote than strangers because strangers at least have the possibility of yet unmade connections.

I stared into the fire until the flames reassembled themselves and my eyes reabsorbed their tears, and when he finally drifted over, I was in an animated conversation with someone else. When I heard the honk of my father's horn, I managed to say good-bye to the group without ever acknowledging Eli's glance, and I made myself skip across the dark grass towards the waiting truck as though he had never crossed my mind.

"Because," I said again, in lame answer to my father's question, "we'll need food."

"I think we're pretty well stocked for a month or so," he said, "especially with the garden doing so well."

"But there's people we should say good-bye to," I blurted.

"Anyone in particular?" I knew he was trying to lighten the blow of having to stop our only entertainment, and normally I would have ignored him, but that night his joking was the perfect seed crystal for my frustration.

"Why the hell didn't you tell us before now?"

"Why, Nell, I didn't know myself until I tried to buy gas again tonight."

"Well, you should have known. If you'd been paying any attention to anything but yourself, you would have known."

In the wide silence that followed I was vaguely aware of Eva's quick gasp. Then my father spoke, and his voice sounded as even and weary as ever.

"You're probably right, and I'm sorry. But don't worry, Pumpkin. Your young man won't forget you. Or if he does," my father continued, "he wasn't worth a spider's fart in a rain forest to begin with."

"He's not my young man and I'm not your goddamn pumpkin," I said, flat and hard and loud. I could feel the truck awash with my father's baffled hurt and my own mean pain, and I have to admit it felt exhilarating to be that angry, to be flooded by an emotion that didn't threaten to wash me away.

I could have fixed it. It wouldn't have taken much—a word, a joke, a gesture. I could have put my hand on his knee, could have laid my head on his shoulder, could have said "I'm sorry." But instead I sat stiff and untouchable, glad that for once I could be the one to shut someone out.

—————

We went to town once more after that awful night. It was at the end of August, less than six months ago, though now it seems as remote as a dream dreamed in another lifetime. Eleven Saturdays had passed since we had last been to Redwood. We hadn't had power in five months, the phone hadn't rung in at least four, but still we talked as though by fall—or winter at the latest—everything would be restored.

For a few days our father had been doing some calculating in the pantry and the garden, and one night as we were eating supper, he said, "Girls, I think we'd better go to town tomorrow. We're running short on supplies and the sooner we restock, the better. I hate to use the gas, but I think we've got enough to make it into Redwood and back. Anyway," he sighed, "we have to try."

That night I heated extra water to wash my hair. I shaved my legs and plucked my eyebrows, and ironed my green sundress as well as I could by warming our electric iron on the stovetop.

As I ironed, Father counted his money.

"Good thing I got this out when I did," he said as he spread four hundred-dollar bills out on the table like a winning hand of poker. "The bank closed two days later," he remembered, and shook his head. "Wish I could have got to our savings account, too."

Eva added seventy-three dollars to the pile. I gave him fifty-nine.

We had no way of knowing if that were a lot or a little.

"Of course I'll pay it back, girls," he said, carefully writing out IOUs for each of us on the backs of old envelopes. "Soon as the bank opens up and I can get at my savings you'll have it back. With interest."

We were all up early the next morning, and when we set off, I felt like a girl out of a fairytale, a country girl going into town for market day, going to see the sights, to hear the music and taste the treats, maybe to buy a ribbon or a new ring, a girl making the long trip to town to see her sweetheart.

There can be no excitement greater than that, no other morning sweet as that one, steeped in pure, declarative joy: I was going to town. The sun was warm. I was wearing my green sundress. My hair was light on my bare shoulders. I would see Eli.

Despite my high spirits, the land beyond our clearing seemed oddly foreign. Already the road was starting to show signs of disuse. Weeds were beginning to grow in the fresh breaks and slides, and down the middle of the road ran a widening wale of grasses that slapped and scratched at the undercarriage of the truck.

Four miles down the road, we reached the house of our nearest neighbors. The Colemans were Fundamentalist Christians, and Father used to claim they were the perfect neighbors for us because we had absolutely nothing in common—not even a property boundary since the state forest land snaked in between us. But their once tidy house now looked ransacked. The windows were smashed, the front door hung by one hinge, and the grass in the yard was sparse and brown.

"Wait here," our father said. He grabbed the rifle, and we sat in the cab while he walked up to the house and called inside.

"They're gone," was all he said when he got back. "Looks like a sow's been farrowing in there."

"Where are they?" I whispered.

He shrugged, "Maybe they've moved to town."

Three miles beyond the Colemans', we reached the paved county road. As the truck picked up speed, we spoke less and less and our voices became hushed as if we were in a museum or at a funeral. Several of the houses we passed were burnt to the ground or obviously looted. A skinny dog ran out barking at us from a house with boarded-over windows. Finally, a few miles outside of town, we saw a tenuous wisp of smoke rise from a chimney.

As we neared Redwood, we saw a few more signs of life, a woman hanging washing on a line, a grim-faced man on a bicycle, a handful of children who stopped their game of chase to watch us drive past. Still, even in the bright summer morning, the countryside had the pinched and stretched feeling of a region under siege.

Finally Eva spoke. "What's going on?"

Our father cleared his throat. "We'll find out."

But there was little enough to find out. Although there were a few cars and pickups parked by the curbs, ours was the only vehicle on the road as we turned onto Main Street. All the shops surrounding the Plaza were darkened. Some displayed "Closed" signs, and some even had little clocks in their windows, with their arms pointing to 10 o'clock, as though tomorrow their well-dressed proprietresses would return and unlock their doors. Other windows were shrouded with sheets of butcher paper or plywood, and a few were broken, their jagged holes opening on emptiness.

As we drove past the Uptown, I peered through its windows to see posters peeling from the walls, the juke box on its side, and the tables upended. Across the street, the Plaza was deserted. Its once lush grass was dry and clotted with weeds and all the streetlights had been shot out. Only the trees still looked the same.

"Where is everybody?" whispered Eva. No one mentioned that our father had said the country people would have moved here, too.

Father said, "Think I'll swing by Jerry's and see what he knows."

Jerry Miller was Redwood Elementary's sixth-grade science and math teacher and one of our father's best friends. Jerry was a large, quiet man who had left a position at MIT because he loved kids and hated politics, and every Friday night for years he and Father had stopped to drink a beer together before Father drove home to the forest for the weekend.

Jerry's wife was a lawyer down in the city, and since she and my mother had never been able to figure out how to spend an evening in each other's company, our families weren't together often, though Eva and I always enjoyed the rare times we spent at their house, swimming in their pool while the adults talked on the patio and their laughter floated down around us.

The Millers lived a few blocks from the grade school in the only really prosperous neighborhood in Redwood. But when we drove down those curving streets, the long front lawns were brown and ragged, and jacked-up or tireless cars were propped by the curbs.

Father swung into the weedy circular drive in front of the Millers' tile-roofed house. He turned the truck off, but before he could open his door, a man came out of the house to meet us. He was scowling, and he held a shotgun pointed down at the ground by his side.

Father leaned out the window. "Howdy," he said in the firm public voice of a grade school principal.

The man nodded.

"Mr. Miller around?" asked Father.

The man shook his head.

"How about Mrs. Miller?"

Again the man shook his head. "Nope," he said.

"Uh-hum," Father nodded, as though it all made sense. "You wouldn't happen to know where they went, would you? Jerry is a friend of mine."

"Think they might of gone south."

"Down to the city maybe? Where Mrs. Miller works?"

"Maybe."

"When did they leave?"

"Don't know. Before we got here."

"And when was that?"

The man shrugged.

"So you're caretaking for the Millers until they get back?"

The man glared and jerked the gun barrel an inch or two off the ground.

"Well," Father said, still casually, "guess we'll be going."

The man nodded.

Instead of driving past him, Father backed the truck down the driveway, and we rode off in silence, trying not to imagine where the Millers might have gone, trying not to imagine what had happened to them or when we would ever see them again.

Finally Father spoke. "I suppose I'd better see how the school's doing," he said flatly, and we drove those few blocks in a dream, dazed by the film of strangeness that overlaid those familiar streets.

When we reached Redwood Elementary, Father pulled up beside the empty flagpole, and we sat in the truck, studying the place that had for years been his second home.

The front doors were chained together, and the long line of classroom windows were boarded over.

"Mike must have done that," Father said, referring to the custodian who had worked there longer than even he had. "Maybe Jerry helped him before they left."

We gazed across the open expanse of schoolyard to the empty play equipment. A rope hung ominously from the monkey bars, and the chains that had once held the swing seats dangled vacantly. There were no children anywhere.

After a long moment, Father put the truck back in gear.

"Aren't we going in?" I asked.

"No," he said, "there's nothing I can do there now. Besides, I think we'd better finish our business and head back home as soon as we can."

After another silence he added, "I'd love to find someone we know and maybe get some news. But I can't think of anyone I trust who lives close by. And we can't afford to waste any more gas driving around—the trip home is iffy enough as it is."

Ever since Father had said we were going to town, I had been cherishing an image of Redwood as the bustling center of a new—if temporary—society. I had pictured the Plaza thronging with people and ringed with booths like an outdoor market. I imagined farmers and tradespeople selling squawking chickens and fresh eggs, homegrown vegetables and homemade breads, and pretty trinkets and used tools. I had pictured street musicians and food vendors, and shoppers with baskets on their arms, stopping to bargain and gossip. I was even imagining carts and horses, as though, while we were waiting for the life we had known to start back up again, everyone had decided to play at returning to a quaint and picturesque older world.

For so long it had been my unquestioned assumption that if only I could somehow travel those thirty-two miles to town, if only I could cover the distance between our clearing and the Plaza, then I would see Eli, and that if only I could see him, everything would be right between us. But the empty Plaza crystallized the realization that had slowly been seeping through me: I wouldn't see Eli. I had no idea where he lived or how to try to find him. I couldn't call him. And I couldn't draft Eva and my father into spending our time and gas searching for him. Besides, I had no idea if he were still in town. I couldn't even be sure he was still alive.

And even if I did manage to find him, what then? The last time I had seen him I pretended to ignore him. Suddenly I realized that all my hopes for Eli had been as unreal as my fantasies about market day. I had no idea who Eli was. All I had known were my fantasies, and now they, too, were gone, choked and withered as the grasses of the vacant Plaza.

It seemed I was watching my final hope for happiness dissolve, and I felt a blinding anger sweep over me. I wanted to strike out, to be as cruel to someone else as life had been to me. I sat stunned, hardly breathing, trying to think of some hurtful thing to say to my father or my sister, trying to think of a way of making them suffer, too. But in the end I said nothing and only sat, anguished and empty, as we drove through the grim streets of Redwood.

Father drove to the Savewell grocery first, but its doors were boarded over, as were the doors of the rival supermarket by the padlocked post office.

"Maybe everything's closed," whispered Eva.

"Could be," our father answered, squaring his shoulders. He glanced at the gas gauge and then drove to the far edge of town, to the Fastco warehouse.

Fastco was the only discount outlet to have ventured into remote little Redwood, and although there were a number of locals who refused to enter it, it drew shoppers enough to keep it crowded. Everything in Fastco came packaged in enormous quantities—dishwashing soap in gallon containers, flour in fifty-pound sacks. Our father called it "Industrial Strength Shopping," and he delighted in teasing Mother about the size of the packages of toilet paper she brought home. When he discovered you had to buy a membership to shop there, he loved to explain that "Here in America, we now get to *pay* for the *privilege* of shopping."

Back in those days, the Fastco parking lot was always crowded with carts and cars and kids. But today, except for a few sorry-looking vehicles scattered across the vast expanse of asphalt, the lot was empty. The store windows were dark, and the signs taped to them advertising sales on canned tuna fish and fresh asparagus and fabric softener were faded and torn. We parked anyway, climbed out of the truck cab, and waited while Father dug a flattened role of duct tape out of the glove box. Together we walked towards the warehouse.

"Is it open?" asked Eva as we reached the unresponsive electronic door.

Father paused for an almost imperceptible second, and then said, "Only one way to find out." He pushed against the door and it yielded, opening into the echoing warehouse, chilly and lofty as a cathedral. We stood just inside the door for a moment, waiting for our eyes to adjust to the lack of light. High above us in the ceiling, beyond the network of steel struts, a few fiberglass skylights let in a faint smear of daylight.

"Is there anyone here?" whispered Eva.

"Anyone here?" called Father.

"You bet," came a hearty voice from the darkness. "There's not much left, but as long as you pay cash for it, it's yours."

It was a shock to see that giant warehouse so dark and empty. The wide aisles were deserted. There were no harried mothers pushing carts filled with cases of disposable diapers and huge boxes of sugared cereals. There were no retired couples stocking up on birdseed or booze. There were no forklifts sweeping around the corners of the displays, growling and beeping as they moved pallets of canned peaches or paper towels or bleach.

And there seemed to be no food. The enormous shelves that reached from the concrete floor halfway up to the distant ceiling were all but bare. What we could make out on them looked more like trash than groceries, some heaps and scattered piles of junk, a few crushed boxes and flattened cans.

"We're too late," whispered Eva. "There's nothing left."

But our father was already at work, untangling a shopping cart from the collection at the front of the store. He pushed it towards the first aisle with a show of his old determination. "There's plenty left," he called back to us with a purposefulness that felt contagious. "We just have to hunt for it. Grab yourselves one of those All-American shopping carts, girls, and follow me."

We began the once-familiar ritual walk up and down those aisles, our steps echoing on the concrete floor, our voices hushed and timid in the gloom. We soon saw that Father was right—here and there, on the great sheets of plywood that served as shelves a little salvageable food remained.

The aisle we entered first had once been stocked with baking goods. Now, strewn at random over the shelves were a dozen or so pint bottles of imitation vanilla extract, some enormous packages of paper liners for muffin tins, and several institutional-sized containers of garlic salt and baking powder.

"These will come in handy," said Father, tossing the baking powder and garlic salt into his cart.

"What else do we need?" he asked, and we looked at each other, unsure of how much of the irony in that question was intended.

"Flour," said Eva, and we pushed past shelves empty except for a sprinkling of cocoa and a broken box of corn starch.

Sprawled in the shadows at the very back of a bottom shelf, we found half a dozen fifty-pound sacks of flour, but when we stooped to heave them onto Eva's cart, we saw they were all half-empty, and when we tried to lift them, we only succeeded in spilling great puffs of flour.

"Thought we might need this," said our father, pulling the duct tape from his pocket. "Nothing's junk, as long as duct tape will fix it," he said, quoting himself in an epigram that used to make our mother cringe.

We helped him patch the sacks with great X's of tape, helped him lift them onto the cart. "This'll last us six months, easy," he said, dusting off his hands and his pants legs, "unless Eva decides to quit being a ballerina and take up Sumo wrestling."

"Shouldn't we leave some for someone else?" Eva asked as we loaded the last unwieldy sack onto her cart. She pointed to the eye-level signs that said *Remember the Other Guy* and *Limit Yourself—Avoid Government-Imposed Rationing!*

For a moment our father looked stricken. Then he said, "We're not going to be back here for a while, so I think this is a fair share. Anyway, no one else seems to be rushing to take it."

At the end of the aisle we found a ten-pound bag of sugar, though it had obviously gotten damp at some point because the sugar inside was as hard as concrete.

"It's no good," I said when I felt it.

"Why not?" asked Father.

"It's hard."

"It would have been snatched up long ago if there weren't something wrong with it, but it's still sweet."

We added the sugar to my cart.

The shelves on the next aisle held a few giant-sized bottles of toilet cleaner, some smashed cartons of dishwasher detergent, several mop handles, a torn package of sponges, and some green puddles from which the scent of ammonia arose. We took a plastic bag which contained a few splintered bars of hand soap, and Father taped up an almost empty box of laundry detergent and added it to our load.

"We need candles," Eva said. But all we could find was a single broken utility candle.

On we went, foraging through the dim reaches of the warehouse, past the aisle-length refrigerators empty except for puddles of dark water, past stacks of boxes containing blank video tapes, telephone answering machines, compact disk players, and computer programs, as we searched for usable supplies and edible food.

Further back in the warehouse, where the dark grew even denser, we discovered overlooked cans of soup, tuna fish, fruit cocktail, and sauerkraut. All of them were rusted or dented and most had lost their labels, but we added them to our cart anyway, along with two ten-pound boxes of crushed spaghetti and one of broken macaroni. We found some half-empty bags of pinto beans. We found a five-pound box of pulverized crackers and three large plastic buckets of peanut butter with tarry black stuff covering their lids.

We couldn't find salt or canning lids or toilet paper. We forgot to look for yeast and deodorant.

Finally Father said we had enough. "I wish we could have found some more canning lids, but even so, we're more than set till the power comes back on, especially with what we'll get from the garden and the orchard this fall."

As we wheeled our carts to the row of checkout stands that waited like sentries at the front of the store, we could see that a man sat at one of the middle ones, reading a paperback by the dim light that filtered through the skylight above him. He looked up as we approached, and I realized I had seen him there before. He was wearing a jacket with the Fastco logo, and the name *Stan* and the words *Assistant Manager* were embroidered over his heart.

"Ready?" he asked, smiling and jumping up from his seat.

"Yes," we mumbled, taken aback by his energy, by the odd normalcy of his being there at all, and by something else, a tiny splinter of craziness in his brown eyes.

"May I see your card, please?"

Our father looked blank a moment, and then pulled his billfold from his back pocket, fumbled through his collection of bank and credit and ID and library cards until he found the bright orange card that proved he was a Fastco member.

"Thank you, sir," said Stan after he had compared Father's face to the photograph on the card.

Then we watched in amazement as he lifted the mended bags and broken boxes and dented cans from our carts and stacked them neatly in cardboard boxes, adding everything up in his head as he went. "That's 3.49 and 4.95, that's 8.44, and 1.95, that's 10.39, and 7.39 is 19.78, and 6.49 is 24.27 and 3 at 1.89 is 29.94."

He seemed to be pulling the prices out of thin air, though I noticed he charged ninety-nine cents for every unlabeled can. It crossed none of our minds to question either his pricing or his addition.

Finally the last smashed can was packed away with the rest of our goods, and he turned to our father to say, "And 11.89 is 404.54. Will that be all, sir?"

Our father cleared his throat. "That's all."

"Then your grand total is 404.54. No tax these days," Stan added with a wink.

Our father counted out his bills and handed them to the clerk, who rubbed them between his fingers, studied them under a magnifying glass, and finally dabbed at a corner of each with a cotton ball he had soaking in a bowl of clear fluid.

"You seeing a lot of counterfeits these days?" asked our father.

"Not seeing much of anything. But you can't be too careful. That's why I have Sheila here to keep me company." He gave us another smile and reached down to pat the rifle we suddenly noticed leaning against the defunct product scanner.

"Sheila's been a real pal. 'Specially back when the looters tried coming around."

He shook his head in a sudden fierce disgust. "People wanting somethin' for nothin'—that's what got us into this mess. But Sheila don't go for that any more than I do, and they all soon learned that only paying customers are welcome here." His fingers lingered on the gun's barrel for a moment before he tucked the money Father had given him into the slot of the locked cash box that sat beneath his chair.

"We live out of town a ways," said our father, trying to keep the conversation casual, but lowering his voice as he spoke. "So we don't hear much news."

"Not much to hear," answered Stan, counting change from his pocket into our father's open hand.

"Where is everybody? The town looks pretty empty."

"Well, lots of people left, of course, following rumors. Some went over to Sacramento. Others headed south. Heard there was work—and utilities—down there. The good life, dont'cha know?" He shrugged. "All those rumors. Seemed too chancy to me, but then what do I know? No one's come back yet. But that could be good or bad, if you see what I mean."

"It happened so fast," I said.

"Yep." He looked pleased. "That's what most folks said. But they always used to tell us at the grocers' conventions how it'd only take three days of interrupted service for the shelves to start emptying. If you think about that, it's amazing we lasted as long as we did."

We nodded.

"Mostly the town looks empty 'cause people've left. But there's been some sickness emptied it out, too. The measles swept through, a month or so ago, took quite a few folks off. Lost my littlest like that.

"Then something else came—some stomach thing—and there went some more. And some around here's died other ways—ptomaine, a couple of cases of appendicitis. Even a cut'll do you, if it bleeds too much or gets infected."

"Where are the doctors?" I asked.

He looked at me blankly for a minute and then said, "Well, they're still around, I guess, some of them. Not that it does much good, now that all their medicine is gone and their fancy equipment is shut down. There's a woman in town does stuff with plants—and some'll go to her when they need help. I don't know, I'd rather take a pill, myself. But I guess that'll have to wait awhile. Knock on wood we won't need any more doctoring till things get going again."

"The people who are still left around here—where are they?"

"At home. Mostly people just keep close to home. You know—doing some gardening, keeping chickens, that sort of thing. Waiting. I suppose they feel safer if they're close to their own houses. Home turf and all."

We nodded our agreement.

"Me, I'm different, I guess," he went on. "I like to get out a little, come here, you know, and keep busy." He shook his head apologetically. "Not much going on, until the government gets back on its feet."

"What news of that?"

"Heard a rumor they may be taxing again by fall. But rumors—ha! Heard a rumor that some folks in Grantsville had built a spaceship and were selling tickets to the moon."

He gave a short, hard laugh, a sound of contempt that made his shoulders rise abruptly and then slump back down, and in that moment his face lost its practiced pleasantness and he looked desperate. "What they're gonna tax then, I don't know. Yours are the first real bills I've seen in a coon's age. Nobody's buying anything. Money's all gone."

"Any gas in town?" asked Father, folding what was left of our money back into his worn wallet.

Stan laughed again, that same caustic snort. "Old Mick Mitter over at Exxon claims he's expecting a shipment any day now. But you know Mick. Or maybe you don't. He likes to talk. Been looking for that delivery ever since May." Stan smiled his Assistant Manager of Fastco smile, though his eyes still held something that seemed both wild and vacant. He set the final box of groceries back onto Eva's cart and asked, "You folks like some help out?"

———

Today is a day worse than Christmas. Today is a day worth abandoning the calendar to avoid. It's a day that can never again mean anything but regret and loss and a sorrow like steel—so hard, so sharp, so cold the very air seems brutal. Breathing hurts. My heart aches to pump blood. Like Midas' Touch in reverse, everything I touch or look at, read or remember turns to dust. Because today is my father's birthday, and every thought I have of him is tainted by my memory of his death.

It was early last September. The mornings were chill with coastal fog, the afternoons heavily hot, and the evenings that followed were wide and mellow, with an air that felt like silk against our bare arms, and pink clouds high in the deepening blue of the sky. The garden was past its prime. The lettuces and spinach and mustard had bolted months ago; we had long since eaten all the radishes and peas, and we were getting to the end of the corn and beets and carrots. The beans and summer squashes and tomatoes were slowing down. Down in the orchard the walnuts were almost ready to harvest.

Father said we were weathering the storm. We would have our power back soon, he promised. The phone would ring again, and he would hike to town for gas. Soon after that, Redwood Elementary would reopen, Eva could resume her ballet classes and take her audition, and I could start preparing in earnest for my Achievement Tests in November.

It felt as though the tourniquet that grief had put on our lives was finally loosening. Father still frequently disappeared upstairs long before the sun went down, but the long hours he spent wood cutting and gardening seemed to lend him a new vigor. He was no longer as remote as he had been, and sometimes he even broke his mourning with a joke.

In the meantime, I found myself reading—or rather rereading—every novel in the house. I had long since worked my way through the final load of books from the library, my language tapes were silent, the computer was a dusty box, the calculator batteries were dead, and so I returned to novels to supply me with thoughts and emotions and sensations, to give me a life other than my own suspended one.

Siddhartha. M is for Murder. The Hobbit. The Golden Notebook. Tess of the D'Urbervilles. Catch-22. The Martian Chronicles. Adam Bede. While I was reading a novel, I was immersed, awash in the story it told, and everything else was an interruption. I could read for hours at a stretch, and any distraction—a question, a meal, the coming of darkness—made me bristle with impatience.

I occasionally found myself daydreaming about Eli, but most of the urgency had drained from those fantasies. His memory was like a worn teddy bear, something I had once depended on but had finally outgrown. I clutched it now and then out of old habit, but I had come to think that Eva was right, that Eli wasn't for me, and I had even begun to imagine his replacement—the boy I would meet at Harvard.

Mornings we canned.

Mother had inherited canning jars from every elderly female relative on both sides of the family, and occasionally she used to put up a few jars of treats—herbed carrots or spiced peaches or tomato chutney. After she died, we found almost a full case of Fastco canning lids in the pantry, and one summer evening, when the tomato plants were burdened with fruit, the beets were bulging out of the earth, and the beans hung like long fingers from their sagging vines, Father sat out on the deck, *The Complete Book of Home Canning* spread open on his lap while he read from table of contents to index. Finally, as the last pink cloud faded to blue-black in the sky above us, he closed the book, looked up, and said, "That does it, girls—this summer we'll eat what we can, and what we can't, we'll can."

After that he woke Eva and me at dawn each day, and all morning we picked and washed and skinned and sliced and packed and processed, until the creases and whorls in our fingers were permanently stained by the juices of tomatoes, beets, and plums, and our faces and arms were reddened and swollen from the kettles of boiling water it seemed we were constantly bending over.

The woodstove had to roar in order to keep the water in the canning kettle at the rapid boil *The Complete Book of Home Canning* required. By mid-morning, the house was so hot that breathing seemed an awful chore. Slowly, the heaps of fruit shrank and the piles of pits and slipped skins grew. Slowly the table was filled with jars of seething fruit, and above the fierce roar of the fire, we could begin to hear the little ping of canning lids sealing as they cooled. And slowly Eva and I would become less and less helpful and more and more sullen, until finally my father would say, "You girls run on, and I'll finish up this last batch. Hey—twenty-one quarts! That's a good morning's work."

Once I snapped, "What the hell are we doing all this for? I thought you said things would be back to normal soon."

"Oh, I don't know," he answered a little too evenly. "I suppose a jar of fruit could always come in handy—for trade, if nothing else. Besides, it seems a shame to let anything go to waste these days."

I scowled, and Eva and I burst from the house into the lesser heat of the day, leaving the worry and cleanup to him. Now I wonder if he didn't know more than he would admit when he insisted that we work every morning until all the jars we owned were filled, less than a hundred lids remained in the case our mother had bought, and even the windfall apples and bee-stung peaches were canned and added to the crowded pantry shelves.

When, at the hottest hour of the day, he finally emerged from the house, it was to work in the garden or to cut wood in the forest.

"I'd planned to reshingle the roof and shore up the utility room this summer," he said, "but right now it looks like firewood and food're more important." He said he wanted us to have at least three years worth of firewood curing by the time the rains came that winter. And he wanted extra wood to sell, too.

"We'll need to be a little ahead of the game this fall," he said once. "Public schools are guaranteed to be the last solvent institution on the block. And I've got two strapping daughters who'll be asking for dowries sometime soon. Or at least toe shoes, tuition, and lipstick. Let's see, wasn't that Kiss Me Quick Crimson or Move Over Mauve? Either way—gotta have us a little lipstick money put aside."

I knew he was trying to make right all that had soured between us, but even as I longed to joke with him, my throat thickened with resentment.

Part of me yearned to hear him tease me, laugh, and call me Pumpkin, but another part bristled, furious he could now be happy, and equally furious that he had ever been otherwise. I clung to the power of my anger, the safety of having the upper hand, and when he saw that his peace offering had once again been refused, he gathered his chain saw and his bow saw and left the clearing, calling over his shoulder as he strode away, "Once upon a time there was a poor woodcutter who had nothing to his name but a little cottage in the woods and two strapping daughters who needed lipstick...."

So he roamed the woods, felling trees that he left to dry in the summer's heat, or limbing the trees he had already felled, cutting them into stove lengths, and stacking them beside the old logging roads, ready to load onto the truck as soon as he had the gas to drive it with.

He had saved a little gas for the chain saw. "It's fuel well spent," he explained when I complained that he had gas for his saw but we couldn't use any gas to drive to town. "A chain saw's one of the most efficient little internal combustion engines there is. And right now I'm afraid we need firewood a whole lot more than we need a trip to town."

As the summer progressed, he used his bow saw and ax more often, but it made for tedious work, and occasionally we still heard his chain saw whining in the distance like a vaguely annoying mosquito.

While he spent his afternoons in the forest, Eva and I stayed in the clearing, halfheartedly weeding the garden, puttering in the increasingly spartan kitchen, or trying to pursue what had once been our passions. But more and more frequently we would abandon all pretense of work, would leave the stifling house for the stunning heat of the day. Side by side we would stretch out on the shade-dappled fir needles up by the water tank. There we would pant and doze, hoping for a wisp of breeze.

We were up at the water tank that afternoon. It was late in the day, almost time for Father to return to the clearing, for us to think about getting some supper. Out of sheer boredom I was painting my fingernails from my little stock of hoarded polish, and I can still feel the cool tickle of the brush, still smell the chemical tang rising from that squat bottle, still see the wet crimson ovals of my nails against my fruit-stained fingers, still hear the chain saw droning away comfortably somewhere just inside my awareness. In my memory of that moment I am too innocent to be anything but happy.

Suddenly we heard a scream.

It was a sound that shattered everything we had come to depend upon as real. For a vast, suspended moment, we could not assign meaning to that sound, and our minds raced, blindly trying to identify the cause of such a noise.

I had never heard my father scream, had never imagined such a thing. Like seeing him cry at our mother's funeral, it made me feel ashamed not so much because of the unexpected weakness it revealed but because I had never even considered the possibility that my father might weep—or scream.

It had to be his scream. There was no one else, though as we ran through the forest, I still could not really believe that sound was his, even when, breathless with fatigue and terror, we burst upon the spot where he lay, his thigh gashed and throbbing blood.

I'll always wonder how we knew to run in that direction. There was a whole forest for him to be lost in, and sound carries strangely between these hills, yet we leapt together from our daydreams and ran unerringly towards the echo of that scream, ran through tangles of poison oak and blackberry brambles, ran oblivious of snakes and pigs, ran to where our father lay bleeding his life into the earth.

His face was white, the skin stretched thin and taut over the bones of his cheeks. His shirt was off, and his tanned and sawdust-covered forearms seemed in sickening contrast to his pale chest. His eyes were dark and already growing distant, and yet he smiled when he saw us and gave me a look so warm and sweet and sad, so loving and forgiving that I sometimes think it is the cause of all my nightmares.

"It's okay," he whispered. "It's okay."

For a moment we hung back as though, even after our headlong run through the forest, we were squeamish, reluctant to get bloody, reluctant to have to witness the meat, the torn jumble of muscle and sinew and fat our father had become. I think we didn't want to recognize what had happened, not out of fear, but out of a wild hope that, if we didn't admit that our father was hurt, then he wouldn't be—if we refused to see his wound, then he would rise from where he lay, and walk back home with us through the fragrant summer woods.

But that moment passed and we were beside him, kneeling on the forest floor in a paste that was pine needles, humus, and our father's blood.

"What happened?" Eva sobbed.

His face was tight and sharp, and words were hard for him to come by. "A branch. Must have fallen. Hit me. From behind. Pushed me over. Onto. The saw."

"I thought it wasn't supposed to do that," I gasped, staring in horror at the blood-smeared saw with its chain of grinning teeth.

He grimaced. "Took. The chain break. Off. Last week. Stupid. Serves me. Right."

"What should we do?" Eva said, though whom she was asking wasn't clear.

Our agnostic father smiled, and with a sound as close to a chuckle as a dying man can make, he answered, "Pray."

"What should we do?" she asked again, and this time she was asking me. My first response—even after all those months of isolation—was to go for help. The numbers 911 leapt into my consciousness, and I saw myself racing back to the house, snatching up the phone, punching those three sacred numbers. Then I heard the blank wall of silence from the receiver that had been dead for half a year.

Next I thought of the Colemans four miles down the road, imagined running to find them. But I remembered their house was abandoned, a littering-place for pigs. I thought of driving break-neck to town for help, but there was no gas left in the truck. Finally I thought of the police whistles our mother had once hung like charms around our necks, and I believe my fingers even groped my chest as though, if only I could find that lost whistle and blow into it as hard as I could, I would shatter the barrier between the living and the dead, and my mother herself would leave her weaving and come running from the house to help.

I wanted someone to save our father. I was afraid to try to save him myself.

"Come on," screamed Eva, "we've got to do something." I fell to my knees beside my father.

"What?" I begged. "I don't know what to do."

I thought of the first aid kit in the bathroom, with its Band-Aids and iodine and emergency manual. "The first aid kit," I said, jumping to my feet and ready to run. "The manual will tell us what to do!"

But Father answered, "Don't go. Nellie. I'd. Miss you. Too much."

I felt like I had when I was eight and my fever had risen to one hundred and five, when my senses were so excruciatingly acute that the whorls of my fingertips looked like mountains and it seemed I could feel the individual grain and grit of reality. I felt as though my whole life before had been only a bland dream, and I had just now awakened—to the scream that had been beneath me all along, a subterranean current of horror running under every day.

The only door of escape, I saw, opened into madness. I could rise, and walk away through the sunny woods and never have my mind again, and some part of me wanted to do that. But it was my father who lay there, my sister who expected me to save him, and so I did what I could, though in the end it was nothing.

He was clutching his upper thigh with both hands, and when I eased his hands away and saw how the chain saw had tangled the denim into his flesh, I gasped. Unthinkingly I clapped my shaking hands against his thigh, trying to reshape his leg, to press it back together so that no more blood could escape.

I think his femoral artery must have been severed. Although it had almost quit bleeding by the time we arrived, every time he moved, a little more blood dribbled between my fingers. At some point I remembered to try to stop the bleeding by applying pressure to the artery. I pushed the heel of my hand against his pubic bone at the place where I hoped the artery ran, and I will never know if he might have lived if only I had thought to do that sooner.

He had begun to tremble, and finally I realized he was in shock. I got Eva to cover him with his shirt and elevate his legs by holding his feet in her lap. But even with his legs up and his shirt spread over him, he shivered as though the earth he lay on was covered with snow.

He said he was thirsty, and Eva reached for his thermos, and I helped him to swallow the last drops it held. But it was all so pathetically little. A little water, a cotton shirt, and our four hands could not heal his leg, and I knew of nothing else to do.

He died as the sun was setting. We held him, stroked his face, and spoke to him the way mothers speak to ill children, promising them it's all right, okay, murmuring the lies that transcend themselves, become a sort of truth simply because of the force of the love or need that causes them to be spoken. He listened to those lies, and tried to rest quietly. "It's okay," he gasped once long after it seemed possible for him to speak. "It's okay." Then he summoned his whole fading self, shifted his gaze to me, and said, "Don't worry. Pumpkin."

Long after his gaze had turned inward, long after even his trembling had ceased and his ragged breaths caught us by surprise, we talked to him. "I'm sorry," I choked out once, as the first tranquil stars appeared in the clear sky. But by the time I was able to say those words, I was speaking to a corpse.

And then we were orphans, alone in the forest, with night closing in. No matter what comes next, no matter what we have left to endure, there can be no worse time than that night. We had to stay with him. We couldn't bear the thought of leaving his body to the pigs, and yet we were terrified of them, and of the snakes and ghosts we were certain the dark was calling out.

It was too late to return to the house for blankets and matches, too late to go for the gun to bolster our courage against the dark, and so we wiped ourselves off as best we could on Father's shirt, though our hands still felt stiff and sticky, and the tang of blood was everywhere. We each found a fallen limb with the heft of a baseball bat, and, hunched together beside the body of our father, we watched the final color fade from the sky, watched the darkness take the land, tensed and waiting for the beasts or demons that would finish us off.

Nothing happened. We huddled together in the chill night, too numb with cold and shock to speak or even weep, fingering the branches in our laps whenever a twig snapped or a tree creaked or we heard the hollow call of an owl. We endured. Hour after slow hour we endured, while inside us life's scream ran on, unstoppable. When the stars began imperceptibly to fade, we were still there, still breathing, and our father was still dead beside us, his face both sharp and slumped.

But perhaps something had happened. For when the forest began to reappear from the blur of darkness, we hardly felt relieved to see it. It was no longer the benevolent place of our childhood nor even the neutral place it had been the day before. The forest that was revealed as the night receded was a hard, indifferent place, a place where a man could pour his life's blood into the soil, and the trees, the rocks, the very bloodied earth would be unchanged. Only the vultures, pigs, and worms cared about what had happened.

We buried him there because we had to, in the midst of that mean wood, covered with the earth his blood had soaked. When the sky brightened enough to be able to see the deer trail that had led us to him, Eva went back for shovels, water, towels, and a clean shirt, while I waited numbly beside his body. When she came back, we gave him a sort of crude laying-out. We washed his face, straightened his limbs, and wrestled the shirt onto his body.

We spent the day digging. We had chosen a spot close to where he lay to bury him, but when my first attempt to dig into the sun-baked earth yielded only a jolted shoulder and a scraping of dust, I was almost ready to give up. Only the thought of what would happen if we left him unburied made me stab my shovel back into the indentation I had gouged.

And so, one hard-earned shovelful after another, we dug our father's grave. We worked at opposite ends of the hole. By mid-morning our blisters had broken and bled, and the absurd crimson enamel had long since chipped off my torn nails. By noon we had drunk all the water Eva had brought, but we kept working, determined to dig a grave no pig would open—while the vultures wheeled high above us, their shadows gliding coolly across our sweating backs.

Only the threat of spending another night outdoors made us stop, for the sun was edging behind the hill when we quit digging. Since we still had to cover him with the earth we had moved, our good-byes were brief. We kissed him, edged his body to the crumbling verge of the grave, and pushed. There was no way to ease him down, no way to make it gentle, to mask the fact that this was a dead body tumbling into a pit. There was no way to avoid shoveling earth over his face, and there was a time, when his body was half-covered with dirt, that it was all I could do to keep the scream from erupting from my mouth.

The sky was growing dusky when we finally finished. We gathered the shovels and towels, the thermos and empty water bottle and bow saw in our broken, shaking hands.

"What about the chain saw?" Eva asked.

I looked down at it, saw the dark smears and clots of blood and shuddered. "Let's leave it."

"Dad would kill us," she whispered. "We might need it."

When we got home, we lugged the mattresses from our beds down into the living room. We bolted the doors, locked the windows, and took brief turns in the chill water of the tub. After we had used a little of our hoarded soap to try to rinse away what would never leave us, we each collapsed, dripping, onto our mattresses, too stunned and exhausted to eat or weep or even dry ourselves.

Then it seems we sat for days, each of us huddled into herself while the weeds took the last of the autumn garden. I think I would almost rather endure having to watch him die than have to face again the emptiness that followed. For what came next were days of complete inertia, when we played Backgammon or assembled puzzles like a couple of Alzheimer's patients waiting dumbly for something they've forgotten, able neither to grieve nor hope.

Somewhere during that time, my nightmares began. Night after night I dreamed my father was torn from his grave. I dreamed the pigs had found him after all, had rooted him from the earth with their brutal tusks. When I tried to shovel the dirt back over his body, I dreamed the shovel melted. When I tried to use my hands to scoop earth back into his grave, they dissolved and my arms turned to stumps. The only way I could bury my father was to cover him with my armless body, and I was afraid to touch him, afraid that touching him would infect me with his death.

But whether I touch him or I run, whether I'm dreaming or I'm awake, on his birthday or on all other days, my whole life has been contaminated with the fact that he is dead.

———

We ate the last of the green beans today. I pried the golden lid from the glass jar, tried both to remember and not to remember the heat, the kink in my neck, and my rich and sullen resentment as I bent over the bowl in my lap, snapping beans, while my father lifted another rack of steaming quarts from the boiling water bath.

———

Today we made a wondrous, marvelous, miraculous discovery! Today we found light and heat and music! We found the source of power and travel, the fluid that changes everything! Today we found gasoline! I could fill this entire notebook with exclamation points and still not show how thrilled we are.

It was midday. We'd been working in the shop all morning, untangling the stuff on our father's worktable and shelves. My fingers were stiff with cold and black with grease. My neck was cramped. My feet were numb. It was time to go inside, time to stoke the fire and rinse our hands and fix something to eat. Eva needed to practice, and I wanted to try to finish the J's before dinner.

I was sitting at the steel table, working through a sodden cardboard box of stuff. I had sorted it down to the final, hateful handful of grimy lock nuts, rusted steel wool, twisted wire, and unidentifiable little pieces of black rubber that might—even now—truly be junk.

Eva had finished with the shelves and was in a back corner, poking through an odious jumble of cans—enamels, varnishes, paint thinners, wood stains, body putties, rust removers, engine oil, axle grease, and canning jars filled with sinister-looking liquids whose homemade labels had long since faded or fallen off. It was the biggest mess we had yet to tackle, and sheer dread made us save it till last.

"Don't start that now," I said. "Help me finish this box, and we'll quit for today."

"I just want to see what's here," she muttered, pushing aside a fruit crate filled with brushes and paint rollers and rusty scrapers.

"It'll wait till tomorrow. Let's go in. I'm cold."

"Just a minute. Come on and help me move this compressor out of the way."

"Eva, it's cold. Let's go in," I repeated.

I could feel the fine grit of impatience in my throat as I spoke. Suddenly she gasped and dove behind the air compressor.

"Oh, Nellie, look!" she said, tugging a red plastic container up from beneath a tangle of garden hose.

"What is it?" I asked.

"I think it's gas!" she answered.

I leapt from my seat. But right behind the adrenaline coursed the fear of another disappointment, and I asked warily, "Are you sure?"

She twisted off the lid, took a whiff, and handed the container to me.

"Smell," she said.

I pulled air in through my nose, and the scent hit my brain like a drug. The raw, sweet, headachy smell of a thousand gas stations bloomed in my head. The smell transported me, resolving not into any one particular memory, but into the total feel of another time. For a moment my body was composed of other cells, cells the encyclopedia says have long since sloughed off me, and I was once again waiting at the gas station while one or the other of my parents filled the car with gas from the chugging black hose and the smell of gasoline permeated even to the backseat.

"It's almost full," Eva said, with satisfaction. "We've got five gallons!"

"I can't believe it," I answered.

And amid the cold clutter of our father's shop, we leapt and hugged and whooped like wild things.

———

But what yesterday promised to save us has now ruined everything, has soured the very air between my sister and myself.

We carried the gas container inside, set it on the table to enjoy as we ate our pinto beans. We were proud as prospectors who had just struck the motherlode. All afternoon our elation buoyed us—we had gas, gas, gasoline! and because of that, all our troubles were as good as solved.

Until we tried to agree how to use it.

"I'm going to go fill the generator," said Eva, as evening neared and our excitement had finally subsided to a warm and solid glow.

"What?" I asked.

"I'm going to fill the generator," she repeated, her hand already clasping the handle of the gas container.

"Right now?"

"Of course, right now," she said. "If I wait any longer, it will be too dark to see what I'm doing."

"But why?"

"For our celebration."

"What celebration?"

"We'll have a party tonight. We'll turn on the lights, take hot showers, wash a load of clothes. And," she added exultantly, "play some music. I'll dance."

"We can't," I said.

"Why not? I'm sure the generator still works."

"I mean we can't use the gas."

"Why not?"

"We've got to save it for the truck. So we won't have to hike to town."

"But we don't want to go to town now, anyway. Remember last time?"

"Yes. But sooner or later we'll have to go, and when we do we'll need this gas."

"There's almost five gallons here. It'd only take two to get to town."

"And two to get back."

"So four. But that still leaves a gallon for now."

"Who knows how far we might need to drive before we can get more. Besides, what if one of us gets sick and we need to run the generator, or we have to use it in the chain saw or something? We might even want it for trade. We can't just use it up."

"We won't use it up—just enough for some music, this one time. It wouldn't be wasted."

"Look, Eva, I'm sorry. But we've got to save it for an emergency."

"And what if it's an emergency now?"

"An emergency?" I repeated dumbly.

She answered in a voice both fierce and desperate, "I need to dance, Nell. I have to dance to music. Just for a few minutes. To give me courage."

I looked at her hands, her long fingers clutching the gas container's red handle. For some reason I remembered my mother's cold hands cradling her tulip bulbs, and for a second I was willing to go along with my sister's madness. But then I relived that moment in the forest when my father was bleeding to death and I remembered the truck was out of gas.

"I want you to dance. Eva, you know I want you to dance. But don't you see—that gas is our life insurance."

"*Our* life insurance?"

"Yes."

"*Ours?* Half mine?" she questioned.

"Of course half yours. Everything is half yours. You know that."

"What if I just use my share?"

"There wouldn't be enough left to do any good. We have to save it all. For when we really need it."

I waited for her next argument, but her face grew flat and closed. "By then it may be too late," she said and left the room, left me standing alone beside the grimy container, hating myself for saying no, hating myself for being right.

———

There's something wrong with Lilith. When I opened the hen house this morning, she was squatting by the door and didn't even move when Pinkie tumbled over her, rushing for the table scraps. I tipped the bucket to show Lilith its contents—a few thin potato peelings and an apple core nibbled down to the stem and seeds—and she looked at them dully. I pushed at her gently with my foot, and she waddled a few painful steps, but then she sank back down into her half-squat. Her vent looks distended and swollen, and there's an ugly discharge leaking out of it.

I have no idea what to do.

When we were little, Eva and I used to pretend we were the twins we felt we should have been, since for three days every year we were the same age. We dressed ourselves in matching clothes, called ourselves by rhyming names, were equal halves of a single thing.

When we were little, Eva and I were like a binary star, both of us orbiting a common center of gravity, each reflecting the other's light. We used to wake in the morning after having dreamed the same dreams so often we came to expect it. We began to menstruate on the same day, and each month we had our periods at the same time, until Eva's became sporadic because of her dancing.

Of course we argued. Almost daily we engaged in skirmishes of what Father called "The Snot-Stew Wars" because of the way we would reduce any dispute to its essential conflict: "It is not," one of us would say, in reference to whatever was the cause of our quarrel, and the other of us would answer, "It is, too." *It is not. It is, too. Is not. Is too. 'S not. 'S too. Snot! Stew!* By then we would be giggling, our delight in the ridiculous litany of our discord putting us back in harmony once again.

But now we can't even agree on what will save our lives.

When I went out to the hen house this morning, Lilith was lying in a heap by the door, and Bathsheba and Pinkie were pecking at her swollen vent. Horrified, I rushed at them, kicking and yelling. They scattered, squawking their indignation, leaving Lilith unmoving on the floor. Her eyes were open, and I could see her rumpled body heave when she breathed. I knelt beside her but I couldn't bring myself to touch her.

I ran to consult the encyclopedia, but by the time I returned with the volume for Poultry, Lilith was dead. I think an egg got stuck inside her.

I can't get along with my sister. I can't even keep a chicken alive.

I wish at least I had been able to touch her.

Eva was practicing. It was raining. The yard was filled with a grim mist of fog and wood smoke that the rain fell through but did not clean. I was trying to read the encyclopedia, pushing my way through the *K*'s as though I were slogging through wet clay, and it was all I could do to keep from cheating by skipping to whatever entry promised to hold my attention.

I rose from my stale place at the table to pace the room. In an unguarded moment I headed down the hall to Eva's studio. But then my memory of the gasoline came crashing back like another cold wave in a rising tide, and I turned away from her door. It had been three days since we found the gas, and still we had nothing to say to each other.

I wandered instead up the cold stairs and into the room that had once been my bedroom. It was dim and chilly and lifeless. It smelled of dust, and beneath that there was the faint sweet scent from some long-vanished sachet. Tacked to the walls were my travel posters—islands and oceans and castles and electrified cities at night. Stuffed animals and hair barrettes and bright strings of beads were scattered on the floor as if whoever had once lived there had left in a hurry.

We haven't yet tried to inventory our own rooms, since we know what they contain, and since they contain so little that will be of help to us. Idly I began poking through the drawers of my dresser, looking at all the clothes there was no longer any reason to wear. It seemed as though they belonged to a stranger, those knotted pantyhose, those anklets edged in lace, those jewel-colored knee socks. I buried my arms up to the elbow in a cool tangle of slips, and suddenly my fingers felt something hard.

I pulled it from the drawer, saw it was a little heart-shaped box my father once brought home for me from a conference he had attended. Almost absently I lifted the lid, trying to remember what treasures I might once have hidden inside. There, on the red satin lining the bottom of the box were a broken charm bracelet, a ticket stub, some brightly colored hairpins, a bluebird's feather, two seashells.

And four pieces of chewing gum.

And a chocolate kiss wrapped in silver foil.

I shut the box. I opened it again, and they were still there—four pieces of gum and a foil-wrapped kiss, put there back in a time when a stick of gum was nothing, when it took a handful of kisses to satisfy a moment's craving, back in a time when I was so wealthy I could afford to forget four pieces of gum and a chocolate kiss.

I wanted to sit down on the cold floor of the room in which I had been a little girl and stuff them all in my mouth at once, gum and chocolate together in a sweet, soft mass. Then I remembered Eva, and for a second I wanted to run into her studio.

But she had yet to forgive me for saving the gas.

I stood weighing the kiss in my open palm. I remembered all the times she used to get angry with me when she saw me eating sweets. *Don't let me see,* she would snap. *If you have to eat that junk, just please don't make me watch you. The smell alone could make me fat.*

By this time I had eased the silver foil off the kiss as though I were teasing the petals of a flower open. The candy inside was pale with age, but it still smelled like chocolate—the deep velvety smell that seemed the essence of all my cravings. I balanced it in the palm of my hand for a moment, and then, before I could think, I lifted it to my mouth and scraped the mottled surface with my teeth. Chocolate bloomed in my mouth, and my tooth-marks scarred the kiss.

Then it was too late to turn back. *Besides,* I thought, *Eva will never have to know I've eaten it. She was too busy, she had her dance. She'd probably be grateful. And anyway, she shouldn't have been so stubborn about the gas.* I thought, *I'll give her a piece of my gum.*

I sat on the cold floor, sucking the kiss, suffused with a profound and earthy satisfaction. I forgot Eva and the rain and the gasoline and ate the whole chocolate in a delicious, ravenous dream.

When it was over, I smashed the foil into a tiny, hard ball, dropped that little silver nugget back into the box with the gum, and tucked the box back into the drawer. Downstairs, I went straight into the bathroom. Facing my reflection, I wiped my lips again and again. Then I rinsed my mouth, drinking and spitting until I spat only clear water.

After a clear morning the March rain begins again. Eva retreats to her studio. I return to the *K*'s, reading so stupidly I might as well be running my hands instead of my eyes across the pages. I would sell my soul for the VCR to flicker on.

Just before dark, Eva comes out of her studio, opens the stove door, and sits on the floor, rubbing her calves and staring at the caged flames.

"What should we have for dinner?" I ask.

"I'm not hungry." She speaks to the fire.

"Rice and tomatoes?"

"I don't care."

"There's one jar of apricots left. We could have those."

"I can't do this anymore," she tells the fire. "I can't keep dancing to a metronome. I was working on my leaps today, and I know I'm not getting the same elevation I used to."

She looks up at me with the ferocity of a trapped animal. "Balanchine said that music was the floor for dancing, and I don't have any floor any more, nothing to push off against. It's like I'm just falling. Like I'll never leap again."

Suddenly she's pleading, "Nell, please let's use some of the gas. Just a little. Just give me ten minutes of music. Please."

I can't respond. I'm terrified to see Eva slumping towards despair, but I'm equally terrified at the thought of using even a drop of the gas.

Finally I say, "Eva, I'm sorry, but we've got to hold on just a little longer."

"I can't," she says dully. "I can't keep dancing like this."

"You've got to," I say, startled by the sudden realization of how much I've come to depend on my sister's dancing.

I grasp at the first idea that offers itself. Like a mother trying to distract an unhappy child, I say brightly, "I've got a surprise. It's not as good as the gas, but I found it yesterday, and I think you'll like it."

She doesn't lift her head as I leave the front room. She doesn't even look up when I come back downstairs with the heart-shaped box.

I thrust it towards her. "Open it!"

When she doesn't respond, I lift the lid, tilt the box towards the fire so she can see its contents.

"Look—four pieces of gum," I say.

"Where did they come from?" she asks, touching them with a tentative forefinger.

"I found them yesterday while you were practicing. In my underwear drawer. There was a chocolate kiss, too."

"Where is it?" she asks.

"I ate it."

"When?"

"When I found it."

"Where was I?"

"In your studio."

"While I was in there trying to dance, you were eating chocolate?"

"I didn't think you'd mind."

"You didn't think I'd *mind?*"

"Well, you were practicing. I didn't want to bother you."

"I can't believe this."

"You never eat chocolate, anyway."

"I still have a right to half of everything in this house."

"But it was my kiss."

"Why?"

"Because I found it in my drawer."

"Does that make the gas mine because I found it?"

"But it was in *my* drawer. *I* put it there. It was mine, back before all this began. Look," I said, teetering between anger and misery, "I'm sorry."

But she had already stormed back into her dark studio and slammed the door.

It's been two days since the kiss fight. I gave Eva all the gum, though whether she's chewed it or not, I don't know. It is no longer a pleasure we can share. Neither of us has apologized, but life dribbles on. Sometimes I want to scream at her, "It was only a stupid piece of chocolate!" Sometimes I want to weep, "I'm sorry, I'm sorry. Use all the gasoline. Forgive me." But I say nothing, and neither does she. We sleep by the same stove, share the same kettle of hot water, eat the same spare meals, and there are times when I could almost believe our quarrel was only another of my nightmares.

Even fighting is a luxury you can't afford if your whole life has been pared to one person.

We were in for the night. Bathsheba and Pinkie were in their coop, the wood was stacked by the stove, the doors were locked, the bath water was heating. Late in the afternoon, the few white clouds in the clear sky had begun to thicken and darken, and when the rain arrived, it was so steady and quiet it seemed almost a comfort. Eva and I still hadn't spoken much since our fight, but the silence was beginning to soften, and it felt as though a new bruised tenderness were developing between us.

We were sitting opposite each other at the table by the window, eating canned beets and shreds of boiled macaroni by the day's last grey light. We were eating quietly, listening to the sound of the rain and the noise of the fire and the hum of the kettle as its water gathered heat, listening to the gentle, familiar sounds that seemed to ease the night in around us.

There was a knock on the door.

It was a light *tap, tap* that tore through us like a scream, left us each paralyzed in a wake of adrenaline. We sat stunned for a moment. And then it came again—three more quick taps against a door that hadn't been knocked on for what seemed like years, the sound that meant either our deepest fears or our greatest hopes had finally arrived.

"Open the stove," I hissed at Eva.

She knelt, eased the stove door open. A little firelight filled the room.

I fumbled in the coat closet and pulled out our father's gun, but I couldn't find the bullets. I didn't know how to hold it or where to point it, so it stuck out in front of me like a stiff third arm, and I was almost as afraid of it as I was of whatever was outside. I slipped to the door, pressed myself against it as if I could feel the intent of the person it hid from us through some pulse in the wood itself.

"Who is it?" I growled—or tried to—through a throat clogged with fear.
"Nell?"

"What do you want?"

"Is Nell there?"

"Oh," whispered Eva, rising from the stove, looking at me.

"Nell? It's Eli. Is that you?"

Suddenly I was wild with relief. I felt the quick stab of Eva's glance, but I
didn't stop to care. A giddy sense of joy flowed down me like a warm rain,
and my fear turned to thrill. In the second it took me to unbolt the door, I
tried to remember what I was wearing, whether my hair was combed.

It wasn't the Eli of a year ago who stood outside. He seemed larger, his
features stronger. His face was wet with rain, and rain dripped from his mat-
ted hair down the poncho that hung to his knees, covering the pack on his
back so he looked like a huge sea turtle.

Perhaps it was just the shock of seeing any person other than my sister,
but for a moment I wanted to slam the door shut, to pretend we'd never
heard that knock, to stay, if not safe, then at least familiar with all that threatened us. But it was Eli, after all, standing in the rain outside our door.

It crossed my mind to reach for him, to touch him somehow in welcome.
But while part of me wanted to, another part was aware of what seemed like
countless layers of change and time that separated me from that girl at the
Plaza, and I remembered with a little flare of resentment what I had realized
the last time I'd seen him—we were so loosely connected, I had no right to
claim even a hug. I moved aside, and he stepped through the door, dripping
water.

"Hi," I said, a little flatly.

He didn't seem to notice. "Eva. Nell." He gave a half-bow, first in Eva's
direction, and then in mine, though his pack and poncho crippled some of
the elegance of that greeting.

Then he reached out a wet forefinger and touched me, fitting his finger
for just a moment into the notch at the base of my throat where my clavicles
meet. It was a curious gesture, more intimate than any way he had touched
me before, and I glanced at him to see if it was another prank. But his face
had lost its pleased and detached look, and seemed solemn, tired. My throat
tingled in the wake of his touch, and I had to restrain my hands to keep from
fingering that spot myself.

"Where's your dad?" asked Eli, trying to peer into the blackness beyond
the stove's dim glow.

We were silent for a moment—stunned, I think, at the effort of having to
reduce what we had lived through to a few spoken words. Finally Eva said,
"He died."

"Oh," he said, still standing just inside the door. "But you're okay?" he asked, looking first at me and then at Eva. "You're not sick or anything? You two are okay?"

"We're fine," I said, wanting to cry.

"How'd you get here?" Eva asked.

He pulled the poncho over his shoulders, shrugged off his creaking pack, shook his head so water scattered from his flung mane, and there was a quick sizzle when the drops landed on the stove. "I started out on my bike, but it got a flat I couldn't fix. So I walked. Started yesterday. I didn't know which house was yours, so I had to try every one. You know you're out here by yourselves? There's no one else on this road for at least ten miles."

I wanted to throw myself against him, to weep myself soft and raw and open, to cry until I could finally sleep, my head still pressed against his chest. But the last time we had seen each other we hadn't even spoken. He had always been a stranger, and now he was a stranger in the place where I lived.

I asked, "Are you hungry?" and bent shyly over our little pots of food, scraping out more than his share onto a third plate.

How different that room seemed with him in it, with another voice to fill the darkness. And how strange it felt to be with Eli away from the spotlight of Saturday night, helping him spread his clothes out to dry, showing him to the bath we fixed for him in the dark bathroom. While he soaked and sighed, I groped upstairs and fumbled through the closets for blankets and an extra pillow.

After he had bathed, Eva stoked the stove so that the flames cast a wedge of light across the floor, and the three of us sat cross-legged at the edge of that trembling half-circle, our knees firelit, our faces shadowed. For a while we were silent, watching the flames. I remembered the Plaza, tried to connect those fires with this one, the aloof and mocking Eli with this quiet man. But the Plaza was a world away, and we were no longer the same children who had once strutted and giggled beneath those palms and redwoods.

"What's happening in Redwood?" Eva finally asked, trying to keep her voice light, the way our father had when he talked with Stan in Fastco.

"Redwood?" Eli's voice was thick, as though he'd been startled awake. He cleared his throat. "Not much."

"Do they have electricity yet?" I blurted.

"No. Not yet." He sounded apologetic or reluctant to speak more.

"What's the news? Any idea when they'll get it?"

"Not really. Someone said they'd heard, well, that there was power back east." He paused for what seemed like a moment of indecision, then added quickly, "But it's all rumor."

"What other rumors have you heard?"

"Not much. People stick pretty close to home. Everybody's real afraid of germs. And there's not much reason to go out. No work. No school. And lots of people are gone. Or dead."

"Who's dead?" asked Eva.

"There was about six weeks this fall when everybody was getting the flu—or something," he said, watching the fire, speaking to the fire. "No one was really sure what it was. No one knew what to do. But lots of people died and it made everyone paranoid. My mother died."

"Your mother?" I asked.

"Yes." He paused for a moment and then rushed on, "The Plaza people—some of them died, too."

"Who?" I asked, though I wanted to know what had happened to his mother, how it had been for him to lose her.

"Justin and Bess. That I know of. Oh, and Big Mike. They think he had appendicitis. I thought you'd died, too, when you stopped coming to town."

"We ran out of gas," I said. "We went in once last summer for groceries, but we didn't see anyone."

"Do you guys have bikes?" he asked.

"No," Eva said, and I explained, "Our father gave them away to some children at his school because we'd quit riding them. They were just kids' bikes, anyway."

"Too bad," he said, but before I could ask why, Eva changed the subject. "So why did you come all the way out here, if you thought we were dead?" I cursed and thanked her and held my breath.

"Like I said," he answered, "there's nothing going on in town. I guess I thought I'd give myself a change."

We forgot to lock the doors last night before we slept. I woke once, shocked at the sound of Eli's breathing in the corner of the room, but the crystal of fear that the sound planted in my stomach melted, and a new warmth spread over me, along with a tingle of town-excitement.

When the morning came, there he was, the muscles of his shoulders and arms bunching and pulling beneath his worn tee shirt when he rose out of his blankets to stretch. He looked over at me, rumpled in the rags of my father's flannel shirt, and said, "I always knew you'd look gorgeous in the morning."

I felt the burn of a blush, hot and tight and dizzy. I couldn't separate irony from honesty in his voice, and the only reply I was able to muster was too long and sad for his quick spar. "At least you still remember how to joke," I said, and rushed to hide in the bathroom.

In that dim sanctuary I fumbled through the cupboard until I found the box Eva and I had labeled *Makeup, Etc.* and grabbed a tiny bottle of French perfume that had once resided on my mother's dresser. It was hardly larger than a quarter and half full of a golden fluid. I had pulled out its stopper before I realized I hadn't asked Eva if I could use it. But the room was already flooded with the smell of my mother on those rare nights when she and our father went out without us, when she was taller than usual in her high heels, and she smelled foreign and delicious when she bent to kiss us goodnight.

I lifted my shirt and touched the stopper to my solar plexus. The sweet sting of perfume rose to my nose. I fitted the stopper back into the bottle, put the bottle back in the box and the box back in the cupboard. I went to the mirror. In the eternally dull light of the bathroom, I looked into my eyes, as though I would be able to see a knowledge there that I couldn't yet feel inside my skull. My eyes met themselves, and I drew back, stunned for the first time in my life by my own face. It was the same face I had barely glanced at the day before, the blue eyes, the light hair, the same wide mouth and bland nose, but today it seemed different, a face worth watching, a lovely face, both soft and striking, with a fresh intensity flaring in the eyes.

At that moment Eva walked in to brush her teeth, and I turned from my reflection with a feeling of embarrassment, as though she had caught me looking at something I shouldn't have seen.

She sniffed the air and glanced sharply at me, but said only, "What do you think?"

"About what?" I lowered my face into the pool of cold water trembling in my cupped hands, savoring its icy shock against my eyelids.

"About Eli."

"It's nice to see him," I said, lifting my dripping face, wondering why I felt reluctant to answer, why I felt duplicitous and confused saying something as innocent—and honest—as that.

She looked at me almost shrewdly for a moment, as though she knew a secret I had yet to find out.

"Well," she said, handing me the towel.

After breakfast, we showed Eli around. During a brief break in the rain we introduced him to Bathsheba and Pinkie, led him through the tidied shop, took him down to the dormant orchard. He clucked at the hens, opened a few drawers in the shed to admire their organization, let me tell him which trees were which, but I could tell we were more eager to show than he was to see.

I asked him when we should start pruning, whether he thought the truck battery would hold its charge, how I might have saved Lilith, but he said he'd never pruned a fruit tree, didn't know much about batteries or chickens. He seemed distracted, as though the life that mattered to him were being led somewhere else.

As I write, Eli lounges in front of the stove, blowing gently on his harmonica. He holds it cupped in his hands like he's whispering his thoughts to it. Every now and then he glances at me, and when he looks away and keeps on playing, it feels as though his music is a secret he's telling about me in a language I don't really understand.

I feel impatient and exposed. I want him to leave. But the rain that began the afternoon before he came continues to fall two days later, and he seems in no hurry to venture back into it. The hens come out occasionally, searching the sodden yard for any crawling or sprouting thing they might have overlooked; otherwise the clearing is empty of everything but rain.

We stay inside, Eli and I in the front room, Eva in her studio with the door closed. She has quit even coming out to check the fire. But feeding the woodstove gives Eli and me something to do, some little bit of business, something other than each other to attend to.

It's hard, after all this time, to have someone else in this house. Yesterday I was thrilled to be alone in a warm room with Eli while the rain came down outside. It was as though in some convoluted way my life were finally beginning to take the shape of my desires. But after a morning of talk as bland and fumbling as it had ever been at the Plaza, I found myself thinking of all those fairy tales whose moral is *be careful what you wish for*. Here I was, unable to sit or stand or speak without feeling like an oaf or a child or a spinster, unable to work things out with my sister, unable to study, unable to do anything but suffer his presence.

So far we've talked a lot about the rain and a little about the Plaza people, though even that subject seems risky, haunted now by the kind of candor our talk could never bear the weight of. Eli paces the room while I sit primly at the table, trying to keep talking, trying not to say anything, wishing he would leave.

This morning Eva was in her studio before Eli or I was up. She hadn't stopped to wash her face, hadn't even stoked the fire. At noon when she came out for a couple of shriveled apples, she smiled distantly, but didn't meet my eyes. Then she rushed back to her studio and closed the door.

Eli looked up from his harmonica to ask, "Is she always like that?"

"She practices a lot," I said, disconcerted by how evenly my loyalties were split, startled to realize how little allegiance I felt towards either of them— Eva still angry because of a few gallons of gasoline and a chocolate kiss, or Eli, a stranger taking up too much space in my house.

"I thought she was friendlier."

"She is friendly. She's just working hard. It's hard to push yourself when you're all alone."

"Why does she do it?"

I started to shrug and change the subject, but suddenly I found I didn't care what effect my words had on Eli. I was impatient with politeness, was tired of being cautious. Suddenly the only thing that mattered was telling my story. Eli was eating our food. He was keeping me captive in my own house. Why not make him endure my sorrows? Maybe if he saw me red-faced and gasping, he would go and leave me in peace to study the encyclopedia and try to get along with my sister.

So I started talking.

I told him how Eva had discovered ballet and how abandoned I felt when she first devoted her life to dance. I told him how I had decided to go to Harvard, and how during all the dark months when my mother was dying, I had focused on my studies and Eva had kept dancing. I told him what I'd imagined I could never tell anyone, confessed those startling moments of relief that I had outlived my mother. I told Eli what had happened on our last trip to town, how Eva and I buried our father, how we had survived since then, how Eva had kept dancing.

I didn't cry.

In a funny way I wasn't even sad or ashamed as I spoke, though I was telling Eli the stories I used to imagine would melt his heart, the secrets I had thought would disgrace me. But I no longer wanted pity or sympathy. In fact the emotion I felt most strongly seemed kin almost to anger. I was sick of my own stories, tired of having lived them, and tired of having had to lug them around with me for so long. Now I wanted to be rid of them, and Eli just happened to be there, in their path. In a way it reminded me of the old Paul Bunyan legend, how one winter it was so cold in Paul's lumber camp that all the words he and his crew spoke froze, and when the spring thaw finally came the air was thick with melting talk as all their frozen words came back to life.

Then it was Eli's turn.

He told me about how it had been in town, and what he told me was worse than I had thought. All this time I've been imagining that our struggles were the hardest, wondering if things weren't easier and safer in Redwood, and worrying that we were making a mistake in not going back to town.

But Eli told me about the hunger and anger and fear, about the revival of suspicion and superstition, how people had finally grown impatient with the grim present and the vague promises of change, how they began to distrust the neighbors they had only recently gotten to know. He told me about the bewildered way that people clung to habit long after habit ceased to make sense—housewives trudging out every morning to check the mail half a year after the last delivery, men polishing their cars on Sunday afternoons even though it had been months since there had been water pressure enough to wash them or gas to drive them. He told me about the cheer and roar in the Plaza one night last fall, and how the bank president was found dangling from a streetlight the next morning, his face the color of a rotten eggplant, his toes just scuffing the browned weeds.

He told me about how the flu came, and the shock and anger and terror people felt when they realized there was no one and nothing to turn to for a cure. He told me about the fear of contagion that settled on the town, how people quit shaking hands and sharing food, how they hid in their houses, and still they died, well one week and gone the next.

That's how his mother went. He told me how they buried her, in a coffin he and his brothers made from an old fence and a broken door while his father sat in the living room, staring at the empty TV screen and drinking the bottle of brandy they had been saving to celebrate the return of electricity.

When Eli finally ran out of words, he sat, inert as stone, looking out on the weary rain. I watched him for a moment, and then, abandoning words myself, I rose, crossed to where he was sitting, and laid my hands on his slumped shoulders, let them wait there, heavy and patient and wiser than I'd known, until he turned to face me.

All our stories vanished in his gold-flecked eyes.

Then the door to Eva's studio burst open, and we jumped as though we had been scalded.

"How's the fire?" she asked, tearing open the stove door and jabbing at the coals. "It looks a little low."

———

That was yesterday. Today I feel shy once more, but today my shyness has a sweetness to it, and our talk, though not as deep, lacks the stumble and sting I used to dread. Today I can study, can even get up to go to the bathroom without agonizing over what he's seeing, what he's hearing, what he's thinking. Today when Eli plays his harmonica I like the sound of his music.

"Just don't get pregnant," Eva hisses when she and I go out together in the late afternoon for firewood.

"What?" I gasp.

"Whatever you do, be careful. That's all I ask."

"What are you saying?"

"The last thing we need right now is a baby. And you know he'd be gone in a minute."

"What makes you think he'll do anything?"

"Not he. *You* and he." She smiles, and I'm so taken off guard I'm unable to read the mix of emotion in her voice.

———

This morning came clear and bright—chilly and damp when I let out the hens but with a promise of later warmth in the air.

Eli was waiting at the door for me when I returned with a load of wood in my arms. "Let's go for a walk," he said.

I knocked on the door of Eva's studio, and when there was no response, I opened it a crack. She was standing at the barre with her back turned towards me, but I could see her face in the mirror, serene as still water. Her hand was laid regally on the barre, and she was doing *grandes battements*, her working leg rising over and over as crisply as an exclamation point.

"Eli and I are going for a walk," I said to her straight back.

"Good," she answered, and her leg rose again as easily as though it were filled with helium.

"See you," I said wistfully.

She turned to face me. "Have fun. Don't eat anything wild." She echoed our mother's words so wryly that I moved towards her greedily, eager to share her joke. But when I met her eyes, I was shocked to see not humor or even irony, but a raw split-second of grief.

Eli and I scampered outside like released children, ran breathless and giggling across the shining, rain-soaked yard. We passed the workshop and as we leapt over the rotting mat of last year's tulips I thought I felt a momentary tug. But I shook it off like a dog shaking water from its coat and entered the forest with Eli.

After all this rain the woods were humid—steaming and voluptuous in the sudden gift of sunlight, and I felt both bewildered and newly awakened, as though I had just arisen after a long illness. Water dripped from every leaf and twig, a bright after-rain that sounded like a far-off stream, while the nearby stream ran riotous with rain. The redwoods' needles were glistening, and everywhere were the hard, tight knobs of buds, like tiny fists or taut nipples. The air washed our lungs. We squinted in the blaze of wet light and headed up the stream.

Even after five days in his presence, I felt as though I were walking with a stranger. We had left behind the fusty room in which we paced and ate and slept and talked, and now—for the first time ever—we were truly alone.

"Where are you taking me?" he asked, as he clambered along behind me over the branches and boulders that edged the stream.

"Why should I take you anywhere?" I teased.

"It's your forest."

I was about to protest that it was not my forest when I remembered the redwood stump Eva and I had once claimed as our own.

I felt a twinge of guilt and wondered if she would say I was betraying her by showing that place to Eli. But then I remembered how many times she had refused to leave her studio when I begged her to go there with me, and I thought, *She won't care. And anyway, it doesn't matter.*

"Okay," I said, "I'll take you somewhere. Come on."

"Where are we going?"

"You'll see." We had reached a place where the wooded hillside sloped steeply upwards, and although there was no path in sight, I started climbing. Knees bent, feet cocked sideways to the hill, I clambered, trying to dig footholds into the litter of oak and bay leaves that blanketed the ground, holding my hands out from my body, ready to balance or clutch.

"Just don't grab the poison oak," I called down to Eli. I could hear him scrambling below me. I could smell the leaf mold my feet disturbed. Once I slipped and fell to my knees, grabbing wet handfuls of leaves and hugging the hill with my thighs until I quit sliding. I was breathing hard when I finally scrambled to the plateau at the top, and the knees of my jeans were wet. I turned to watch Eli climb the last few feet.

"What's up here?" he asked, panting.

"Forest."

"All that climbing for more forest?"

"You'll see," I teased.

We stood side by side for a moment while our breathing settled, and I tried to get my bearings. That far above the stream the forest begins to open up a bit. There's less undergrowth, although the trees are still dense enough to make it hard for your eyes to know where to focus, dense enough to make you long for a stretch of open sky. The trees are bigger and here and there a circle of redwoods rings a wide depression that is the grave of some ancient giant tree.

"So what am I supposed to see?" Eli asked.

"Come on," I said. "You'll know it when you see it."

He gave me a bow, and we set off again.

Once we began walking, my self-consciousness returned. I remembered when Eva and I used to pretend we were Indians, and to crack my shyness, I tried to teach Eli to walk as stealthily as possible through the ankle-deep leaves and over the tangled snags. Finally he decided I was quieter than he was. He pushed me against a fallen tree, and the game turned to chase. So we ran through the sparkling forest, panting and laughing, loud as the stream.

"Eva and I used to play up here," I said when we had finally stopped and were standing close together, trying to catch our breath.

"You came here when you were kids?"

"All the time. We practically lived up here."

"Why'd you quit?"

I felt the smile leach off my face. I shrugged. "Eva started dancing. And then my mother got sick. We grew up, I guess."

Eli raised his head, looked at me for a minute, but changed his mind and didn't speak. Instead, he took my hand in his and we walked on through the dripping woods.

It isn't easy to hold hands and walk through a forest. There are branches to duck, logs to climb, trees to skirt. But we managed. In the distance I could still hear the roar of the stream, as insistent as ever, but muted now by a million leaves. I thought of my sister, working in her studio in the silent house, her face blank, her back straight, her hand resting on the barre as though it were floating on water, her leg soaring over and over again into the quiet air, while far above her in the chill fresh forest, I was happy with someone else.

Several times I got confused, whether because of Eli or because the forest had grown and changed, I don't know, but none of the trees looked familiar, and I was almost ready to give up. I was planning the joke I would make of heading back downhill when suddenly I heard the tune of nearby water. Veering towards it, I recognized the little rill that ran near the stump.

I led Eli upstream for a hundred yards or so, and there it was, appearing as unexpectedly as it always had, so that one minute we were surrounded by a tangle of trees, and the next minute we were twenty feet away from a hollow redwood stump the size of a shed.

We stopped, hand in hand.

I had forgotten how massive it was, how solid. It looked more like stone than wood, and yet it seemed alive. Its outer walls were covered with dense little forests of mosses and lichens. On the north side there was an opening wide enough to let two children enter hand in hand, and I led Eli through it. The walls inside were charred from some ancient fire, blackened and lichened and weathered hard, smelling faintly of a smoke so old there may be no one still alive who could possibly remember the flame.

I watched as Eli stood in the soft litter of last year's leaves, spread his arms, and slowly turned around. The walls were always at least two feet beyond his reach.

"Is this what you brought me up here for?" he asked.

"What do you think?"

"It looks like the kind of thing you'd want me to see," he said, and before I could sort out what he meant by that, he reached for me, pulled me to him. Then I was too busy being shocked by the unexpected softness of his lips to fret about any other meanings.

We could have grown roots, we stood there so long. We could have grown wings and risen like angels up through the tunnel of the stump and out into the sky, still talking in that mute language we suddenly discovered we shared, the fluent and precise language of tongues. At times it seemed the forest went about its own business, and at times it seemed it drew closer, hovering over us.

We made love, though *fumbled* is probably a better word for what happened between us. There was a confusion of buttons and a tangle of shirt sleeves and pants legs, exposing selves shy, greedy, and riddled with goosebumps. We spread our clothes over the leaves, and there, on the chill floor of the forest, where a redwood tree had grown for a thousand years, we did what we could with each other.

For me, the biggest revelation of sex was not Eli's penis, which seemed almost girlish somehow, it was so smooth and eager, springing from its tangle of auburn hair and bouncing between us like a puppet on a string. Instead it was the surprise of his whole, full skin against mine, with its exquisite gradations of texture and temperature and pressure. The biggest shock was not our differences but our sameness.

We worked for a long time trying to get him inside me, and whether it was his inexperience, too, that added to our dilemma, I don't know, but it seemed that both of us were unsure of not only the mechanics, but also the etiquette, of what the encyclopedia calls *penetration*. For a long time he stuffed himself against me, until even I realized he needed help, and finally, flushed more with embarrassment than lust, I tried to assist him. But then there were two hands fumbling between our four legs.

I was trying to think of a polite way to call the whole thing off when suddenly I felt something give, felt a new, wet, slick dimension to myself. There was a blur of pain, another level of resistance, and he was moving inside me. I have to admit it felt more odd than good, though at the end there was a moment when he cried out with such a pure sound I felt I had just heard the voice of his soul.

When it was over, we lay together for a moment, and then Eli slugged out of me, and there was a messy wetness between my legs. We sprawled on the tangle of jeans legs and shirt sleeves, sharp oak leaves sticking to our backs and elbows and knees, redwood fronds love-knotted in our hair. I opened my eyes, looked up through the stump to the sky beyond the braid of branches, and it seemed I could hear the sap rushing up through the ghostly wood.

It was strange coming down the hill, my clothes still rumpled, my hair prickly with leaves, my crotch tender and sticky, Eli holding my hand.

Eva was in the kitchen when we got home, rinsing our breakfast dishes. She looked up from the sink and asked, "Did you have a good walk?"

"Nell showed me the stump," Eli said, in another effort to be friendly. For a moment Eva looked stricken. Then her face grew closed, and turning to me she asked, "What stump?"

The next afternoon Eli and I were again lying together inside the stump. We had just finished making love and were lolling in that languorous afterwards, dozing and teasing, and smiling vaguely past the charred walls to the breeze-blown sky. I had my head on his chest and was listening to the sure, firm openings and closings of the valves of his heart.

But at some point my languidness vanished like mist in the morning sun, and I sat up to face him, to watch him tell me that all our waiting was finally over. Because back East, he said—around Boston—things have started up again. He said they have electricity back there. The phones work. People have jobs. There's food in the stores.

"How do you know?" I asked, teetering between delight and disbelief.

"A friend of my uncle's told us."

"He's been back there?"

"He's been to Sacramento. He just came back last week."

"But how—"

"When he was on his way home, he met a man, and they walked most of the way together. This guy had family up by Grantsville somewhere. Anyway, he must have liked Charlie because just before they got to Redwood, he told him all about it, said he was on his way home to get his family and take them back to Boston before next winter."

The man from Grantsville had said that for a while things were awful back East, even worse than they ever got here. The rioting was horrible, and it seemed that gangs were providing the only order there was. Many, many people died from starvation or exposure or disease. But Eli said that has all run its course by now. He said the people who are left are living like kings.

They're rebuilding Boston. They've established a temporary government and set up a system to allow people to file claims on the deserted buildings if they will agree to repair and occupy them. Boston is a boom town. But those who are already there are trying to keep it all quiet. Eli said, "If the whole country heard about it, Boston would be mobbed. That's why Charlie walked a hundred miles with this guy before he said a word because everyone who hears is bound to pack up and head East."

"It's the Gold Rush in reverse!" I said, leaping up. "Why didn't you tell me sooner?"

He grinned, elbowed himself to his feet. "I had to find out who you were first."

"What do you mean? Who am I?"

"The woman I want to go with me."

Even standing naked in front of him, with the leavings of our love beginning to drip from me onto the forest humus, it came as a shock to hear him call me a woman.

"What do you mean?" I repeated.

"I want you to come with me."

At those words some flat, empty thing inside me inflated like a new lung. I wanted him to stop, to luxuriate in that, to celebrate—with me—what he had just said. But he raced on.

"We've got to start soon," he said, "so we don't end up spending the winter someplace in South Dakota. Every day we waste means that someone else is getting a head start on us."

"What about Eva?" I asked.

"She can come, too."

His brothers are going. And their cousin. With Eva, there will be six of us. "Six is a good number," said Eli. "Not so many we have a hard time keeping track of everybody, but enough so that we can take care of ourselves.

"But we have to leave soon," he repeated, "now that spring is coming. It's already mid-March, and it'll take us another day and a half just to walk back to town. Mike and Adam said they could only wait two weeks for me, and I've already been here one."

It was odd to hear someone talking in weeks again, to think that somewhere they still existed, five workdays pivoting around a weekend. I remembered how significant *Monday morning* or *Saturday night* used to seem. And I realized with a spike of something like lust that those words have regained their meanings, back in Boston.

Just the thought of all of that made me feel expansive, generous, awake, alive. I imagined Boston, ablaze with lights. I imagined grocery stores and gas stations, museums and malls, restaurants and arcades, theaters and shops. I thought of what it would feel like to quit hoarding and cowering and grieving, and for the first time in my life I wept for joy.

"You're crazy," said Eva when we told her that night as the three of us sat around the open stove. "You'll never make it."

"Of course we will," said Eli, poking at the coals in the firebox while we stared at the flames with the same mesmerized intensity with which we used to watch TV.

"You'll walk to Boston?" she said, and I winced at the scorn in her voice.

"Yes," said Eli.

"Before next winter?"

"Yes."

"What if you don't get that far?"

"Then we'll hole up somewhere."

"Where? Who would take an extra half dozen people in for the winter?"

"We'd earn our keep. Joe's got a rifle. And a reloader. And if you guys come, there'll be your gun, too. We can hunt and cut wood. We'll be fine."

"Do you know how to hunt?"

"Sure," he grinned. "Why not? I'm a fast learner."

"And Boston's got something we don't have?"

"Yes."

"What?"

"Power. Food. Jobs."

"How do you know?"

"I told you. My uncle's friend—"

"What if he's wrong? What if it's just another rumor?"

"If it were a rumor, do you think this guy would have kept it a secret for so long? He and Charlie'd walked a hundred miles together before he even mentioned it. Does that sound like a rumor? Besides, Charlie's smart. He'd know if this guy was a fake."

"How?"

"He'd know. But look. Even if he is wrong—which he isn't—still, we won't be any worse off than we are now. At least we'll be there when things do start up again."

"If you're so sure Charlie knows what he's talking about, then where are the planes?"

"The planes?"

"That's right. Why hasn't someone flown out West—or driven, for that matter? If things are back up back East, why don't we know more about it?"

"Look, Eva," he said with an elaborate patience, "of course there aren't planes. Those lights aren't running on gas. The gas is long gone. It's alternatives—everything's solar or wind. There's no planes. Besides, no one wants the secret to get out. There isn't enough for everyone."

"So why are you going?"

"To seek my fortune. To get on with my life." He was silent for a moment, and sadder than I had ever seen him. "It's been a hard time in Redwood."

"Oh, Eva," I blurted, "you can dance. There'll be music. And teachers. You can join a dance company—and I can go to Harvard."

She met my eyes straight on then with a look that seemed like a warning, but her message was too dense, and I was too enraptured to try to decipher her meaning.

"Eli's brothers are making a handcart, and they're trying to find a horse," I said.

"That's crazy," Eva answered.

Eli said, "No crazier than staying here and waiting for the lights to turn back on. No crazier than hiding up here in the hills, counting nails and rubber bands, and watching the pantry empty. What's going to happen to the two of you if you stay here?"

"Nothing. We'll be fine."

"Nothing. That's right. Nothing will happen—if you're lucky. If you're lucky, the lights will come back on before your food runs out, or before one of you gets hurt or sick, or before the house catches fire. *If* you're lucky.

"And suppose you are that lucky. Suppose you do manage to survive out here until the power comes back—then what? You're still thirty miles from town. Thirty miles from a goddamn ghost town. Even before all this happened, Redwood was a place to leave. I thought you'd understand that, Eva."

She bristled. "Of course I do. But when I leave it's going to be for something real. Not just craziness."

"Leaving's less crazy than staying here."

"At least if we stay here we'll stay alive," said Eva dryly, "which is more than I can say for you, if you try to walk three thousand miles before next winter."

"You two run more risk out here by yourselves than you do coming with me." Eli's voice softened. "Eva, please. It's an adventure. Come with us. And it's not fair to Nell."

"She's her own person." Eva turned away from us, bent over her fire. "Nell will go if she wants."

———

I did want. More than I had ever wanted anything I wanted to walk to Boston with Eli. But Eli is gone. Eli is crossing the country without me, headed towards the lights of a living world, and I'm back here as though I never left, writing about traveling while Eva dances and another rain falls.

My socks were darned, my jeans double-patched. The mildewed Army surplus backpack we found in Father's workshop had been cleaned and mended and filled, the load arranged and rearranged. I had my letter from Harvard, a copy of my SAT scores, my dead calculator, this journal. I had considered and reconsidered each sweater, each match, each pencil stub and spool of thread and grain of rice, balancing its value on the trip against its weight and bulk, and adding into that equation how much Eva might need it here.

We split the money, but I left her the magnifying glass and the last two teabags. And the gas.

"I'm sorry I wouldn't let you use it before," I said, and added wistfully, "maybe we should stay another day so we can have that party and watch you dance."

She shook her head. "No, if you're going to go, you'd better get on your way."

She gave me the hiking boots we had found at the back of Mother's closet. And she insisted I take the rifle.

"You'll need it," she said, "more than I will—"

I interrupted her to thank her, able at that moment to feel nothing but my own delight. I was seventeen years old, strong, free, and suddenly beautiful. I was a woman venturing out into the world with her lover. Despite everything, I was finally going to Harvard, and no sour sister could possibly curdle my joy.

I have to admit there were even times when it seemed it would be a relief if Eva stayed behind, so that I wouldn't feel constrained by her unvoiced observations. Staying, there was only isolation, worry, fear, and a distant sister. Going, I had Eli, adventure, the future I had worked for so hard. Besides, I was still half-convinced that at the last moment she would change her mind and come with us, that the trip would make us allies again. As I sorted and organized and planned, I kept waiting for the moment when she would finally give in and start to pack.

But in the chill light of that final morning, while Eli was out gathering a last load of firewood and Eva and I were sitting at the table with our cups of tasteless tea, she was still adamant. "No, Nell. I'm staying. It's a crazy trip."

"But what about your dancing? All this time you've managed to keep dancing when no one else ever could, and now you're going to let it all go?"

"I'm not going to let it go. I'll keep dancing."

"But Eva, this could be your only chance."

She flinched, and then answered so quickly I could tell she had been thinking the same thing herself. "Maybe that's not the most important thing."

Trying to keep the fear out of my voice, I asked, "Then what is?"

"I don't know."

I reeled for a moment, but then I saw the bulging packs waiting like promises beside the door, and I tried again. "We're all the family either of us has got left. We've got to stick together."

"No, we don't." She shook her head at me, to keep me from softening that blow. She said, "It's okay, Nell. We've both made our choices."

"You can't stay here alone."

"Why not?"

Eli came back in then, his arms burdened with wood, and Eva and I fell silent. We pretended to eat. We talked about the chickens and the weather, made frail jokes. Finally Eli broke our inertia, stood up in a way that was both reluctant and businesslike. "Well. Sure you won't change your mind, Eva?"

"Yep," she said, lightly. "I'm sure."

"Stubborn, aren't you?"

"Yep," she said. "I'm stubborn."

They smiled at each other with an understanding so strong and amused and certain that I felt a little jealous of them both, as though each of them had, without even trying, usurped the place to which I aspired. Eva turned to face me, took my hands in hers, and looked at me so lovingly and long that even then I expected she was going to change her mind. But she said, "Good-bye, Nellie. I'll always be your sister." To lessen the sorrow she added, "Don't take any wooden nickels. And write when you get work."

I nodded stupidly, hugging her for the first time since we had discovered the gas. I watched as Eli shrugged his pack across his shoulders, picked up the rifle, and opened the door. Finally, when there was nothing else I could do to postpone it, I hefted my pack off the floor, slung it around to my back, and followed him out of the house, out into the blaze of early morning light.

It was a glorious morning. The air was cold, but the distant sun was bright. My eyes watered, and my breath left my lungs in glowing puffs. When we reached the edge of the clearing, at the point where my mother's withered ring of tulips intersected the road, I stopped, turned, lifted my arm to wave good-bye.

Eva stood in the open door, her face serene. Smoke seeped from the chimney on the roof above her, and the air around it seemed to thicken and tremble. We faced each other across the clearing for a full moment and then she raised her hand to me. Behind that simple gesture was all her dancer's grace and prowess, and when I turned my back on the clearing, my eyes were hot with tears.

But I caught those tears before they fell, and their sting seemed only to intensify the keenness of the moment. In that instant I was a bride, an adventuress, a pioneer. The damp trees blazed with light from the freshly risen sun, and bright phantoms of steam rose from the road. The forest smelled of bay and fir, and we could hear the tidy chirping of birds. Beyond us I could see the mountains rising blue and hazy and full of promise, and I knew I had only to cross them and keep on walking to catch up with all my dreams.

When we reached the bridge, I stopped and looked down between the splintered boards to the trickle of water far below. For a moment time itself seemed to become fluid—wavery and dreamlike as the air above the chimney. I remembered how, when I was little, that bridge had been the boundary of my world, and I paused.

"It was sturdy enough when I came up," said Eli after I had hesitated another second, and I nodded and crossed, though I felt as if I were breaking my way through spider webs or that quiet hands were nudging me back.

Then I was on the other side, and every step took me that much further from the source of all my ghosts, that much nearer to all I had ever been promised. I had followed that road for seventeen years, yet never before had I traveled it on foot. It felt like an unfamiliar road I was walking, as though Eli and I were already exploring new territory together. Each bend revealed a place it seemed I had never seen, and everything was glowing with sunlight and green with rain and so beautiful I couldn't keep in mind that I was walking through it to leave it behind.

Eli set a fast pace. Mother's boots felt foreign on my feet, and I was soon sweating to keep up. But even so, it was a pleasure to try to match his steps, to finally be working for something again. I felt, as we reached and passed each new place, that I was accomplishing something, that I was getting somewhere at last.

The winter had been hard on the road. Without my father to keep the ditches open and wrestle the blackberry brambles from the culverts, the rains had gouged deep channels into the roadbed. There were places where the hillside had slumped across it. At one spot, a section of road the length of our house had eroded away, leaving a car-wide trail that hugged the hillside.

"I wonder if our truck could even make it out," I said, peering down into the gorge where the road had once been.

"Hard to tell," answered Eli, striding on ahead.

We passed the Colemans' house while the air was still almost cool, and we reached the county road before midday. It was a little unsettling to see asphalt again, and I found myself speaking more quietly, glancing over my shoulder, and occasionally hushing Eli to listen for the car I was certain I had heard—but which never came.

At lunchtime, we stopped for a few minutes beside the creek to drink stream water and eat some of the beans I had cooked the day before. As soon as we had eaten, Eli jumped up, picked up the rifle, swung on his pack, and led off again. All afternoon we walked, while Eli planned aloud what we would do once we got to Redwood, and I nodded and dreamed of Boston, and my pack straps rubbed raw spots on the skin above my clavicles.

Eli was right—the houses we passed that day were empty, and as we neared them, it was I who picked up the pace, who averted my eyes and hurried us past, trying to ignore the threat of their empty windows and untold stories.

We camped in the forest that night, in a little flat we found between the road and the stream. Eli built a stick fire, and I heated the rest of the beans, which we ate with a sprinkling of powdered cheese. Afterwards, I rinsed our forks and our cooking pot in the stream while Eli made a nest of our sleeping bags beside the fire.

Side by side, we lay back on our bed, and watched the stars bud in the moonless sky. Eli wanted to talk about the trip—about what sort of wheels would work best for the handcart, how we could get more ammunition for my gun, where it would be easiest to cross the Rocky Mountains. I found I was yearning to talk about what it was I had just left, about all I was walking away from. I think, too, I was hoping we would make some kind of ceremony there beneath those blossoming stars, something to acknowledge what it was I had just done. But the words I wanted us to say to each other never came, and we talked instead about how long my mother's boots might last, what kind of roads it would be best to follow, and when next winter's snows might first hit Ohio.

Our talk dwindled as the fire died, until finally we were left staring in silence at the full-blown stars. My thoughts were my own then, and they turned to Eva. I figured she, too, would have eaten by now. She would have locked the doors and stoked the fire, and I imagined her sitting in the dark house, watching the burn of her solitary fire. I wondered what she was thinking, how it felt to be so alone.

I felt my resolve to leave her waver, and to bolster it, I reminded myself how distant and different we had become, how it was best for both of us that I had gone. I reminded myself of all of our disagreements, remembered indignantly how chilly she had been to Eli, how harshly she had warned me not to get pregnant.

A new thought occurred to me, and turning towards Eli, I said, "You've never said anything about birth control."

He lay silently beside me for so long I was beginning to think he hadn't heard. Then he sat up, reached for a stick, and stirred the fire, poking at the embers so they seethed and crumbled. When he answered, he sounded almost wary, "I thought you'd take care of it."

"How?"

"Well, I don't know. You did, didn't you?"

I found I, too, was sitting up, prodding the fire with a redwood branch, and watching intently as the foliage flared and curled. For some inexplicable reason my first impulse was to pretend that it had only now occurred to me what might result from our lovemaking. Finally I said, "When we first got our periods, our mother showed us how to figure out when we were ovulating. I think it's been pretty safe."

"Good," he said, patting my thigh. "I thought you'd be careful."

"What would you have done if I hadn't? Or if it doesn't work?" I asked, trying to keep my voice light.

"I don't know," he answered. "But I don't think you could make this trip with a baby."

He leaned towards me, kissed both my eyes so that the warm pressure of his lips against my eyelids relieved me of all my need to see. Then he kissed my mouth until I felt no more urge to speak.

When we made love it was so dark I could not make out his face, though it was only a breath above my own. I watched the stars instead, saw them grow brighter and swoop nearer until it seemed they were just above us, that if I wanted I could lift my hands from Eli's shoulders and sweep them into new patterns. But suddenly what was happening on earth demanded all of my attention. I closed my eyes, felt a new galaxy of stars blossom inside me.

Later, we roused ourselves to check the fire and rearrange our rumpled bags and then, huddled against Eli, I slept.

I dreamed I was back at my father's grave. It was exactly as it had been on the day we buried him—there was the hole I had dug with Eva's help, there were our two shovels, the bloody chain saw, even his shirt. I could see his blood on the earth beside the grave, and I walked helplessly towards its edge, dreading what I would have to see next. But when I looked inside the grave, what I saw was even worse than what I feared—the grave was empty.

Frantically I called for my father, searched the woods, desperate to find even his mangled body. But he was gone. *I must tell Eva,* I thought. But although I hunted and shouted until my throat was raw, I could find no trace of her.

I woke at dawn with tears of loss streaming down my cheeks—and no sister near to promise I had been dreaming. I looked over at Eli, still asleep beside me. He was so beautiful, lying there in the day's first light. I thought how lucky I had been that he had come for me, how hard it would be to tell him what I had woken knowing I must say.

I rose without disturbing him, dressed, went behind a tree to squat and pee, and then down to the stream to splash cold water on my tears. Eli was sitting up when I came back, stretching and yawning in the strengthening light.

"If we make as good time as we did yesterday, we'll be in Redwood by midafternoon," he said. "How's that sound?"

I gulped air, and said what I had been dreading, "I'm not going."

"What?" he asked, rising abruptly from the tangle of our sleeping bags.

"I'm not going," I repeated.

"You're not going?" he asked, his face clouding with disbelief.

"No," I answered.

"Why not?"

"I don't know. I just can't."

"You're afraid of the trip?"

I shook my head. "It's not that."

"You don't want to be with me?"

"No, I do—"

"Then what?"

"I guess I can't leave Eva."

"She said she'd be okay."

"I know."

"Nell—she'd leave you."

"No, she wouldn't."

"Well, she wouldn't come with you."

"That's different," I said helplessly.

"Oh."

"I'm sorry," I said. "I'm so sorry."

"Look—you've already left her. You've come with me. You can't go back now."

"Oh, Eli—"

"I'll tell you what. We'll go East and get established and send for her. It won't take long."

"How long?"

"By summer after next you'll be together again."

I thought of how much time that was, thought of how little was certain and how much could change.

"I wish I could," I answered, "but I just can't."

"Of course you can. You're saying that you won't."

"Well, then—I won't," I said.

I could see him mustering fresh arguments. But suddenly he stopped and looked at me as though he were seeing something new. Quietly he said, "Like Eva said—you're your own person."

"I'm sorry," I said again, but he had turned away, was already gathering his clothes. He dressed in silence, and in silence we rolled our sleeping bags, loaded our packs. In silence he kicked dirt over our dead fire while I stood watching him with a misery so deep it seemed an effort to pull air into my lungs.

Finally there was nothing left to do. He swung his pack onto his back, handed me the gun.

"Good-bye, Nell."

"Good-bye," I echoed, holding the gun awkwardly between us. Then I pressed it towards him, adding, "Why don't you take the gun?"

He hesitated for a moment, and answered firmly, "No. The gun stays with you."

He reached to touch my cheek. "Take care," he said. "I'll love you however I can."

He turned and strode away, left me standing beside the cold char of our fire with the words I had been longing to hear ringing in my ears, so that I had to bite my lips shut with my teeth, bite them until I tasted blood, to keep from calling after him.

Much later, I turned back up the road. Shivering from the chill, and squinting through my tears against the brightness of the morning sun, I began the long walk home. Mile after mile I stumbled, the pack heavy on my back, my mother's boots leaden on my feet. I walked all day, stopping for nothing but water, while the boots chewed blisters into my heels and toes and my mind grew blistered, too, rubbing and rubbing against the same rough surfaces.

It was dusk when I finally reentered the clearing. The house was a monolith against the darkening forest, and in the open doorway stood my sister, her tears shining on her face like a gift.

So he's gone, walking all the way to Boston, and who can tell what he will find, whom he will meet. Who knows what miracles it would take for me to see him again.

Now the days ring an ever-widening silence. Now the nights are longer than ever. Sometimes my despair at the thought of having left Eli is so enormous I can hardly breathe. Other times I feel a flush of shame for having loved him at all, for ever having writhed and wriggled against him. Then that passes, and I long for him again.

The only thing that returns is the rain, unseasonable and unwelcome. Outside the buds huddle coldly at the ends of their twigs. Inside, Eva dances and I try to study, plunging on into the L's. The fire smolders sourly on wet wood. In the pantry, the sacks flatten, the cans disappear, the jars empty.

I think it has been like this forever.

Today I discovered a spot of blood in the crotch of my ragged underwear, and I felt a wash of relief so intense that for a moment I thought I would faint. I realized that some part of me had been preparing for the next disaster. But along with the reprieve I felt at the sight of my own blood, I have to admit I also felt regret, for now my body has sloughed off all traces of him.

My blistered feet have healed. Eva took them into her dancer's hands and tended them so carefully that already I have fresh pink skin on my heels and toes. These days Eva and I are kind to each other, but it's a distant sympathy and seems to be born more of remorse and loss than any current connection. We don't speak much, and although I long to talk with her, I feel too timid or too tired to interrupt our silence.

———

Somewhere, in a book I have long since returned to the closed library, I read that the peasants in China who grow tea cannot afford to drink it. Instead, they drink cups of hot water that they call *white tea.* Tomorrow our tea, too, will be white.

Tonight we drink hot water made tea by the final scraping of dust from the bottom of the Fastco box. It imparts a tint and scent and taste so frail to the steaming liquid in our mugs that a person who didn't know she was drinking tea might think it was only water.

But we know this is tea. And we know tomorrow there will be no more.

Now it seems as though all of life is a series of lasts—this last cup of tea weaned to the clarity of water, the last quarter-spoonful of sugar rubbed between our tongues and the roofs of our mouths until each grain has dissolved and the syrup has seeped drop by drop down our throats. The last slivers of macaroni. The final lentil.

We ate the last jar of applesauce for lunch today. When Eva wasn't looking, I buried my face in my empty bowl and licked it clean. I hate to use anything now. Each sip, each bite, each scrap is agony, a needle-prick tattooing my awareness with an indelible image of loss and need. These days entering the pantry is an act of courage. The arithmetic, the simple multiplication and subtraction that will show how much we eat in a day, how many days' food we have left, is an equation I can't face. My mind stiffens and goes blank when I try to figure out how many cups of flour in fifty pounds or how many meals are left in the last sack of pinto beans.

I never knew how much we consumed. It seems as if we are all appetite, as if a human being is simply a bundle of needs to drain the world. It's no wonder there are wars, no wonder the earth and water and air are polluted. It's no wonder the economy collapsed, if Eva and I use so much merely to stay alive.

I sometimes think how much better it would be if we were to still our desires, slough off our needs for water and shelter and all this food. Why do we bother? What does it matter? What purpose does it serve? It just keeps us gasping a little longer.

————

Eva and I have been teetering on the edge of argument all day, snapping and poking at each other as though we have both already forgotten how I abandoned everything to stay with her. Part of me longs to snarl at her, tear into her, to blame her for the bare cupboard and the eroded road and all my loneliness. But another part cringes at the thought of a disagreement, wants desperately to get along with the only person I have left.

————

Last night Eva wanted to open the final jar of tomatoes to flavor our rice. But ever since I read about limes in the encyclopedia I've been worrying about scurvy.

"I think we should save it," I said. "That jar of tomatoes is the only significant source of vitamin C we've got left."

She gave me a withering glance and opened the pantry door, saying over her shoulder as she entered, "Save it for what—our funeral?"

"Save it till we really need it," I answered, following her into the pantry. "We don't know how much longer we'll be here."

"Exactly," she said, reaching for the lone jar on the shelf above her head, "that's why we need a treat every now and then."

"Eva!" I cried and caught at her arm, and in that split second of imbalance, the jar slipped between us, exploding on the floor in a welter of glass and fruit.

For a long moment we stared at the tomatoes that might have cured us— or at least lessened the monotony of a meal—now larded with shards of glass, their juices pooling like blood.

"Smooth move," Eva hissed, and suddenly my shock and remorse were supplanted by rage. I found myself scanning the pantry shelves, looking for something hand-sized and hard—something to hit her with. I wanted to hurt her, to kick and punch her, to claw her hair. I wanted to scream, "Now look what you've done! You've ruined everything once again."

I had snatched one of the bottles from Father's wine cellar shelf and was savoring the heft of it in my fist, when the meaning of what I intended to do struck me like another blow.

I gasped and sank to my knees beside the shattered tomatoes.

"What are you doing?" Eva asked.

"I don't know," I said, shaking my head. "I don't know."

"What have you got in your hands?"

"What have I got?" I repeated, dazedly. The bottle was brown and cool and slightly tacky with age. I turned it in my hands and read its label.

"Grand Marnier," I answered.

"You're going to clean up with Grand Marnier?"

"No," I said, and started to giggle.

"What's so funny? A minute ago you were determined to save those tomatoes, and now that you've ruined them, you're laughing."

"Let's drink it," I suggested. I was suddenly elated, suffused with an exquisite upwelling of relief that I hadn't killed my sister.

"What?"

"Isn't Grand Marnier made with oranges? Let's drink it. Maybe it's got some vitamin C in it."

"Well, then according to you, we had better save it," said Eva.

"For what?" I scoffed, ignoring the sarcasm in her voice. "'Snakebite, frostbite, or childbirth?' Besides, there's still the sherry. Come on," I urged, quoting our father once again, "'The best occasion is no occasion.'"

I grabbed Eva's arm to lead her from the pantry, but she shook free and reached for the broom.

From the living room I could hear the sound of sweeping and the chatter of broken glass. I was suddenly eleven again, and Eva was too busy practicing to go to the woods with me. I hesitated and then twisted the lid off the bottle. The smells of orange and alcohol filled the air, and I lifted the bottle defiantly to my mouth. The first sip was sweet, like orange syrup with a backfire. I drank again.

"Eva?" I called.

"What?"

"Want some?"

"No."

"Why not?"

"I'm trying to get the glass out of the tomatoes you spilled."

"I didn't spill them—we did."

"Like hell."

"Come on," I urged. "Try some of this."

"No."

I took another drink, and the unbearable weight of my loneliness pressed in on me. I drank again.

"It tastes like orange suckers," I called.

I heard her sigh wearily. She entered the living room a minute later, carrying a bowl of tomatoes. Sitting by the window where the light was best, she began to poke at the fruit with a fork, to rub the shreds of tomato-flesh between her fingers.

"What are you doing?" I asked.

"Trying to get all the glass out before we eat it—even though you did want to kill me."

"Oh." I drank again. "I'm glad I didn't," I added. Already I could feel the familiar tingle in the back of my throat, the warmth in my belly, the loosening in my brain.

"Eva?"

"What?" she asked, impatience sharpening the final "t" to a knife's edge.

"I do wish you would share this with me. Please. I've missed you."

She sighed elaborately, and then was silent a long time, bent over her bowl of broken tomatoes. Finally she stood up, carried the bowl back into the kitchen. When she returned, her hands were clean. She sat down at the table across from me and reached for the bottle. She raised it to her mouth as though she were performing another chore and drank.

"Well?" I asked.

"What?"

"Doesn't it taste like orange suckers?"

"I guess." She took another drink and handed me the bottle.

So the Grand Marnier passed silently back and forth across the table as the last light leached from the sky. When it was no longer light enough to see the bottle, Eva rose to feed the fire and left the stove door open. By that dim light I studied the curves and hollows of my sister's face. I thought of all that constrained us, all I needed to ask or say to bridge the distances between us, and the longer I watched her still, sad face the more impossible it seemed that I could ever bring myself to speak.

Eva handed me the bottle, and I drank. Finally she said, "Hmm."

"What?" I asked eagerly, pouncing on any possibility of talk.

"I was just thinking—what would Father say?"

"About what?"

"Drinking the Grand Marnier."

"'Pass the bottle,'" I said.

"You've got it," she answered.

"What?"

"The bottle."

"No, that's what he'd say."

"What?"

"'Pass the bottle.'"

We started giggling, and the giggling felt so good. It felt so easy to giggle—so impossible, somehow, to stop—that our laughter grew, took on its own life and momentum until we were laughing in great spasms, until our bellies hurt and our eyes were flooded with tears.

"You've...got...it," Eva blurted between bursts of hysteria.

"What?" I gasped.

"The bottle," she answered, and we laughed until the muscles at the tops of our cheeks ached.

"I'm going to pee my pants," Eva moaned, and that was the funniest thing yet.

"Remember," I spurted, when I could again breathe enough to speak, "when we got the giggles like this when Dad's superintendent came all the way out here for dinner?"

Eva was rolling on the floor, roaring and clutching her stomach.

"And you," I blurted, "you squirted milk out your nose—"

"All over the salad," she shrieked.

"And Mother—"

"Oh, don't, don't," she begged, as though I were holding her down and tickling her feet.

"Took it back in the kitchen, and picked the milky pieces out—"

"And put it in a different bowl—"

"Because that was all the salad there was—"

"Oh, don't. Stop. Please!"

"—and we were having steak and he'd just said he was a vegetarian."

"And she brought it back out again—"

"But the only person who ate any—"

"Was the superintendent—"

"And he ate thirds!"

Finally we laughed our way to silence. I handed the bottle to Eva, which stirred up a final cloud of giggles. She drank, tilting the bottle lazily above her head.

"What would Mother say?" I asked meditatively.

Eva answered immediately. "She'd say, 'A dancer doesn't drink.'"

"Is that why you never drank at the Plaza?"

She nodded.

"That's it? I always thought you were mad at me. I always thought you thought you were better than the rest of us."

"Well, maybe I did, a little. You all got so silly."

"It was fun," I said defensively.

"I know." She sighed, and this time her sigh seemed weary and sad.

"Can I ask you a question?" I said.

"What?"

"Will you answer?"

"I don't know. Maybe."

"Why didn't you like Eli?"

"I did like Eli."

"But—"

"But I didn't like the way you liked Eli."

"What—"

She shrugged. "That's the best I can say it. It's like you're not your own person when you're with him."

She reached for the bottle, took a long swallow, and said, "My turn."

"For what?"

"To ask you. Why did you come back, if you liked him so much?"

Why did you come back? It was the question I had scourged myself with a thousand times, the question to which I thought I had no answer.

Why did you come back? I asked the deep glowing darkness of myself, and the reason came welling up, simple as water. "Because you're my sister, stupid."

She reached across the table to slug me in the shoulder, and then we sat for a long time, listening to the fire.

At last I reached for the bottle and asked a final question. "Eva, why do you keep dancing?"

She shrugged. "What else am I supposed to do with all my time?"

She was quiet then, silent for so long I assumed she was thinking of something else, but suddenly she spoke. "I'll tell you a secret." She flopped her head back for another drink. "The bottle's empty," she said when she had swallowed.

"That's a secret?"

"No—that's a shame."

We giggled a little more, and then she went on, "This is the secret—I couldn't keep dancing if it weren't for the gas."

"The gas?" I echoed guiltily.

"That's what keeps me going. I keep dancing because I know we have that gas. And anytime I really, really had to, I know we could use it for music."

There was a hint of questioning in her voice, and I answered it immediately, with a generosity born of love and alcohol, "Of course."

She paused for a moment to absorb my gift. Then she went on, "That gas keeps it all close enough to believe in. Do you know that sometimes I sneak it out just to look at it? Sometimes I even open the cap and dab a little on me like perfume, so that later, when I'm dancing, I can smell it.

"It's only that gas that keeps me going."

———

Even though I could hear her sobs, my first thought when I saw her lying on the dirt by the chopping block was, *She's dead, my sister is dead. Now I am truly alone.*

I rushed to her, threw myself over her, held her while she trembled and moaned. "Eva, Eva, Eva, what happened? What's wrong?" I pleaded, but she wept and would not answer.

When she finally lifted her face to me, her mouth was swollen and bleeding, and her eyes were the eyes of someone I had never seen.

"What happened?" I asked again, and finally she was able to say it, to force the words out through her split lips. "A man—he raped me."

I eased her to her feet, helped her inside, and built up the fire, using a whole sheet of newspaper in my haste. I gave her a few precious sips of sherry, covered the stovetop with kettles and pots of water. Finally, while the water was heating, the story spewed out of her. She turned her back to me to tell it, and sometimes her voice trembled and cracked, and sometimes she spat the words out in a flat, hard voice that did not seem to be her own.

She had been in the yard. She was chopping wood, enjoying the easy swing of the ax, proud of the way she could dance the logs apart. The sun was bright, warm. There was a breeze.

She never heard him coming, never felt his presence until he was almost next to her.

She gasped, but he held out his hand to quiet her, to steady her as though she were an animal he didn't want to scare off. "It's okay," he said.

He said he was headed north to friends in Grantsville, but that he must have taken a wrong turn. He said he heard her ax and smelled our smoke and thought he'd see who was so far out here, thought he'd stop in and introduce himself.

He never told her his name.

"How're you folks making out?" he asked, his gaze traveling around the yard. "Looks like you've got plenty of wood."

She was so unused to talking to anyone that she felt a little awkward, but she wasn't afraid.

She leaned the ax against the splitting stump and asked him, "Have you heard any news? When will we get our power back?"

He said, "Who knows?"

She said, "We heard that things were starting up again back East."

INTO THE FOREST

"Who told you that?"

"A friend."

"You've got friends out here?"

"Not now. He came to see my sister. But he's gone."

"Yeah. I heard that stuff about Boston, too. Even heard there were some fools who took off, chasing rumors across the country. They won't last long."

Eva said, "That's what I said, too!"

They shared a smile. Then he said, "You people sure have a good-sized woodpile there."

"Yes," she said.

He studied the wood and his eyes narrowed. "You didn't cut all this wood by hand, did you?"

"My father cut it," she said.

"Your father?" he said sharply. "Your father's around here?"

"Yes," she answered, surprising herself by the ease with which she said it. "He's around."

"Where is he? I'd like to talk to him, see what he knows."

"You'd have to wait awhile," she said, her voice level, neutral. "He's out in the woods."

"You folks have any spare gas?" he asked, craning his neck to eye the house.

She wanted him to leave. She answered, "Sorry."

"Sorry what?" he asked. "Sorry you don't have any gas, or sorry you won't share it?"

She shrugged, and started to reach for her ax, ready to continue working.

Just before her hand touched the ax handle, he grabbed her wrist, twisted it so that her arm was yanked behind her back.

"Listen, bitch," he said, "if you think you're saving that gas for an emergency, you'd better consider this one. Where is it?"

When she didn't answer, he spun her around to face him. His face grew flat and hard, his eyes narrowed, and the tiny muscles beneath them jerked and trembled. Even so, she glared back at him. Tearing one shoulder free from his grasp, she aimed a knee at his groin.

She missed—although she hit his thigh with so much force he gasped and tripped. Grappling and struggling, they landed on the ground together. Her dancer's strength might have saved her if he hadn't hit her full across the face, a blow that tore open whole rooms of pain inside her skull, blinding her for a crucial moment, and so confusing her that all she could say when he asked, *Where is it?* was *No, No, No.*

When it was over, he rose, stood above her for a cruel moment, buttoning his pants, fastening his heavy, clanking belt buckle, while she lay huddled at his feet. Then he spat on the ground next to her.

"I sure am sorry I can't stay until Daddy gets back," he said. "But you tell him thanks for the hospitality." He left the clearing, left her lying on the earth with her ax next to her, paralyzed with shock and horror and pain, left her where I found her when I returned from cleaning out the spring.

When the kettles of water were finally hot, I filled the tub and led her to the bathroom. She stood still as a child as I undressed her, examined her hurts. Bruises were already flowering on her arms. Her face was torn and swollen, and her thighs were streaked with blood.

She shuddered when she climbed into the steaming water, and I thought she might weep again, but she seemed to relax just slightly into the heat and wet. She spoke for the first time since she had told me of the rape—"Is there any soap?"

"There's the Christmas soap," I said. "I'll get it."

A tiny, cracked lump of unnatural forest green, scented with a fragrance that must have once passed for pine, it was the last soap we owned, the last of a little wicker basket of soaps we had found among our mother's things. We had eked the others along to nothing, rationing them until only this was left—a splinter of soap the size of a dime, the scrap we had agreed to save for our triumphal trip to town.

When I put it in her hands, she lifted it to her nose, inhaled its fading perfume, and then, looking at me, she asked, "But don't you want to save it?"

"No," I said, cringing at the innocent recrimination in that question. "Use it now."

She asked for a washcloth and when I gave it to her, she attacked herself, scrubbing her skin so viciously I thought she would surely bleed, going over and over every inch of her body, first with soap, and then, long after the last of the soap had vanished into the cooling water, with the washcloth. She winced when she first touched herself between her legs, and I saw tears rise in her eyes, but she clenched her teeth, bit back her tears, washed herself clinically, thoroughly, washed thighs and stomach and breasts, washed her shoulders, her elbows, her wrists and fingers, her knees and shins and ankles and between each toe. Gingerly she daubed water on her misshapen face.

Finally she turned towards me and made a move to climb from the tub. I helped her out, wrapped her in the towels I had laid by the stove to warm. I led her back to her mattress, folded a mug of white tea in her hands, made her swallow the final aspirin.

When I handed it to her, she protested. "We should save it."

"It's okay. Take it."

"We might need it later. Maybe I should just take half."

"Half wouldn't do any good. You'd waste the whole thing if you cut it in half," I answered, wondering what a single aspirin could do against a rape.

She swallowed the aspirin and watched in silence while I took the rifle from its hiding place in the coat closet and inexpertly fit a bullet into the chamber. I checked the safety half a dozen times, stoked the fire, and then sat on the floor next to her mattress with the gun across my lap.

Towards morning she slept, while I stayed awake beside her, staring at the fire, cringing at the wind, afraid to breathe.

There is no place we feel safe. Going outside for wood takes all the courage I can muster, and still I cringe and wince, every moment expecting to be attacked. Inside we feel both exposed and trapped. A dozen times an hour I find myself glancing out the window, scanning the forest, expecting to glimpse the figure I know is waiting for us there.

It changes the front room to have the rifle in it, leaning like a warning against the door frame. A gun is a mean thing. Rather than comforting me, its cool barrel, heavy stock, and slender trigger scare me as much as everything else, reminding me there's violence everywhere.

There is no escaping. Even the fire in the stove seems menacing. Sap boils out of the crackling wood, the flames snap and spit. We're surrounded by violence, by anger and danger, as surely as we are surrounded by forest. The forest killed our father, and from that forest will come the man—or men—who will kill us.

Yesterday I forced myself to go outside and search through the junk pile behind the workshop until I found some sheets of corrugated tin. I nailed them over every downstairs window except the one in the front room. While Eva lay unmoving on her mattress, her swollen face turned to the wall, I nailed the door from the kitchen to the utility room shut and barricaded the washing machine in front of the door that leads outside.

So now we have only a single window and one entrance to our house, but all that means is we will be able to hear him breaking in before he reaches us.

Despite the bright weather and lengthening days, Eva and I stay inside the cavern of our house. Hour after hour we sit at the table by the unboarded window that is our only source of light. For breakfast we share a cup of rice, eating not out of hunger but out of habit. Lunch is half a jar of home-canned fruit, dinner a bowl of beans. Those three events shape our lives.

I try to study, but the words slip senselessly past me, snagging my attention only when they remind me of what I'm missing, of what I have yet to see or do or have or hear, where I have yet to go: *Lindos. Liszt. London.*

I dream of picking up rocks, rough chunks of dirt-colored shale on a cold plain beneath a grey sky, and wake to a despair so heavy it is an effort to move.

After *London Stock Exchange* comes *Londonderry*. After *Londonderry* comes the *Lone Ranger*. And after *Lone Ranger* comes *Lone Woman of San Nicolas Island.*

In 1853, an Indian woman was discovered living entirely alone on an island seventy miles off the coast of Santa Barbara. According to contemporary accounts, in 1835, while her tribe was being removed from the island on orders from the Mission of Santa Barbara, a strong wind sprang up. In the confusion, a child was left behind. When its mother discovered its absence, she swam back to the island to look for it, but while she was gone, the gale grew more threatening, and the captain gave the order to set sail without her.

Eighteen years elapsed before the Lone Woman was discovered by a crew of sea otter hunters. Although no one could speak her language, she used signs quite eloquently. She indicated she had never found her child, and feared the wild dogs had eaten it.

She returned to the mainland with the hunters, and was greatly disappointed to learn that none of her tribe could be found. She died seven weeks later.

And so the inexorable order of the encyclopedia speaks to my life yet again, this time making me face the worst truth of all: *There will be no rescue.*

Ever since this began we have been waiting to be saved, waiting like stupid princesses for our rightful lives to be restored to us. But we have only been fooling ourselves, only playing out another fairy tale. Our story can no more have a happy ending than the Lone Woman's did. The lights will never again come on out here. The phone will never ring for us. Eva and I will live like this until we die, hoarding and cringing and finally starving—if we aren't lucky enough to get our throats slit first.

However we die, we'll die here. Alone. There will be no matriculation at Harvard, no debut with the San Francisco Ballet. There will be no travels, no diplomas, no curtain calls. There will be no more lovers, no husbands, no children. No one will ever read this journal unless the damn chickens learn to read.

Of course this sort of thing happens all the time. I've studied enough history to understand that. Cultures topple, societies collapse, and little pockets of people are left, remnants and refugees, struggling to find food, to defend themselves from famine or disease or marauders while the grass grows up through the palace floors and the temples crumble. Look at Rome, Babylon, Crete, Egypt, look at the Incas or the American Indians.

And even if this isn't another two-thousand-year-old civilization coming to an end, look at all the minor devastations—the wars and revolutions, the hurricanes and volcanoes and droughts and floods and famines and plagues that filled the slick pages of the news magazines we used to read. Think of the photographs of the survivors huddled among the rubble with their desperate eyes and swollen bellies. Think of South America, South Africa, Central Asia, Eastern Europe, and ask how we could possibly have felt so smug. Think about the Lone Woman of San Nicolas Island and ask why we ever assumed we would be saved.

Our parents thought they were raising us well. They thought they were preparing us to be happy adults, intelligent, creative, productive, generous, secure. They thought we were going to grow up, move away, and lead interesting and successful lives. We were going to find mates who were our equals, were going to enrich the world with our very presence. Here we are instead—living without light or soap, abandoned in the forest with nothing to look forward to but the end.

———

The tulips are blooming, a brilliant, worthless wall, separating us from the forest, dividing nothing from nothing. If I could feel, I think they would make me angry. They are a gesture so futile that now I think I was right not to help my mother plant them, for what are they but a hoax, a fraud, another lie?

Here I sit in the cave of a room where once, in another lifetime, I ate popcorn and watched videos with my family. Now I look out at my mother's tulips and contemplate suicide.

It's a physical urge, huger and stronger than thirst or sex. Halfway back on the left side of my head there is a spot that yearns, that longs, that pleads for the jolt of a bullet. I want that rage, that fire, that final empty rip. I want to be let out of this dark cavern, to open myself up to the ease of not-living. I am tired of sorrow and struggle and worry. I am tired of my sad sister. I want to turn out the last light.

I could do it.

I could rise from this chair, say, *I'm going out for wood.* Eva would give her mute little nod, but she wouldn't look up, not even to see me lift the gun from its post by the door.

I could open the door. I could step outside, could close the door forever behind me. Break through the ring of my mother's tulips. Enter the twilit woods, the gun stiff at my side. Push a new path through the forest. In some dim circle of trees, I could sit down on the earth. Take off my shoe. Work my toes into the cold ring of the trigger guard. Fumble the trigger until it gave.

I am my own person, after all.

———

I stood up. I took the gun and opened the door. I was standing at the threshold, looking out at the fading sunset beyond the black trees, when I heard her voice, cracked with fright.

"Where are you going?"

"Just out. For wood." I didn't face her. The forest air was cold on my cheeks and hands.

"Why do you have the gun?"

"It's almost dark."

"But why take the gun?"

"Because I want to, all right?" I growled, turning on her with a ferocity so intense it startled us both. She met my eyes, held them, her face bruised like the darkening sky.

"All right," she said finally.

I stepped outside, closed the door, went trembling into the yard. The gun was cold and long and heavy. I circled the clearing, walking just inside the ring of tulips, their petals like dark flames, like cups of velvet. But beyond them the forest seemed solid, impenetrable. I could find no way to enter it. I stood in the clearing beneath the lurid sky, watched the purple and yellow fade, watched until the first mute stars appeared.

In that darkness I gathered an arm load of wood. In that darkness I reentered the house.

Once again my sister kept me from going where I wanted to go.

———

The days creep by. I think we're somewhere in the middle of April, but I have lost track of time. Weeks have passed since I've written anything in here, and when I try to match the blank squares of my calendar against the days we have just endured, I can figure no way to sort them out.

We breathe and another night arrives, so I suppose time continues. But my calendar is obsolete.

———

Last night I dreamed that someone was standing at the edge of the woods, threatening and taunting us while Eva and I cowered in the workroom beneath Mother's loom. I was holding a pair of shears and whispering to Eva that if he came too close we could cut off his hair. Suddenly the walls dissolved and I was aiming the rifle across the clearing.

I'll shoot! I screamed at him. I felt a surge of ecstatic power. *I'll kill you, I'll kill you, I'll kill you!* I cried. Triumphantly I squeezed the trigger. Nothing happened. In desperation I pulled it again, and saw that instead of a bullet, maggots were oozing from the barrel.

I woke tangled in panic, but even before I calmed enough to convince myself it was only a dream, the dream's meaning had crystallized. I stared up at the window where a faint starlight filtered into the room, and knew I had to learn to shoot the rifle.

This morning I took it out on the deck and tried to remember what little my father had shown me about guns. I was afraid to waste bullets, so over and over I practiced loading, releasing the safety, and aiming at the forest. Finally, after more than an hour of pretend, I stuck a man-tall stick by the side of the road at the edge of the clearing and set an old pickle jar upside down over it. Then I went back to the deck and, bracing myself against the railing, lined up the sights and pulled the trigger.

There was a blast so loud and hard I thought I had shot myself. My shoulder stung, my ears rang, and tears ran unbidden down my face. When I recovered, I was standing three feet back from the railing, the pickle jar was intact, and Eva was cringing at the doorway.

"I'm sorry," I said. "I've got to do this."

"I know," she whispered through stiff lips and vanished into the house.

I forced myself to try again. This time I was anticipating the punch of the stock against my shoulder, and I aimed too hastily, shying from the jolt of the gun before I even pulled the trigger. The barrel swung up wildly and the shot tore into the air.

I resolved to make myself do it right. I decided to try to trick myself into not flinching by easing the trigger back so slowly I would never know the moment at which it fired. The brunt of the recoil slapped my shoulder and the barrel remained level, but the shot vanished into the forest, and the jar stayed on the stick.

It seemed to me that somewhere I had heard you should always sight a little high, so for the next shot I aimed in the air above the jar. Once again I avoided flinching, but once again the shot sped harmlessly into the forest.

I felt as though I had been beaten. My shoulder was weak and aching. My head was ringing, my hands were wet, and I thought I couldn't endure having to pull the trigger another time. But the pickle jar taunted me from the edge of the clearing, as menacing as the man in my nightmare.

Desperately, I reviewed my knowledge of trajectories and parabolic curves and reasoned that before a bullet could fall, it must first rise. I sighted a little low, and pulled the trigger as gently as I could. In a blink the pickle jar exploded, leaving me trembling with elation and terror.

———————

Her face is mending, but day after day my sister remains silent, not sullen, but with a helpless sweetness that reminds me of our father's dying smile. She seems almost apologetic, as though she would gladly leave her shock and fear behind, shed them like a worn skin, if only she knew how. She's begun tending the fire again, but I do the few other things that get done. I give her food, and what she doesn't eat, I eat myself, or save for the next meal.

"Want to play Backgammon?" I asked once, but she shrugged so listlessly I knew it was useless to set up the game.

She hasn't entered her studio since the rape.

"Why don't you dance?" I urged yesterday.

Startled, she looked up from her lap. It was as though I had asked her why she didn't play the bagpipes, or why she didn't fly.

"I can't," she said.

"Let's use the gas," I said, "so you can hear some music again."

But her body remained passive and no desire brightened her face. "No," she answered. "No. We'd better save it."

———————

This morning I woke with the sun full on my face and the headache I've been battling for days finally gone. I felt light as an angel, suffused with the sort of shaky energy that follows an illness. My lungs felt flat, my muscles limp, but my body was eager to be used. Taking the gun with me I went outside to sweep the deck. Then I rinsed out a pile of clothes and hung them on the line in the sun-scented wind, feeling—between my furtive glances at the forest—full half-seconds of pleasure in the sweep of the broom and the warm tug of the breeze.

On my way back from the clothes line I passed the garden. It was a mess, and I felt a stab of failure and guilt. We didn't even finish harvesting last fall. We never pulled plants or saved seeds or mulched. We hadn't pruned the orchard. We should have started seedlings indoors by the stove back in February. We should have planted the cold weather crops last month. We should be planting tomato, pepper, cucumber, and melon starts now. But the last time either of us held a shovel was to dig our father's grave.

I opened the gate and entered the garden. Slowly I walked the perimeter of the plot, just inside the chicken wire deer fence, trying to remember everything I had ever resisted learning about gardening. Underneath the snarl of pungent, tough, sticky weeds, I thought I could see the leaves of a volunteer potato plant. I dropped to my knees, set the rifle down beside me, grabbed a clump of weeds in one tentative hand, and pulled. They resisted, and I thought of hair—handfuls of hair rooted in a scalp. I shuddered, gritted my teeth, and tugged harder. Finally the roots gave, and I almost tumbled backwards as they tore free. The little circle of bare soil they revealed was dark and damp. I worked my hands into it, felt it press under my fingernails, crumble through my fingers. Suddenly I was pulling weeds, plunging my hands into their lush midst, tearing them out by the fistful, until my palms were stained and reeking with their green musk.

The sun felt like a hand on my shoulders, birds called at the edge of the clearing, and once a butterfly landed on the naked soil next to me. It sat still for a moment, and then closed and opened its flat wings and flew on. I forgot to scan the forest for intruders.

I remembered the seeds. Springing up from the garden, I jogged to the workshop, found on a top shelf an airtight plastic box crammed with a jumble of paper envelopes. Some were commercial packets, but most were envelopes salvaged from old bills, labeled in our father's handwriting, and filled with the lumps and beads of home-grown seeds. Back inside the deer fence, I spread the packets on the ground and shuffled through them, intent and absorbed, plotting a garden.

When I quit at noon, a strip of soil the length of the garden was weeded and turned and ready to be sown.

The encyclopedia reminds me that a flower's whole reason for being is to produce seeds. All that color and scent and nectar exist solely for the purpose of transporting pollen, solely to attract the attentions of insects or to take advantage of the wind. The reason for flowers is these inert, unremarkable little specks and knobs, these palmsful of chromosomes that may one day feed us.

I planted pumpkin seeds this morning—three to a mound in a row across the west side of the garden. Scrawled in my father's handwriting on the envelope in which I found them was a single word—*Pumpkin*. For a wild moment when I first read it, I thought he had addressed the envelope to me. But when I tore it open and saw only seeds like those we used to scoop from jack o'lanterns, tears I didn't want to own bullied their way into my eyes.

Still, there's a lucidity that sometimes comes in that moment when you find yourself looking at the world through your tears, as if those tears served as a lens to clarify whatever it is you see. As I stared at the word my father had pencilled there, I saw that perhaps it was a message to me, after all.

———

I hurt so much it's hard to hold this pen. My hands are throbbing with blisters and scratches, stiff with the soil it seems that no amount of scrubbing can ever wash completely clean. My arms and legs and back ache as though I had the flu. I never realized what hard work gardening is.

So far I've planted over half the seeds, and tomorrow I'm going to take down the deer fence so I can expand the garden all the way to the shed. We've got to have that much space at least, if it's to keep us alive.

———

"I need help," I said this morning as I blew the steam off the surface of my white tea and took a sip. "In the garden."

Eva looked down at her untouched rice.

"I can't set the new fence posts by myself. And it's almost impossible for one person to stretch out chicken wire. It keeps rolling back on itself."

Eva said, "Maybe tomorrow."

"It's as safe as staying in here," I reasoned. "Safer—because I've got the gun and there's more ways to run."

"I just—I don't feel like going out there today."

"But Eva, the garden won't wait until you feel like it. We've got to get the rest of it planted as soon as possible. Besides, if we don't have it fenced again before the seeds I've already planted come up, the deer will eat the sprouts."

"It doesn't matter."

"What?"

"It doesn't matter what we do. It doesn't matter if the deer eat the sprouts."

I felt as though I had been hit. Her words stung in the blisters on my hands, punched my aching back and thighs. I took a drink of the scalding water in my mug as though I could use its heat as inspiration for my fight. But before I could begin to protest, her words had reached my heart.

"You're right," I answered quietly.

She looked up in surprise. "What?"

"You're right. It doesn't matter. We'll probably get killed before these seeds even sprout."

She bowed her head. In that silence I finished my rice and water, and tried to plan how I could set the redwood posts I had cut for the fence by myself, how I could unroll the chicken wire and tack it tight without my sister's help.

But when I stood up from the table, Eva stood, too, and followed me out to the yard she had not entered since the rape.

I had already limbed and topped half a dozen small trees, and dug the holes for them with Father's rickety posthole digger. Eva followed me to the shed, watched as I heaved the half-full bag of cement mix into my arms, and then trailed me back to the garden. While I tried to empty the bag into a bucket, she stood meekly by, her hands hanging heavily by her sides.

"See," I said, to fill the silence, "the bottom half of this bag must have gotten wet, but hopefully there's still enough for six holes, especially if I break some of the hard stuff up. Can you hold the bucket for me?"

She darted a glance at the forest before she bent stiffly and steadied the bucket. As soon as I had dumped in enough cement mix for the first batch, she straightened up as though her job were done. She looked ready to race back to the house. To keep her with me I began to talk.

"Good," I said, "now we've got to mix it. Why don't you find something to stir with while I get the water?"

She returned with a stick, and I continued talking. "I'll pour while you stir. That's it—all the way to the bottom of the bucket. Let me add a little more water. Okay, I'll lift this first post into the hole, and hold it straight. You wedge some of these rocks down around it. Good—that's good. We need to pack the cement down over them now. Can you get me some more rock?"

Step by step we set the posts, me explaining and encouraging and Eva woodenly responding to my requests. By noon three new fence posts stood along the west side of the garden.

At lunchtime I had to open a second jar of peaches, and by the end of the day, when all but one post on the east side was set, she was anticipating the work's needs, and even offering a little advice.

Eva ate all of her breakfast rice this morning. Out in the garden, she offered to mix the cement while I gathered rock to wedge around the post in the final hole. But when I bent to lift it into place, something seemed to give in my lower back. I lurched forward onto my knees while my muscles screamed and twisted.

"What is it?" asked Eva, bending beside me.

"My back," I gasped. "It hurts."

"Lie down," she said, with an authority I had not heard since she last danced. "On your back. Flat. Bend your knees. You want the whole spine to touch the ground. You've got to rest it before you do any more damage. Didn't anyone ever tell you not to lift with your back?"

I lay still until my muscles quit their spasms. But when I tried to sit they clenched again and I had to wince in pain.

"Lie back," Eva commanded. "It takes awhile. But if you rest now, you'll probably be able to dance—I mean work—tomorrow."

"We were almost done," I moaned, "and the lettuce is beginning to sprout."

"I'll finish it," she said. "The deer can grow their own damn lettuce."

So while I lay with my spine pressed against the soil, Eva set the final fence post and wrestled a ring of chicken wire around the extended garden.

"We can stretch and tack it tomorrow," she said when she had finished. "It's makeshift," she added with a satisfaction that sounded like our father's, "but I think it'll keep the animals out for one night. Come on, Nell. We've got to put you to bed."

———

Next morning my back felt fine. But Eva insisted on giving me a massage before we went out to the garden.

"If we don't take care of it now, it'll plague you for a long time. I know," she said, pushing me down on my mattress with an imperiousness that delighted me.

To please her, I lifted off my nightshirt and then lay still, marvelling at how quickly her hands found sore spots I had not even been aware of. I sighed and relaxed into her ministrations, giving the remnants of my pain up to her fingers. Her hands felt so capable, so intelligent and caring, and I luxuriated not only in their feel, but also what it implied, that the sister I loved so much still existed, might finally be returning.

"There," she said at last. "How's that?"

I moaned my pleasure, and she moved away, leaving me lying on my mattress, eyes closed, arms outstretched, a puddle of happy flesh preparing myself for the day ahead, anticipating the needs of the garden that had absorbed my attention and devotion since I pulled the first handful of weeds.

"Ready or not," I said when my plans had crescendoed and it seemed I could no longer lie still, "here I come!"

I pushed myself up from my mattress and was looking for a tee shirt when I caught sight of Eva.

She was sitting at her place by the table, and silent tears were rolling down her face, the first tears of hers I had seen since I found her bruised and weeping in the yard.

"Oh, Eva," I said. "What is it?"

She shook her head as if to shake away her crying, but when the tears continued to course down her face, she answered, "I get so scared, I can't stop it. It's like black waves, and I'm a little cork. I bob to the surface and think I'll do okay, and then another wave comes and I'm drowning again."

I went to her, bent over her, pressed my naked arms around her. She sat motionless, her face glazed with tears. Then suddenly she turned, sobbing wildly, and buried her face against my chest. She cried until my breasts were slick with tears, while I held her, rocked her back and forth in my arms.

"My turn," I whispered, when her crying had finally begun to wane. She tried to laugh a protest between her sobs, but I took her hand, pulled her from her chair and led her to her mattress.

"Lie down," I said. "Let's see if I learned anything."

I winced when my blistered palms first met her skin. At the touch of my hands, she began to weep even harder. "It's okay," I told her. "You can cry now, all you need."

At first I simply stroked my sister's back. *See,* my hands said, *here is Eva's neck, here are the curves of her ribs, these are her sad shoulders, and the lovely vertebrae of her spine, here is the tender bowl of muscle that is the small of her back.* Then, starting just below her occipital bone, I massaged the strong trapezii that run down her neck and across her shoulders, rolling them like ropes between my fingers, the symmetry of my hands matching the symmetry of her back. Over and over I pinched and eased and soothed those clenched muscles while she wept into the sheet on which she lay. I forgot about my oozing blisters, forgot even about the moist soil waiting outdoors, and concentrated entirely on how my hands were speaking to her shoulders.

Gradually I teased and rubbed and urged the pent-up sorrows from her shoulders. Finally I felt those muscles begin to give, to ease, to loosen so imperceptibly I would have thought it was my imagination if it weren't for the fact that her crying, too, began to quiet. She sighed, and my hands began forays down her back, across her ribs, along her spine.

When it seemed she had softened back into herself, I dug deeper, pushing and kneading and squeezing the horrible memories and new habits the rest of her body harbored. She shuddered and winced, stiffened and struggled, and each time finally gave way, relaxing even more profoundly as her muscles discovered there was no need to cling to all that pain.

Slowly my sister softened, grew passive and spent, until at last every muscle in her back was loose, and when I lifted her arm, her hand flopped limply. For the first time since the rape, her flesh was not afraid, and I felt a joy rise in me, through my hands, up my arms, swelling my heart because it seemed it was in my power to make my sister well.

I began caressing her softly then, my hands working as gently as breath across her back, telling her good-bye, that my work was done. I touched her the way I would touch a fledgling bird, treasuring and tendering what I could hardly believe had allowed itself to be held. But even as I stroked her to wean her from my touch, it seemed I could feel new tension enter her body. For if her flesh was now relaxed, it was also vulnerable and open to intrusion, and I could sense her fear that I might leave her.

So I continued to stroke her, waiting for the time when her body would tell my hands it no longer needed their touch. I loved her so—my sweet, sweet sister—loved in her all else I had ever loved, loved all of her I knew and all I knew I could never reach, loved this dancer, this beautiful woman beneath my hands, sister with whom I had once peopled a forest, sister with whom I had suffered so many awful things, sister whom I could leave for neither love nor death.

I love you, my hands said. *Remember this is yours,* they told her. *This body is yours. No one can ever take it from you, if only you will accept it yourself, claim it again—your arms, your spine, your ribs, the small of your back. It's all yours. All this bounty, all this beauty, all this strength and grace is yours. This garden is yours. Take it. Take it back.*

I ached with love for her. My hands trembled across her back. I wanted to save her life, wanted to call her soul back from the dark place where it crouched. I loved her so much, loved each swell and plane of her, each quirk and quickness, loved the eager way her lungs drew air, the way her spine arched as my hands floated the curve of her hips, wandered down the twin columns of her thighs to the hollows of her knees, and then retraced their path, to meet at that shadow where her legs converged.

When she turned to face me, I could see she had returned at last. She was alive with a longing that so shook me that I quailed. But before I could pull away, she began, with fingers and palms and breath and tongue, to teach me more than I had just showed her about the sanctity and rapture of being flesh.

We made love, my sister and I. Together we resurrected the joy of both our bodies. Together we learned that not all force is violence, and when Eva, who had huddled into her shame and silence and pain, arched and opened, and cried out, I knew that something precious had been redeemed.

We cuddled like babies until we slept, and later we woke and rose together from her mattress, dressed and drank water and went outside together to plant the new garden.

———

It must be almost June by now, though that's only the roughest of guesses. These days we spend all our time in the garden. In the gray dawn we drink our cups of white tea and eat our meager breakfast. By the time the sky has begun to blossom with color, we're outdoors, shivering in the chill air as we open the gate with stiff fingers. We thin and weed while the sun rises, our breath coming in white puffs, our bodies loosening, warming into the work. Later, when our hands can stand the cold, we start to water. First we use a hose to siphon out the old claw-foot tub our father set up to collect water in after the electric pump quit. When the tub is empty, we begin our endless trips to the stream, carrying water to the garden a bucketful at a time.

We've planted every seed we've got, every seed our father left us, even those unidentified ones that sifted down into the bottom of the box. We're fertilizing every volunteer, pleading with every plant to live, to thrive, to blossom into food.

Digging, weeding, watering a careful pailful at a time, we work until the sun is above us. We stop for lunch and a rest, and then we work until the light begins to thicken and the cool air brings its swarms of mosquitoes. At night when I lie in bed, my muscles tremble and my calloused hands ache. I close my eyes, and I see dirt. But I have no dreams.

We still glance towards the woods more often than we did before, and we don't venture outside the clearing, beyond the withered ring of tulips. We still jump when a hawk calls or a jay squawks or a deer crashes through the forest. I carry the rifle with me wherever I go, and we still retreat indoors well before nightfall. Long before they're ready to roost, we lure Bathsheba and Pinky into their coop with garden thinnings. And once we are inside, we triple-check the boarded windows and move an elaborate assortment of furniture in front of the door before we begin to fix our dinner. But all that has begun to seem more like a ritual than a strategy for survival—I am almost certain the man who shattered our lives is not lingering in the forest, that we are safe at least until the next one wanders in.

I worry about the seeds my father saved because they are the result of last year's hybrids, and I worry about next year, when all the seeds we plant will be open-pollinated. I worry about when to plant and how to fertilize, and whether or not we'll have enough water. I worry about low germination rates, and diseases and insects and accidents. But I haven't wanted to be dead since the day I entered the garden.

Eva still doesn't dance. But she works as hard as I do, and sometimes she laughs in the morning when we greet the rows of new seedlings that have pushed through the earth while we slept.

We have begun to hold hands for a moment before we eat, our faces bowed over our plates of food, and though I can't really say what we mean by that gesture, we find we do not want to eat without first reaching for each other's hands. That is the only time we touch.

———

Eva threw up yesterday morning. My first reaction was stark horror as I thought of ptomaine poisoning, dysentery, cholera, *Giardia*, the flu that killed Eli's mother. I insisted that we take her temperature. But it was normal, she didn't have diarrhea, and she hadn't eaten anything I hadn't also eaten.

"I'm okay," she kept insisting, "just a little queasy."

Finally she sent me on to the garden without her.

"I'm fine," she said. "I just need a nap." And when I came in at noon, she had fixed me lunch.

But this morning she threw up again, and again I had to go to the garden without her. I watered the carrot sprouts, weeded the potatoes, and was splitting firewood, the ax raised above my head, when an explanation for her sickness popped into my head, and my arms let the ax come tumbling down in stunned disbelief. It glanced against the upended log, and the log rolled off the chopping block onto my feet.

By noon Eva said she felt better, and she worked in the garden until dusk. But tonight I find myself watching her surreptitiously, sneaking glances at her belly, her breasts, sneaking glances at the encyclopedia: *In addition to the physician's tests for raised levels of chorionic gonadotropin, pregnancy is first recognized by the symptoms of nausea, swollen breasts, and missed menstrual periods.*

Not that, goes the voice inside my head in a dead-end prayer, a mantra of despair. *Not that. After all we've been through, please, please, please—not that.*

———

Abortion, the spontaneous or induced expulsion from the uterus of the nonviable fetus. Purposeful abortion techniques have been practiced by almost all cultures, with or without social countenance.

What techniques? How have they been practiced? I don't need a definition or a vague sociological treatise. What I need are facts. Details. Descriptions. Directions.

What I need is an abortion manual.

There's got to be a way. I think about it constantly. Bending under the sun, crawling across the earth between the frail green rows that sprout our future, I think about abortion.

Eva keeps throwing up and saying she's fine. Her periods were always so inconsistent because of her dancing she may not have realized it yet herself.

———

This morning we were pulling weeds, moving side by side down the rows of beans whose green seed leaves were unfolding from the earth like pairs of wings. I had just finished breakfast, and Eva had again refused to eat.

"No food," she said, when I had offered her a hard-boiled egg just larger than an avocado seed, the first the hens had laid for months.

But now she was crawling along beside me on the moist dirt, our paths separated by a line of tender plants. In a funny way it seemed almost holy, to be inching along on our knees, breathing on the plants, tending to them. The earth was cool, the sun warm, the birds were busy, and I realized with a sudden shock that for the first time since my being with Eli I had just had a moment of unabashed and easy happiness.

"If all this grows," I said, sweeping an arm around the expanded garden, "the two of us just may make it through next winter."

Eva had stopped, too. She rocked back on her haunches and said, "There'll be three of us."

For a disconnected moment I thought she meant Eli was returning, and then I saw we were talking about that other thing, and I wanted to keep weeding. But she sat there watching me, waiting for me to speak.

"What do you mean?" I stammered.

"There's a baby coming."

"I've been afraid of that."

"Yes," she said, working her hands into the chocolate soil, "there is. I wasn't sure before. But now I am."

"What do you want to do about it?"

She looked at me quizzically as she squeezed a handful of earth in her palm. "What can we do about it?" she asked.

"Well, I'm not sure yet," I answered, "but there's got to be a way. We'll figure it out."

"Figure what out?"

"You know."

"What?"

"How to stop it."

"Stop it?" She opened her fist so that the clump of dirt lay on her palm, ridged and whorled with the pattern of her hand. "Why?"

"But Eva—you can't have it."

"Why not?" she asked, as if she had never spent all those years in her studio, fighting something as basic as gravity.

"Are you kidding? How will we take care of it?"

"I don't know. We'll find a way. Anyway," she shrugged lightly, "it's started. We can't stop it."

"Of course we can. There are lots of ways. The encyclopedia doesn't say much, but I think we can figure it out. There're hot baths and hard exercise and maybe herbs. We could try the rest of the cough syrup."

"Do you know what you're saying? There's going to be a baby. You can't just stop a baby."

"It's not a baby yet. And you can stop it if you have to."

"Why would I have to?"

"Eva," I gasped. "You were raped."

She flinched and grabbed her abdomen as though she could protect it from those words.

"That has nothing to do with it."

"What?"

"That has nothing to do with it."

"But Eva, it's his baby."

"Whose?" she asked sharply, and for a second I swear she really had no idea who I meant. Then she scoffed, "That man's? Do you really think he could possibly make a baby?"

She rocked forward onto her hands and knees, resumed her slow crawl beside the beans. "And even if that was when this started," she said, as she drew a weed from her path, its roots tender white veins in the sunshine. "Even if it did start then," she repeated, lifting her eyes to hold mine, "how could this baby possibly be his?"

"Well, genetics—"

"Genetics!" she snapped the word out as though it were her rapist's name. "Genetics. Did that ever make sense to you, Nell, that a woman could be pregnant and carry a baby inside her for nine months and then nurse it and care for it and change its diapers, and a man could claim it was half his?"

"Our father changed our diapers."

"Then he earned his share in us. Besides," she pulled another weed, her voice strong, gentle, and as sure as I had ever heard it, "how can this baby even be mine?"

"What do you mean?" I asked.

"It's its own person," she answered triumphantly.

———

So my sister is going to have a baby. Several times in the days between then and now, I've been swept by a worry so strong and cold it felt like getting caught in an ocean wave, tumbling in a wash of icy water and gritty sand, unable to breathe, fighting to find which way is up.

Then the wave recedes, leaves me dry and standing on my feet, watering squashes, weeding tomatoes, staking up beans, making preparations for whatever future we may have left.

Last night I dreamed that Eva and I were sitting on the ground beside the redwood stump where I first made love with Eli. A bear came shambling out of the forest towards us. Stiff with fear, we watched it approach, saw the easy shift and roll of the powerful muscles beneath its fur. As it loomed closer, I noticed the bloated ticks ringing its eyes, saw the shocking length of its unsheathed yellow claws, and I was sick with fear.

It approached me until it stood directly in front of me. It opened its mouth, and I saw its thick teeth and the naked pink of its tongue. A terror as great as any I have ever known settled over me like a suffocating blanket, and I closed my eyes, surrendering myself to those jaws. But next I felt not the rip and tear of teeth, but the wet scratch of a tongue and the rank wind of bear's breath on my face.

A moment later it left me, and shambled over to lick and breathe on Eva, enveloping her face, too, in its wide jaws. Then it disappeared into the woods, and I sat by the stump, thinking, *So that's how babies are made.*

———

The encyclopedia doesn't say a lot about pregnancy and childbirth, though there are long articles on conception and fetal development and a worthless entry about the types of drugs obstetricians use during labor. There is a section called *Abnormal Changes During Pregnancy* and another on *Accidents During Labor,* but I can't bring myself to read those yet.

It does say, *A woman's strength and general physical health are several of the many factors affecting labor length and outcome.* And also, *Walking is considered the exercise of choice for the parturient woman.*

Even armed with the machete and the rifle, we felt as though we were going to our doom, when we left the clearing and entered the forest for our first walk. Despite the midday heat, we wore boots and long pants and we felt a tight sense of foreboding as we followed the dirt road away from the house.

The forest looked lush and safe, but we jumped at the sound of each other's footsteps. Even the breeze made us wince. We had rounded the first curve in the overgrown road when something started in the underbrush and went bounding and crashing up the hill away from us. A little sheepishly we agreed we had gone far enough for the first day and we headed home.

But we went out again the next day and ventured a bit further down the road. The day after that we inspected the orchard and the following day we walked to the bridge. On the way home I realized with a shock I had left the gun in the garden.

After a hard winter and an uncertain spring, both hens are laying again and we are rich in eggs, most of which we scramble with parsley, rosemary, and basil from the garden or hard-boil to eat with sprinkles of our hoarded garlic salt.

The garden is doing pretty well now, too, although not a single melon or broccoli seed ever germinated, the corn seems to have stopped growing, and the last row of lettuce I planted produced only a few ragged plants. But we're already eating chard and spinach and peas, and tonight we had a salad of beet green thinnings.

I never realized what a lovely flower garden a vegetable patch is. The squashes sport wide golden blossoms, tomato flowers are scattered like white stars among the green vines, and the bean plants are decorated with lavender buds.

Down in the orchard, the fruit trees are loaded with small, hard fruit, and the green knobs of nuts fill the walnut tree.

Eva's flat stomach has begun to show a tidy bulge, though there are still moments when I can't believe she is really pregnant, when I'm sure it was all a dream, when I'm certain her fickle period will still arrive. She has regained some of her old grace and moves like herself again, though she still does not dance.

Nothing seems to bother her these days. She forgets to lock the door at night. She doesn't give a thought to the emptying pantry. She hardly notices the ragged holes in the chard leaves, the stunted pepper plants, the scruffy cucumbers, or the puny corn. She doesn't worry as I do about F1 crosses or sterile seeds. She has never thought to count the canning lids or wonder what will happen if the spring runs dry.

But I worry for both of us. I worry about pests and diseases and accidents. I worry about fire and marauders. I worry about the hens and the orchard, about the broken shingles on the roof, and the sagging utility room. At night I lie awake, staring into the blackness, and wonder how we will ever get a baby out of Eva and how on earth we will manage once it's here.

———————

I still read the encyclopedia sometimes, not for the Achievement Tests or Harvard seminars but in the same way I once read novels—for the stories it contains. I read only at night now, in those few minutes after the day's work is done and before the last light fades from the room. I have abandoned the alphabet, and I skip and skim, sprawling on my mattress with the volume propped up beside me and reading whatever catches my fancy until my weary body drags me into sleep and the final sentences mingle with my dreams.

Redwood (Sequoia sempervirens), *the coast redwood is the world's tallest tree and one of the most long-lived. In favorable parts of their range, coast redwoods can live more than two thousand years. Although only one seed in a million becomes a mature redwood, only wind and storm and man pose any threat to a full-grown tree.*

Even when redwoods are toppled or otherwise injured, they have a remarkable adaptation for survival. Wart-like growths of dormant buds called burls are stimulated to produce sprouts which grow from a fallen or damaged tree. It is common to see young trees formed from burls encircling an injured parent tree.

———————

We hadn't intended to go there when we set out on our walk this afternoon. At first we just headed down the road, and then, right before we reached the bridge, we decided to turn off onto a game trail we discovered a few days ago. It led us through a thicket and across a flat space where the forest canopy was high above us and there was little undergrowth. After a while the trees began to grow smaller and denser again, and we found we were hiking uphill. Following the narrow trail in single file, we climbed slowly and steadily, each of us absorbed in the clean sound of our breathing, the honest burn of the muscles in our thighs.

When I realized we were walking through the same part of the forest we had torn through to reach our dying father, my first thought was to turn back. But that impulse passed and suddenly I felt an urgent need to see his grave. I wanted to face it, to know for certain what had happened. I wanted to see if my old nightmares were true.

I wanted that so intensely I felt reluctant to mention it, in case Eva would decide to turn back. I was following her, and just as I was beginning to feel guilty for tricking her into going where she might not want to go, I saw her pace slow. A second later, she squared her shoulders and kept walking. Later, when we passed a patch of purple wildflowers, she stooped to pick a few.

By the time Eva led us into the glade, my hands, too, were filled with flowers, and I was panting and hot and ready for a rest. Even so, I entered that place hesitantly, ready to wince and run.

There was our father's grave, closed and quiet. Despite a winter's worth of rain and oak leaves and fir needles, it seemed barer than the ground around it. But it was not opened. We faced only warming dirt and not the torn earth or strewn flesh of my nightmares.

I have to admit I felt a sense of accomplishment looking at that quiet mound. Somehow we had known what to do. We had dug deep and filled it well, so that now, after one winter, our father's grave lay closed, healing cleanly like a well-tended wound.

We lay our flowers on the mound, and then sat beside it in a deep silence as though we were sitting beside an old friend with whom words were no longer needed. I pressed my palms against the soil that covered my father's decomposing cells and thought of maggots, rot, and worms, remembered all the nightmares I had woken to in the darkness of our house, all those images that left me stiff and wet with dread and guilt.

I imagined my father's face bloating, collapsing beneath its load of dirt. I imagined the writhing insects, the thick liquids, the putrefaction. And yet, that held no horror. *So what?* I thought. *We shit when we're alive, rot when we're dead. That's nature. That's our nature.*

In that gentle wash of early summer sun, I dozed, dreamed again, felt in the sun on my head the weight and warmth of my father's hand. I remembered how when I was a little girl he used to come into my room at bedtime, how he would sit on my bed for a joke and a moment of talk before he bent to kiss me, to say, "Sweet dreams, Pumpkin," and leave me warm and safe in the benevolent night.

It came to me then that I could take comfort in knowing my father and my mother were dead, that death's mystery had already embraced them. Whatever happened when a person died had happened to them. They had gone on ahead, had broken the trail, and because of that, death seemed a little cozier, a little safer, a little less terrifying. Because my parents were already there—in death—I saw I could afford to enjoy the sunlight for as long as I possibly could. Sitting beside my father's grave, I was glad—and unafraid—to be alive.

Then Eva, who had been rummaging in the weeds on the other side of the grave, said, "Look at this."

"What?"

"Aren't these strawberries?" she asked, holding out a few berries the color and size of drops of blood.

"I guess so," I answered.

"They look ripe," she said, lifting them to her mouth.

"Eva!" I gasped before she could taste them.

"What?"

"You can't eat them."

"Why not?"

"They might be poisonous."

"Strawberries?"

"They might not be strawberries."

"What else could they be?"

"I don't know. But you can't take a chance," I said, pointing at her belly.

She looked down at herself, shrugged, and held the berries out to me. "Okay. You try them."

Wild plants can kill you, I heard my mother say as Eva poured the berries into my palm. But they looked so innocuous, so sweet and innocent, and before I could think, I tossed them into my mouth. The seeds felt like tiny grains of sand between my teeth and the tang of strawberry burst on my tongue.

"What do they taste like?" asked Eva.

"Strawberries," I answered, "only stronger. Strawberries to the tenth power."

I bent to look for more. "If they're going to kill me," I said, "I want to make sure they do a good job."

"Hey!" cried Eva. "Don't hog them all."

We left our father's grave and nibbled our way home, foraging from one patch to the next, grazing mindlessly as cows, greedily as kids, following the faint, meandering trail of strawberries that seemed to spread from that quiet glade through the whole forest.

Tonight it came to me, as we sipped our bedtime cups of white tea—surely there is more than just an afternoon's treat of berries in the woods. Surely the forest is filled with things to eat. The Indians who once lived here survived without orchards or gardens, ate nothing but what these woods had to offer.

But I have no idea where to begin. I have studied botany. I know about plant morphology and physiology. I know how plants grow and how they reproduce. I can recognize a plant cell under the microscope, can list the chemical reactions that cause photosynthesis. But I don't know the names of the flowers we left on our father's grave. I don't know the names of the weeds we pull from the garden or even what kind of leaves we use for toilet paper.

I can recognize poison oak. I can tell an oak tree from a redwood. But all the other names—Latin or Indian or common—are lost to me. I can't even begin to guess which plants are edible or how else they might be used. *That bush*, I say, *that flower* or *those weeds*. And how can bushes or flowers or weeds feed us, clothe us, cure us?

How can I have spent my whole life here and know so little?

————

"There has to be a way we can learn about wild plants," I said to Eva this morning, after having said it to myself all night.

She looked up from her plate of eggs to ask, "How did other people do it?"

"What do you mean?"

"How did anyone ever learn which plants were good to eat?"

"I suppose someone had to try them."

"So?"

"We can't do that—it might kill us."

"What does your encyclopedia say?" she asked, rising from the table.

"Nothing."

She carried her plate into the kitchen and was at the front door when she turned to say, "I thought Mom bought a book about the plants around here—so she could try dyeing with them."

Entering our mother's workroom was like entering the airless darkness of a tomb. With the window boarded over, there wasn't even light enough for me to read the titles of the books crammed into the bookshelves that covered two of the walls, so armload by armload I carried them into the front room, and then armload by armload I returned them to their shelves—books about educational theories and weaving techniques, car repair manuals, murder mysteries, histories, biographies, novels. I rejected the Bible, and *The Age of Innocence,* and *The Life of Einstein*, hauling each out into the light and then returning it back to its place on the dusty shelves.

Finally I went out to the workshop for the claw hammer and the crowbar.

"What're those for?" called Eva from the garden as I passed.

"I need some light," I answered.

The nails squealed and protested, the hammer slipped and gouged the window frame, and I sliced my hand on the corrugated tin, but finally I got it down and daylight resumed its residence in my mother's workroom.

I found *Native Plants of Northern California* wedged on a top shelf between *Madame Bovary* and a book about the Spanish Civil War. Although my mother had written her name inside the front cover, its spine was unbroken and its pages pristine, as though she never had a chance to read it before the cancer stole even her love of color. I opened it eagerly, drawn not by a quest for color but by the lure of food.

It was a disappointment. I think unconsciously I had been expecting a friend, a guide, a grandmother. I had been imagining a wise woman who loved us and who knew how much we had suffered, who would rise from the pages of that book and lead me into the woods, kneeling by the stream to show me herbs, poking her stick into the bank to dig up roots, patiently teaching me where to find, when to harvest, and how to prepare the forest's bounty.

Of course there was no such woman, only entry after entry of Latin names and botanical descriptions and vague black and white sketches or out-of-focus photographs. *Native Plants of Northern California* is as dense and confusing as the forest it is supposed to describe. All day while Eva gardened, I pushed grimly through its pages, trying to connect the weeds in the woods with the grainy photographs and spindly drawings, trying to rekindle meaning in words I had once memorized—*petiole, umbel, raceme.*

Tonight I am more confused than ever. I feel as if I'm trying to learn a new language without the help of tapes and books, a language for which there are no longer any native speakers, and for the first time in my life, I wonder if I can pass the test.

———

There is a little plant that grows beside the workshop that I think is sheep sorrel. The encyclopedia doesn't mention sheep sorrel but *Native Plants* has a description that seems to fit, though there's no illustration. The dictionary says sheep sorrel has pleasantly acid-tasting auricled leaves. "Auricled" means ear-shaped, and I suppose those lobed leaves might be considered ear-shaped, though they look more like arrowheads than ears to me.

I can find no other description that fits any better, and surely, I reason over and over again, if the dictionary says sheep sorrel is pleasantly acid-tasting, it can't be poisonous—though the dictionary's definition for deadly nightshade says nothing about poison.

What an act of courage and faith and luck it is to pluck and taste a little green leaf. With Eva standing beside me in the cool evening and our mother's warnings buzzing in my brain, I felt as though I were recreating the history of humankind as I bent, picked a leaf, brushed a delicate coating of dust from its surface, and took a nibble, so tentatively I think I expected it to burn my lips. But it had a cool, delicate, clean taste. It tasted sour and green, like chlorophyll, pickles, or the evening air. It was a little tough, almost like lettuce that's bolted—but fresher, more alive.

"What's it like?" asked Eva, watching me.

"It's good," I said, "a little sour."

We went inside to our dinner of beet greens, peas, and boiled eggs. I woke once in the night with a little cramp and lay awake a long time, wondering if I were going to die and wanting desperately to live.

———

There's not much that's at its prime in the forest in midsummer. The spring greens have turned so tough and bitter we can't eat them, and the autumn fruits and nuts and seeds aren't yet ripe. But so far, I've tried watercress, purslane, plantain, shepherd's purse, soap plant root, redwood sorrel, lamb's quarters, amaranth, wild mustard greens, and a late patch of miner's lettuce.

Slowly I'm beginning to untangle the forest, to attach names to the plants that fill it. The leaves we use as toilet paper are mullein. The plant with the tiny daisy-like flowers that grows by the workshop is pineapple weed—a cousin of chamomile. The weed in the garden with the triangular leaves is lamb's quarters. All these years, the bushes that line the roadside have been hazelnut bushes. And the flowers we laid on our father's grave were blue-eyed grass—the root of which is supposed to reduce fever and ease an upset stomach.

Native Plants says the maples in these woods will produce sugar sap, that coltsfoot leaves can give us salt, that the Indians who once lived here used Spanish moss for diapers, California poppies as a painkiller, and molded acorn meal as an antibiotic. There are plants to stop fevers, plants to relieve colds, plants to soothe rashes and menstrual cramps. There are plants to strengthen Eva's contractions and ease her pain in labor, plants to make her baby strong, plants to help her milk come in.

There are teas. For months now we have drunk hot water when we could have been drinking wild mint, wild rose, blackberry, bay, mountain grape, black mustard, pennyroyal, manzanita, fennel seed, sheep sorrel, nettle, fir needle, madrone bark, yerba buena, black sage, pineapple weed, violet, wild raspberry.

And there are acorns. *Native Plants* says, *Worldwide and throughout history, acorns have served as a staple part of the diet of many peoples, including the Japanese, Chinese, early Mediterraneans, and North Americans.*

Acorns have been prized as a food source both for their abundance and for their nutritional value. In the Western United States, for example, several of the varieties of oak favored by the indigenous Indian tribes could yield from 500 to 1000 pounds of acorns per tree per year. Although the bearing season for oaks is only a few weeks, it has been estimated that an industrious individual, work-ing eight hours a day, would be able to collect over four tons of nuts. Such a harvest could feed a family of five for more than a year, yielding over 5000 kilocalories and 50 grams of protein per day per person.

I've lived in an oak forest my whole life, and it never once occurred to me that I might eat an acorn.

———

Before, I was Nell and the forest was trees and flowers and bushes. Now, the forest is *toyon, manzanita, wax myrtle, big leafed maple, California buck-eye, bay, gooseberry, flowering currant, rhododendron, wild ginger, wood rose, red thistle,* and I am just a human, another creature in its midst.

Gradually the forest I walk through is becoming mine, not because I own it, but because I'm coming to know it. I see it differently now. I'm beginning to see its variety—in the shape of leaves, the organization of petals, the million shades of green. I'm starting to understand its logic and sense its mystery. Everywhere I walk, I try to notice what's around me—a clump of mint, a cluster of fennel, a thicket of manzanita, or a field of amaranth to gather from now or return to later, when the need is there or the season is right.

Why did we ever buy flowers—great, gross, hulking things in plastic con-tainers from the Buy-n-Save parking lot—that we watered, fertilized, fenced, and sprayed, and that still finished the summer ragged from slugs and snails and grasshoppers? Why didn't we let the flowers grow where they would, healthy and strong and in their own time?

I wish my mother were alive so I could tell her that we didn't need those Buy-n-Save petunias, didn't need even her ring of tulips. *Clarkia. Columbine. Red Clintonia. Blue-Eyed Grass. Woolly Paint Brush. Wood Rose. Red Thistle. Owl's Clover. Calypso Orchid. Golden Fairy Lantern. Globe Lily. California Poppy. Miner's Dogwood. Buttercup. Windflower. Solomon's Seal. Lupine. Vetch. Moun-tain Iris. Ceanothus. Fireweed. Shooting Star.*

We were surrounded by flowers all the time.

———

We're eating like queens from the seeds our father saved, from the gar-den we hoed and mulched and planted and weeded and watered. Summer squash and zucchini, cherry tomatoes, carrots, beets—each picking is a feast, a gift, a windfall.

But already hybridization is going awry. We've got some plants that pro-duce round zucchinis and others that yield weird green gourds. None of the cabbage, eggplant, or radish seeds germinated, and some of the tomato plants that I thought would do the best because their foliage grew so vigorously have set no flowers.

And there are other worries. The corn is still puny-looking, and it may be my imagination, but I think both the creek and the spring are beginning to slow. In the meanwhile, the cupboard empties. Only a cup or two of wormy flour is left in the pantry, and only a quarter of a sack of pinto beans. The rice is gone. The Fastco cans are gone. There are three more jars of our father's beets, two more jars of plums. At night my mind throbs with questions: *What if the beans fail? What if the corn won't grow? What if the rest of the tomato flowers don't set? What if the spring runs dry or if pests get into the garden? What will we do when we've used the last canning lid?*

And the biggest and most enduring worry of all—*what will we do with a baby?*

———

The other day I was in the woods behind the house, harvesting yerba buena to add to the pantry's growing assortment of herbs. I felt calm and dreamy, crawling across the sun-dappled forest floor, snipping sprigs and tucking them into the old Easter basket I've started to use for gathering herbs.

I pinched a shiny leaf, rolled it between my fingers, held it to my nose, and closing my eyes, I inhaled the brassy smell of mint. I remembered that *Native Plants* said the California Indians used yerba buena as a sedative. For a long moment I was happy breathing its scent, but just as my lungs had finally filled and I knew I would soon have to interrupt my pleasure to exhale, another thought jabbed at me with such urgency that I forgot about the crushed leaf in my hands.

The Indians—I thought—*what about them?*

Tonight, work-weary and half-drowsing, a cup of *yerba buena* tea steaming on the floor beside me, I opened the encyclopedia, reread what I had read last winter, back when it mattered only as information to memorize for the Achievement Tests: *The Indians who came to inhabit the region of Northern California now known as Sonoma, Lake, and Southern Mendocino counties are referred to as Pomo, although they did not comprise a single tribe. For at least ten thousand years before the arrival of the Spaniards, the Pomo enjoyed a rigorous but relatively peaceful life.*

Because they seemed to practice a sort of primitive birth control, and because of the temperate climate, and the abundance of game, fish, and native plants in that region, their population was well maintained in relation to their resources.

Famines were never reported. Even in years when the acorn crop was light, there were always other food sources to fall back on....

Today California's native population is of only vestigial importance. Between 1769 and 1845, the Indian population of the state decreased from an estimated 310,000 to 150,000. By 1900, there were fewer than 20,000 Indians living in California.

Suddenly I remembered another book, a paperback collection of stories, songs, and interviews from California Indians. I had skimmed it once years ago, when Eva and I were trying to figure out how to build a teepee, but I abandoned it as soon as I discovered that none of the tribes it mentioned lived in teepees. I found it again tonight on the crowded shelves in Mother's workroom. I carried it out to the living room and sat with it in front of the stove, reading the words of the people who inhabited our forest before us.

"The following is from an interview with Sally Bell, one of the last of the Sinkyone. She was over ninety years old when she gave this account in 1928 or 1929."

Massacre at Needle Rock

"My grandfather and all of my family—my mother, my father, and me—were around the house and not hurting anyone. Soon, about ten o'clock in the morning, some white men came. They killed my grandfather and my mother and my father. I saw them do it. I was a big girl at the time. Then they killed my baby sister and cut her heart out and threw it into the bush where I ran and hid. My little sister was a baby, just crawling around. I didn't know what to do. I was so scared that I guess I just hid there a long time with my little sister's heart in my hands. I felt so bad and I was so scared that I just couldn't do anything else. Then I ran into the woods and hid there for a long time. I lived there for a long time with a few other people who had got away. We lived on berries and roots and we didn't dare build a fire because the white men might come back after us. So we ate anything we could get. We didn't have clothes after a while and we had to sleep under logs and in hollow trees because we didn't have anything to cover ourselves with, and it was cold then—in the spring."

That is what the encyclopedia means when it says, *by 1900, there were fewer than 20,000 Indians living in California.*

———

I was down at the stream looking for watercress when one stone among the scatter of pebbles, rocks, and sticks in the streambed made me stop and lift it from the water. It was a cylinder of grey granite just shorter than my forearm. Heavy and smooth and perfectly tapered from one blunt, broad end to the other, it fit so snugly in my palm I knew at once that mine was not the first hand to have held it.

At first its weight and size made me assume it had been a weapon, but then I remembered that power is necessary for many chores, and I decided it must have been a pestle. It feels like a gift.

—————

The Pomo divided the year into thirteen moons and named them mostly for the kind of food available under each—the moon when you can get clover, the moon when the fish begin to run, the moon when the acorns come.

I am no longer certain what month this is, but last night the moon was full, and we canned our first batch of tomatoes today. At dawn Eva built a fire in the stove while I went out to pick tomatoes in the chilly garden. When I came inside, the stove-warmed room felt wonderful, and when I poured boiling water over the first bowl of tomatoes and picked one up to slip its skin, the heat felt welcome on my cold hands.

But soon the room was blistering hot, and my fingers were throbbing from scalding water and tomato acids. I remembered my father saying, "It takes more boiling water to can a tomato than it does to have a baby." In my palm, the flesh of each skinned fruit felt like a heart, and I thought of Sally Bell and shuddered.

We worked until noon, until the last ripe tomato had been processed and the house itself felt like a quart jar that had just been lifted from the boiling water bath. Finally we left the jars to cool and the fire to die down, and we escaped to the orchard to harvest plums. When we reentered the house at dusk, there were nineteen quarts of tomatoes waiting on the table, only one of which hadn't sealed.

Tomorrow we will can plums, and the next day we'll start on the peaches. We've only got eighty-three lids left, so all too soon this hot work will be over, and everything we can't cram under a lid will be left to rot in the summer sun.

I wish we could eat it all now and hibernate all winter.

—————

We had spent the afternoon on the ridge above the house, picking the waxy manzanita berries I've just learned how to steep for juice. We were on our way home, walking silently through the hot forest, enjoying the thud of the berry bags against our backs and the occasional wisps of air that came to tease us like a phantom breeze.

I was thinking only of what obsesses me now—the way our pantry is filling. I was estimating the number of quarts the bean crop would yield, calculating meals, and planning what to can next, when suddenly Eva plopped her bag down and veered off through the woods.

"I'll be right back," she said, following the water-sound of the little stream that parallels the road at that point. "I want to cool off."

"Wait for me," I said, setting my bag beside hers.

The summer heat had reduced that tributary to little more than a trickle, but the water felt like cold silk against our naked feet. I stood on the mud and gravel of the streambed and felt the press of the current against my ankles, felt its coolness rise up my dusty shins. I forgot about counting canning lids.

But then I caught sight of something that made the whole world grow taut and still.

"What is it?" Eva asked when she heard my gasp.

Wordlessly, I pointed to a track in the quiet mud.

It was broad and blunt, shorter than my own foot but wide as my outstretched hand—a thick-heeled footprint crowned by five toe-marks. My first thought was, *He's come back,* and I froze, standing in that stream like a stunned rabbit, waiting for the drowsy afternoon to be rent by a final blow and scream.

Then I noticed the pock-marks in the mud beyond each toe, realized they had been made by claws, and felt a brief sweep of relief that no human being had left that track. A second later I was wheeling and listening, scanning the forest for the new danger it contained.

The forest was unchanged. It was as candid, quiet, and impenetrable as it had been a minute ago. Only we were different.

"Bear?" Eva whispered.

I nodded, "I think so."

"I thought they were all gone," she said, clasping her abdomen as though by protecting it she could keep us safe. "I thought the bears left when the settlers came."

"I guess they're back," I answered, straightening up and hurrying on.

Which is worse? I wondered as we raced down the road towards home with our jostling bags of berries—*a bear or a man?*

Black bear (Ursus americanus), *the most prevalent bear in North America and one of the largest mammals. Once the black bear enjoyed an extensive habitat of wooded land, though in recent times both its range and numbers are much diminished.*

Like man, all bears are plantigrade, walking on the entire foot and commonly leaving a track showing the large palm and sole pads, and, in some cases, the claws. Unlike its fiercer North American relative, the grizzly or brown bear, a black bear will rarely attack humans, generally preferring retreat to confrontation.

The black bear is omnivorous; besides animal prey, it eats insects and a variety of vegetable matter. Given the opportunity, it will also raid garbage dumps and campsites. In Northern regions the black bear spends the winter sleeping in a den, but unlike such animals as the ground squirrel or chipmunk, it is not a true hibernator.

Last night we smelled smoke.

It had been a hot day, hot with the sort of oppressive late summer heat that takes your breath away. We'd managed to spend both morning and afternoon in the garden, pulling the bolted lettuce plants and collecting their seeds, weeding the potatoes and pumpkins and watering the panting plants.

We had eaten our garden supper out on the deck—sliced tomatoes with basil, steamed green beans, and summer squash—and were lingering outside with our glasses of manzanita juice, watching the light fade from the western sky, and trying to catch a sweep of breeze before darkness chased us back into the hot, locked house.

We'd decided to can another batch of tomatoes in the morning, and I was fretting about our dwindling supply of canning lids, wondering what sort of risk we would run if we tried to reuse them, while Eva fanned herself with a languid hand.

The breeze we had been longing for finally came—a puff of air so frail it didn't even stir our hair. I found myself remembering autumn, the chill mornings, the golden light, the maples' yellow leaves. I was thinking about the whimsy of memory when the breeze returned. At first I thought the fickle evening air was somehow pulling the scent of smoke down from the chimney, but when it came again, it didn't have the old creosote tang of a cold chimney.

Suddenly I was on my feet, sniffing the air and pacing the deck in the coming darkness, sniffing and sniffing.

"What is it?" asked Eva.

"I think I smell smoke," I said.

In an instant she, too, was up and sniffing. There were long minutes when I was sure we were imagining it, when I felt impatient or bored and was ready to go to bed. But then one or the other of us would say, "There!" and the air itself seemed to stiffen with our fear.

"Do you think he's come back?" asked Eva. "Is that his campfire?"

The evening was so still, the breeze so inconsistent, that it was impossible to pinpoint any direction, impossible to guess how far that smoke might have traveled to reach us.

"I don't know," I answered, and went to get the gun, though it suddenly struck me that a forest fire seemed the worst menace there was. A man might possibly be reasoned with—or shot. A bear we could try to elude. But a late summer forest fire would destroy everything we must have if we are to have any chance of survival. It would ruin our house and our water tank, would scorch our garden and all our stores of food. A late summer forest fire would leave us abandoned at the mercy of the woods.

"What should we do?" I whispered to Eva after we both said, "There!" almost triumphantly because we had again caught that faint, sinister smell.

"I suppose there's nothing we can do," she said, "but wait and see what happens."

"What if it is a forest fire?"

"We'll leave."

"Where can we go?" I asked.

"To the stream," she answered and I thought of the two of us trying to flatten ourselves into that eight inches of cold, black water, while above us and around us on all sides the forest blazed and roared and toppled.

It was an awful time. We were afraid to stay outside after dark, and yet we were afraid to go indoors, where we couldn't keep track of the breeze. We sat on the deck on either side of the open front door, twitching like startled deer at the night sounds, gulping at the breeze when it wafted by, waiting for the crescent moon to clear the treetops, waiting for the blaze to sweep down around us.

I said, "Maybe we should try to save some things."

"How?" Eva asked from her post at the opposite doorjamb.

"We could carry some stuff down to the creek."

"What would we take?" she asked, and I fell silent. We couldn't take what people used to take when there was a fire. We couldn't take the photograph albums and family letters, the artwork or heirloom silver. We would have to take the things we needed. But we need it all. If we are to survive, we need everything—every jar and nail, every piece of clothing, every scrap of paper and scraping of food, all our father's junk. And most of all, we need the things we couldn't possibly carry to the stream. We need the woodstove, the workshop, the water tank and garden, the orchard and truck. We need the house. If those things burn, we might as well burn with them, for we will surely die.

So we stayed where we were, sitting on our deck in the pleasant summer night, listening to the crickets, watching the moon and stars, imagining tongues and walls of fire, imagining trees screaming, flames soaring, imagining that horrible light.

At dawn we were still there, huddled under the blankets I'd dragged outside when the warmth had finally seeped from the air. Our clearing was still green, the garden was growing, the house stood. At first we felt sheepish for all our worry—until we noticed the fine white twists of ash scattered across the deck like fairy bones.

"At least it's not a campfire," Eva observed.

It was a strange day, ominously normal except for our exhaustion and the flecks of ash. The sun shone. When we went out to pick the ripe tomatoes, the garden was full of its own grandeur, and the tomatoes yielded themselves easily into our hands, heavy and rank-smelling and with the night's chill still in their flesh.

But when Eva knelt to start a fire in the stove so we could heat the water to can them, I felt a shiver of worry.

"Maybe we shouldn't can today," I said.

"Why not?" she asked.

"For one thing, we won't be able to tell if the fire's getting closer if we're smelling this smoke, too."

She said, "I suppose you're right."

I looked at the bowls piled with crimson tomatoes, tomatoes hefty with the promise of food next winter, and said in desperation, "I don't know. Maybe we should go ahead and can anyway. We can't let them rot."

"We could dry them," offered Eva.

"Dry them?"

"Like raisins or prunes. It's going to be another hot day. Why not use the sun? Anyway, you've been so worried about those lids."

She was so placid I wanted to choke her. Of course we could dry the tomatoes. And the apples. And apricots. And pears. And peaches. And plums. And why not onions and peppers? It will stay hot almost until the winter rains arrive—day after day of dry heat. We could probably even dry pumpkin and chard and beets, if we wanted to.

In the back of the workshop we found two aluminum screen doors and, as we hauled them out into the sunshine, I remembered the day our father brought them home.

"I thought you went to the dump to get rid of things, not to collect more," our mother had said when he drove up. "What on earth do we want with someone else's old screen doors?"

"But Gloria," protested our father, pleased with both his doors and his wife, "darling. These are fine doors, first rate doors. Their frames aren't bent and their screens aren't torn. The person who threw them out was either immoral or a fool. Besides, I thought they might do for the hen house."

That silenced my mother long enough for him to lug them into his shop, and there they had stayed, lost behind other, more recent bones of my parents' fond contention, until we resurrected them to preserve our winter's food.

Together Eva and I rinsed away the dirt and cobwebs and left the doors on the deck while we went inside to slice the tomatoes.

"The thinner they are, the faster they'll dry," said Eva with sudden authority, and so we cut them thin. We dealt the slices out on the screens, row after row, like coins, and then went to work in the garden. But when we came back at noon, the slices were swarming with wasps, and their juices had begun to eat into the screening.

"We've got to find something to lay them on to protect them from the metal, and we need something to cover them with to keep the bugs off," I said.

"Like what?"

"I don't know. Something like cheesecloth or net."

"Sheets?"

"Too thick. The air won't circulate underneath them and they won't get enough sun."

"I've got an idea," Eva answered and ran into the house, while I worked at prying the discolored tomatoes off the corroded aluminum.

When Eva returned, she was lugging a long garment bag.

"Will this do?" she asked, unzipping the bag to reveal our mother's wedding dress, with its yards of white netting and voile skirts. "We could spread the net under the slices—and cover them with it, too."

Tentatively I lifted the dress from its dusty bag, remembering, as I held it up and squinted against its whiteness, how at some point in our childhoods, each of us had claimed it was the dress we would wear for our own weddings.

"I don't know," I said, handing it back to her. "Wouldn't it just stick to the screens, too? These tomatoes are pretty juicy."

"Oh," answered Eva, unconsciously holding the dress to her shoulders, smoothing it down over her hips and across her swollen uterus. "What if we made frames from wood, and stretched the net across them?"

I lifted the hem of the dress, caressed the gauzy fabric between my earth-stained hands, and remembered how the Unicorn Tapestries had been used by peasants to keep their potato crop from freezing during the French Revolution, how after the Reformation, stones from England's cathedrals were built into pig sties and door stoops, and books from the monastery libraries were torn up—page by page—in outhouses.

I wondered if those people, too, had felt regret at what their need had driven them to do. Then I said, "Let's try it," and went back to the house for scissors.

All afternoon we worked, searching through our father's heaps of lumber for useable boards, measuring and cutting and hammering frames, tacking the net across them, and stopping occasionally to sniff the hot, still air and scan the sky for smoke. The fire remained invisible, though occasionally we caught its scent. Even so, its existence permeated our work, threatening to make it futile. We sliced tomatoes, spread netting, and moved the drying racks to follow the sun with a fresh sense of urgency.

By the time the sun had left the clearing, our fingers were puckered and stinging with tomato acids, and the first slices we had set out had shriveled to half their size. They looked like wizened scabs on the stained netting of our mother's wedding dress, but they felt leathery and the bits we nibbled were sweet and intense, a concentrate of tomato and sunshine that seemed certain to blaze through the wettest winter days.

We carried the racks indoors for the night, locked up the hens, ate supper, and settled down again for our vigil on the deck. Eva went to sleep at once, but after a night of sleepless worry and a day of work, I was tired with the sort of gritty exhaustion so far beyond sleep that sleep seems impossible. When I closed my eyes I was haunted by rows of tomato slices, so for a long time I kept my eyes open, studying the night for signs of fire.

But the only fire I could see was the distant burn of the stars as—one by one—they became apparent in the clear sky. Just above the dark treetops at the northern edge of the clearing I found Ursa Major. I remembered what the encyclopedia had said about the great antiquity of that constellation, and how, although it had been called a dipper or a coffin or a plough because of the configuration of its seven stars, cultures as widely disparate as the ancient Chaldeans and the Iroquois Indians had claimed it was a great she-bear, lumbering across the sky in search of her children or running from the hunters who wounded her so that every autumn she stained the forests with her blood.

After a while I gave up trying to see a bear in that kite-shaped group of stars and traced the path from Ursa Major up the sky to Polaris. I found Ursa Minor and Cassiopeia, and from there my gaze wandered out through the gardens of stars whose names and patterns I have yet to learn.

When I awoke, it was so late that the reel and throb of cricket-song had ceased, and the clearing was wrapped in the endless velvet of a summer night. The stars had shifted. Cassiopeia was above me and the Great Bear was hidden in the trees.

I glanced at Eva and saw that even in her sleep she held her belly cradled in her arms. I tested the air for smoke, but all I smelled was the clean tang of fir and bay and dew. It seemed the immediate danger was past, and I suppose we will never know how close that fire came to razing our lives.

———

The garden harvest is coming to an end. We used every canning lid we had and the pantry shelves are packed with jars of tomatoes, green beans, beets, plums, applesauce, peaches, apricots, pumpkin, and pears. Strings of dried fruit and peppers and beans hang from the ceiling, along with bunches of herbs from the forest. Dried onions fill one tattered grocery sack, and our meager harvest of dried corn fills another. The winter squashes are piled in a corner of the pantry, and a box of potatoes is stacked beside them.

It looks like a lot of food, but when I think of how much we eat, I wonder if that pantry can possibly be full enough to keep us alive.

———

A mile or so to the east of us, the forest begins to break up. First the redwoods disappear, and then slowly the firs and maples drop out. Finally the madrone and bay vanish, too, and the land opens, levels out onto a wide ridge where only oaks are left—coast live oaks set so solidly across the land they appear more like monuments than trees. Away from the clutter and tangle of forest, they grow massive, their trunks thick, their branches spreading with a vast graciousness above the golden grasses. They are old, quiet trees, laden with tough, curled leaves and clusters of honey-brown nuts, and it is to them we went to learn about harvesting acorns.

If you want to gather acorns, you have to crawl. You have to go down on all fours like an animal or a suppliant and crawl through dust and duff, crawl across the earth on your palms and knees, sorting among the sharp leaves and empty hulls for ripe acorns.

There's more skill to it than I would have imagined, and already I'm learning tricks to make it easier. Yesterday I had collected a whole sackful before I realized that even the tiniest pinprick of a hole in the acorn's shell means there is a little white worm writhing inside. This morning I had to take the time to inspect each nut for holes before I could add it to my sack. But by afternoon I could almost always tell if an acorn would be sound simply by how it felt when I picked it up.

Our hands are busy, but it is slow work. To circle a tree can take hours of careful labor, beginning at the trunk and spiralling out to the drip line. It's hot and dusty, hard on backs and knees. But there's a rhythm to it, slow and dreamy. After a while, it's almost like prayer.

The crickets sang as though the day itself were breathing, a song inhaling and exhaling in the heat, expanding and shrinking and circling back on itself. Sometimes there was the blessing of a breeze. Deep in the sky above us, three buzzards wheeled and soared so elegantly I could almost have been persuaded there was something sacred about eating carrion.

For a long time Eva and I worked in silence, filling our canvas sacks and pillow cases. By the time the sun was overhead, all our containers bulged with nuts. Leaning our backs against the trunk of the oak we had been working under, we ate boiled eggs and apples, looking out across the silent, sundried hills.

"We could be the only people left in the world," said Eva in a voice that held no fear or sadness. I nodded a little dreamily, answered her in the same tone, "We could be."

I dream of the bear. Once again, it shambles out of the forest. Once again, it approaches me, and I can see the powerful heave and shift of muscle beneath its dense fur. But this time, although I am wet with fear, my fear has a different quality, and I realize that either I do not expect the encounter will kill me or I don't mind the thought of dying quite as much as I once did.

Again the bear bends over me. But this time, instead of licking me, it opens its jaws over my face, so wide that my whole head is inside its mouth and I am looking down the dark tunnel of its throat. I feel its teeth meet through my neck, and I know it has bitten off my head. But when it lifts its mouth from my empty shoulders, I can see the world as well as ever—in fact, things have a lucidity I had never before imagined, and I think, *What an effort it was to have to lug my head around with me for so long.*

The acorns produced by most oaks contain tannic acid, which, although it serves as a natural preservative, causes the nuts to be unpalatably bitter. Consequently, making most species of acorns fit for consumption involves one of a number of processes of leaching the tannin from the nutmeats.

A fresh acorn tastes like earwax. It puckers your tongue, draws the saliva from your mouth, and leaves a bitterness that lingers long after you've spat it out.

The Cahuilla Indians said that in the beginning acorns were sweet, but there came a time when human beings so angered their creator that the acorns were made bitter, and ever since then people have had to sweeten acorns for themselves.

It took a few days before I worked out a process for drying, shelling, skinning, pounding, leaching, and cooking acorns. At first I used the pestle to try to grind them on a flat stone Eva had helped me heave up from the creek. The blisters on my hands had broken, and I had wasted a lot of nuts before I conceded that grinding acorns only turns them into a paste impossible to leach because water won't filter through it. Finally I figured out that acorns have to be pounded instead of ground, and although my arms still ache from the hours I have spent lifting the pestle and letting it fall, I have learned how to produce a usable meal a little rougher than coarse-ground cornmeal.

I used an old coffee filter to leach it, pouring boiling water through it again and again until the tea-colored liquid that dripped from the filter had turned clear, and the meal tasted mild, almost empty of flavor, like unseasoned beans. I mixed the leached meal with fresh water and simmered it until the mush was soft.

I'm sure a Pomo would have laughed at my methods, but I have to admit I was proud when Eva and I sat down to supper last night. We held hands for a moment across the steaming bowl, and then we ate. It was bland and hefty—like rice or bread—slightly nutty, a little earthy, a food as enduring as oak.

———

I used to shudder when I cut into an acorn and found a worm writhing there. Then I read that the Pomo considered worms to be a delicacy, and now I feel ashamed when I cut them out. I wish I, too, could eat those larvae that in my dreams mean death. I wish I could bite into them, chew them up, swallow them down. I want to learn to eat worms.

———

Up beyond the redwood stump, we found a grove of valley oaks loaded with the fattest acorns I have ever seen. But when we tried to haul them home, the hike was so strenuous that after a day's worth of trips up the hill and back, we were exhausted, and we hadn't collected nearly as much as I'd hoped.

We'd almost decided to concentrate on the scantier and wormier harvest closer to home when Eva suggested we dry the acorns in the forest and store them in the redwood stump until we needed them this winter. So this morning we dragged our drying racks up to the stump, along with eight thirty-gallon plastic barrels we'd once used for what we thought back then was garbage.

I don't think we had been to the stump together since we were twelve or thirteen, and as we scrambled up the hill with our first load, trying to maneuver Eva's unwieldy belly and our equipment up that steep slope, I felt oddly disoriented, clogged by too many memories, and confused by the novelty of the present—by my pregnant sister huffing behind me, by our urgent need for acorns.

When I finally reached the stump, I felt a reluctance to reenter that place I had been last with Eli. But as I was hesitating, Eva came panting up. She threw down her load with a gasp, and, rubbing the broad slope of her belly, she looked around.

"I guess it'll do," she said, "though we'll have to cut some of those saplings to let in enough light for drying. What'd you and Eli do up here, plant more trees?"

We laughed together a little ruefully, and then Eva hiked on up to the oaks with the gathering sacks, leaving me to arrange the barrels inside the stump and cut three of the scrawny firs that choked the space in front of it. As each one crashed through the tangle of branches, the circle of sky widened and a little more light entered the clearing. By the time Eva came back with her first load of nuts, I had the drying racks laid out and waiting in a new patch of sun in front of the stump.

We worked all afternoon, gathering acorns, spreading them on the screens, moving the racks to follow the migrating sunshine. On one trip we found a mountain of blackberry bushes still laden with late berries. We harvested a basketful of them, too, and spread what we didn't eat out to dry beside the acorns.

The air began to thicken and cool. Suddenly it was dusk, and we wanted to be out of the forest and back at home. We poured the acorns into one of the barrels to keep the dew off them, but the berries were still too juicy to move without turning them to jam.

"Let's just leave them out for the night," Eva said, bending over the rack and testing first one and then another between her purple fingers. "The dew won't hurt them much, but we'll ruin them if we try to move them now."

"Won't the squirrels or birds get them?" I asked.

"At night? We'll be back first thing in the morning."

We left before the dusk grew any denser.

Just after dawn we scrambled back up the hill, huffing and laughing in the bright mists, carrying cups, plates, a cooking pot filled with ashes and live coals. We were planning a breakfast of mint tea and acorn mush and blackberries over the campfire we were going to build, and I think we were both feeling almost as lighthearted as the children we had once been, happy to be playing together in the forest again.

I reached our new clearing a step ahead of Eva and gasped, too shocked to turn and run.

The racks were tossed in opposite directions, their screening hanging in shreds, their frames twisted and bent. The stained lengths of wedding net were tattered and strewn. A few berries were scattered among the forest duff.

We drew together. The forest was quiet except for the domestic chirp of birds. If it weren't for the mute violence of the torn drying racks, there might have been no bear.

Then there was a choice to be made, another decision about how we would live, about what risks were worth taking. We had to decide what to be most afraid of. We had to choose between our fear of a hungry winter with a new baby and our fear of a black bear in early autumn. We had to weigh what we could imagine of the dark drizzle of winter—when the pantry had been emptied and we were reduced to boiling shoe leather and eating the cambium of trees—against the claws and muscles of a bear.

In the end we chose to fear winter. *The encyclopedia says black bears are shy,* we reasoned. *It says they're only aggressive in the spring, only when they're hungry and their cubs are young. We'll just make sure we never leave food out overnight again.*

Although we constructed logical arguments and elaborate justifications, it wasn't logic that finally persuaded us, but the fact that it felt good to be out in the woods, gathering acorns, drying berries, drinking our wild teas, and cooking our meals by the daytime fires Eva kindled in front of the stump.

Every morning now, as soon as our chores in the fading garden are finished, we head to the woods. All day we gather and dry acorns, and in the evening we add our harvest to the barrels. We fasten their lids with bungee cords, block the doorway with sheets of plywood, and as we hike home in the twilight, down through the forest that's grown so wild it now harbors a bear, I feel a secret elation. In some unfathomable way I feel less alone.

———————

Now that the garden is almost done, we seem to spend more and more time at the stump. We've opened up a pool in the creek for collecting water—which I insist we boil before we drink—and well away from the stream we've dug a latrine.

We finished harvesting a few days ago. For our work we have five barrels full of acorns and a quarter of a barrel of dried blackberries. We've decided to leave them all up at the stump for now and to fill the other two barrels with dried food from the pantry. That way, whatever happens, we'll always have a cache in the woods.

To have even one barrel full of acorns is to have an immeasurable wealth. When we had emptied the last sackful into the fifth barrel, I bent over it. I worked my hands down through the sleek, cool nuts until my arms were in up to my elbows, and laid my cheek against the acorns in a kind of embrace. I smelled their faint dust, thought of all the rain and darkness and hunger they would forestall, and felt fiercely proud.

The good days linger, though they're shorter now, and cooler—an Indian summer before the winter rains arrive. The hens stopped laying awhile ago, and the garden is just about gone, although we still get a few thick-skinned, watery tomatoes, a few final peppers, and some chard. All the barrels in the stump are filled with food, a cache I hope could see us through the winter if it had to. I spent the last two days nailing a roof of plywood and corrugated tin over it, so that now it looks more like a hobo shack than the fairy cottage we used to pretend it was.

Eva's belly has begun to dwarf her, a firm globe where she once had a plane of sheer muscle. Sometimes I can see her whole stomach heave beneath the workshirts she wears. "It's a dancer," she'll laugh, "practicing its *frappés*." But her moving stomach sickens me like the paintpots we saw when we went to Yellowstone the year I was eight, the slow, hot mud bubbling stupidly, more threat than life.

She has complained of feeling sick recently. She's pale and tired and doesn't eat much. She says she is queasy all the time. When I make mint tea for her, she smiles and claims she feels a little better.

Maybe more time has passed than I had thought. Maybe her labor is coming soon.

I finally made myself read through the sections in the encyclopedia about *Abnormal Changes in Pregnancy* and *Accidents During Labor* this evening. I read about *gestational diabetes, heart failure, eclampsia, epilepsy, placental cysts, placental inflammation, hydatidiform moles, toxemia, hypertension, polyhydramnios,* and *placenta previa, abruptio,* and *accreta.*

I read about *premature births, breech, posterior and transverse presentations, umbilical cord accidents, cephalo-pelvic disproportion, cervical edema, posterior arrest, shoulder dystocia, uterine rupture or inversion, fetal distress, retained placenta, postpartum hemorrhage,* and *neonatal apnea.*

When I began, I was sitting at the table across from Eva, but after a paragraph or two, I found I had to get up and move away from her, out to the deck, where I sat in the chill dusk and read with a horrified fascination.

I never guessed that having a baby was such a risky business. I can't stop thinking about it. It's like the itch of poison oak—when you try to relieve that raw agony by scratching, it only intensifies the pain.

———

Last night I stacked a huge load of firewood just outside the door and made a little nest for a newborn out of blankets and a dresser drawer. Then, in a desperate attempt to prepare myself to be an obstetrician, I tackled the encyclopedia once again. I was skimming past the drawings of female reproductive organs, past sections with titles like *Anatomic and Physiologic Changes in Non-reproductive Organs and Tissues During Pregnancy*, when the word *anemia* snagged my eye: *If fatigue and nausea are present in the second or third trimester, anemia may be suspect; however, only a hematocrit can ascertain the type and severity of an iron deficiency. The parturient individual suffering from anemia has a much increased risk of labor difficulties, as well as postpartum hemorrhage. In addition, macrocytic anemia, caused by a lack of adequate B-12 in the diet, is associated with brain and nerve damage in the neonate. However, since B-12 exists in adequate quantities in almost all dairy and animal products, this type of anemia is typically a threat only to strict vegetarians.*

I felt the same sort of satisfaction I used to know when I pressed the final piece of a puzzle into place—we haven't eaten meat since we finished the last can of tuna fish sometime last winter, haven't even had eggs for almost a month. And Eva is nauseous, pale, and listless.

Labor difficulties. Postpartum hemorrhage. Brain and nerve damage in the neonate. If I had to, I suppose I could kill Bathsheba or Pinkie. But they seem like friends after all this time, and anyway, how much B-12 would one old hen contain?

———

Both feral hogs and wild boars belong to the species Sus scrofa, *which evolved in India some thirty million years ago. Although Columbus brought swine with him on his second voyage in 1493, it was really the conquistadors who were responsible for introducing boars to the New World. When domesticated Spanish pigs escaped into the American wilderness, they adapted rapidly to their new environment, losing, within a few generations, their barnyard features, and re-*

verting to the erect ears, long snout, straight tail, broad shoulders, and prominent tusks of their wild ancestors.

Wild boars are quite fierce, although they seem to enjoy contact with their
own kind. They are intelligent, have a keen sense of both smell and hearing,
and are remarkably swift of foot. Wild boars are omnivorous and consume a
large variety of plant materials, although they have been also known to eat
snails, snakes, mice, insects, eggs, and carrion, as well as certain types of soil and
rock from which they obtain minerals and other nutrients.

There would be a lot of meat on a wild pig—lots more than on a black-
tailed deer. Smoked—or dried in the last of the autumn sun—a boar could
last us a long time. Besides, there's not much to love about a pig—they're
blunt and ugly and tough, rooting up bulbs and making muckholes in the
creeks. It wouldn't be like killing a deer, with its soft eyes and dancer's legs.

I think I could kill a pig.

I think I have to try.

Killing a wild boar is harder than it sounds.

I guess I had thought that once I resolved to do it, I could just pick up the
rifle I've never used on anything but pickle jars, go for a little walk, and
shoot the nice, obliging piggy that was waiting for me by the side of the
road. But even when I'm not hunting them, I hardly ever glimpse a wild pig.
All day I wandered through the forest, nervous and jumpy, seeing nothing
but sparrows and squirrels. The gun awkward on my shoulder, I scrambled
up and down the steep hills, breaking my way through the tangle of skinny
branches, ducking and climbing and twisting through the trees, looking for
the pigs who entered these woods with the first Europeans. I followed the
narrow grooves of animal trails up and down the hillsides, but I found nothing but more trees.

Finally I sat down in that forest just where I was—halfway up another
hill—sat on the earth with my gun by my side, surrounded by a tight
weave of light-starved trees, and tried to think like a hunter, tried to think
like a pig. I sat a long time, unmoving, watching patches of light open
and fade on the leaf-littered floor, listening to the sound of a distant wood-
pecker.

I wanted to get up, to go home. I thought, *I can't do this.* But a kind of
inertia kept me sitting. Finally I rose, climbed up the hill and past our stump
to the little stream. I hiked upstream until I came to the wallow I thought I
had remembered there. It was a hole large as an old-fashioned bathtub, its
black muck churned with the cloven prints of pigs' feet.

I sat in the underbrush above the wallow with the rifle balanced on my knees until the light began to fade, but nothing came except a late hatch of mosquitoes.

The next day I went back before sunrise. In the dim first light, I hid on the bank above the wallow in a thicket of hazelnut bushes, determined to wait until a pig came.

I crouched there until noon, till my fidgets had come and gone and come again like a fever that rises and falls and returns, until the juncos were confident enough to go about their business at my feet. Once I heard a distant crashing. Adrenaline jagged through my stomach and brain, but nothing else happened. The crashing veered off and faded away. I sat until my butt ached and my back was stiff and my legs screamed, but nothing came.

"Maybe they're nocturnal," Eva said at supper.

"I don't know. The encyclopedia doesn't say."

"Why don't you give up?" she asked listlessly. "We've got plenty of other food." She poked at her stewed pumpkin and tomato slices and applesauce while I ate. Finally she pushed her plate towards me, asking, "Do you want this? I'm feeling a little queasy."

I thought, *Labor difficulties. Postpartum hemorrhage. Brain and nerve damage in the neonate.*

I said, "Maybe they smell me."

The next morning I hiked up to the wallow carrying the tee shirt in which I had been sleeping. It was one of my father's, worn shapeless and soft from years of use, and it reeked pleasantly of my own night smells. I spread it carefully on the mud of the wallow, and I came away.

A day later, it still lay stretched and flat across the mud, though brown water had seeped into the fabric, leaching across it like patches of mold. I stared at it for a moment before I turned and left, a harsh sense of failure biting into me.

When I reached the wallow the morning after that, I was so prepared for more disappointment that at first I thought the shirt had simply vanished. But then I noticed a clot of cloth trampled into the mud. For a second it was a shock, a tiny violation, to see my father's shirt—the shirt I had worn as I slept—torn and filthy and wadded in the muck, but a moment later I felt an elation so fierce I had to restrain myself from shouting. Instead, I unbuttoned my threadbare jeans, took off my ragged underpants, and laid them on the mud. Then I squatted and peed and went back home.

The following morning my underpants were churned into the wallow.

"I'm going to take a nap," I told Eva when I got home.

"Are you okay?" she asked.

"Yes. I just need to rest. I'm going to climb a tree by the wallow tonight and wait for them."

"At night?"

"Sure," I shrugged, saying it before I could think about it. "Why not? The moon's full," I added, as much for my benefit as for my sister's. "I'll be fine."

I set off just before dusk. In the pack on my back I carried our father's whetstone, the boning knife from our mother's kitchen set, the hatchet, and a bottle of water. My jacket pockets were bulging with dried apple slices and bullets. The rifle felt companionable on my shoulder as I climbed up through the cooling woods, past the hulk of the stump with its trove of food, and up along the streambed until, just as dark was falling, I reached the wallow.

I looked around for something to climb, but none of the trees had branches I could reach. The trees closest to the wallow were the tanbark oaks that grow on these crowded hillsides, tall, slender, and almost branchless until they reach the forest canopy. Beyond them were redwoods whose lowest branches were thirty feet above my head.

Slowly I circled between their trunks, thinking, *Well, I tried. It's not my fault there were no trees I could climb. It's not my fault Eva's pregnant. She probably doesn't have anemia, anyway. I'm just being paranoid. Her labor will go fine. The baby's probably fine. Or if it isn't, it isn't. It's too late to fix it now.*

Light was failing quickly, and perhaps the thought of trying to make it back home in the dark kept me where I was. I didn't want to spend the night on the ground, so finally I tackled the most promising tree I could find—an oak that grew uphill of the stream and curved back over the wallow. I slung the rifle behind my back alongside the pack and set my hands on either side of the oak's trunk. It felt chilly, damp, and raw. It was surprisingly solid.

I heaved myself up. The first branches were little more than twigs that snapped in my hands as I tried to hold them. But I was able to reach one sturdy enough to act as a ballast. I held it and pulled myself higher, the gun barrel bumping my cheek. Finally I reached a branch thick enough to hold my weight. I clambered onto it, straddling it as though it were a horse. I was higher up than I would have liked, and skewed to the wrong side of the tree, so that I had to lean out and twist my shoulders to face the wallow directly. But it was too late to try anything else.

Clinging to the trunk, I wiggled until I had the gun off my shoulder and cradled in my lap. I loaded it, triple-checked the safety, worked out a way of bracing my elbow and shoulder against the branch I was perched on, and then practiced sighting down at the wallow. When it got too dark to see my imaginary target, I wedged the rifle between me and the tree and reached in my pocket for a slice of dried apple.

The last light fell. I was alone in the dark with a mouthful of apple pulp, perched in an oak tree above a muddy hole in the middle of a forest whose edges I no longer knew, with all the night pressing down on my shoulders. Above me there was a dark web of branches, and beyond that I could see a few specks of starlight. I felt a tickling on my shin and reached down to slap at it, trying not to think what it might be. The forest floor had vanished. I clung to the smooth, cool body of the oak and waited for the moon to rise above the treetops.

It seemed to take forever. I hung in the darkness a long time, listening to the distant weary chirping of a few final crickets, stiffening at the occasional scuffling or crashing beneath me, brushing at real or imaginary spiders. My legs began to grow numb, and I started to worry that the pigs might come and leave before the moon would let me see them. Then I became afraid the moon wouldn't rise at all. Maybe I had been confused about what phase it was—or maybe there was an eclipse. Perhaps the moon had simply vanished.

The shadows began deepening in the darkness. At first I thought my eyes were just inventing something to look at, or that they were only adjusting to the night, but finally I was sure it was the moon coming after all.

A full moon is much dimmer when you're in the middle of a forest than when you're standing in a clearing. Cool and imperturbable, the light the moon cast was broken by the ceiling of trees so that it fell in silvery patches, leaving the shadows thick and black.

I eased my hand in my pocket for another slice of apple. I tried to shift my weight off my thighs, tried to shrug the pack on my back into an easier position, tried to lean against the branch that cradled me, twisting and shifting until I was momentarily almost comfortable. I watched the moon ease itself into an open circle of sky, and, to pass the time, I tried to review everything I had learned about it. I remembered that the moon orbits the earth at an average distance of 238,000 miles, that its surface area is about the same as that of North and South America, that its albedo is only seven percent, and that the basalts in the Sea of Tranquility are 3.7 billion years old.

But I have learned something the encyclopedia doesn't know—if the moon is waxing, you can reach up and cradle its outer curve in the palm of your right hand. If it is waning, it will fit into your left palm.

A little wind shivered through the leaves. *Rock-a-bye baby,* a voice in my head sang. *In the treetop.*

When the wind blows, the cradle will rock.
When the bough breaks, the cradle will fall,
and down will come baby, cradle, and all.

I uncurled my fingers from the gun and dug in my pocket for another slice of apple. My legs ached, and I tried to remind myself what I was doing, clinging to a tree in the middle of the forest in the middle of the night. I remembered my sister and the baby she would be having. I realized I always thought of it as a girl, and tonight I felt certain my intuition was right. I knew Eva was carrying a daughter, and I was even beginning to feel a grudging fondness for that little girl who will so complicate our lives. I imagined that she would be a composite of my sister, my mother, and myself. We would name her for her grandmother, I thought, and once again a Gloria would inhabit our lives.

I imagined the stories I would tell that little girl about the way things used to be, when lights could be switched on at midnight, when there were boxes that made music and washed clothes and cooked food, when people could travel while sitting down. I imagined the games we would make of gathering acorns, digging potatoes, planting seeds. I imagined showing her wildflowers and herbs, and which hand holds the waxing moon.

Eva would teach her to dance, I thought, and I would teach her to read and write, and as I clutched the oak and planned my niece's future, it seemed I could feel generations of women receding behind us and stretching out ahead of my sister and me. I felt a connection with both my foremothers and with the future, and I knew—despite all odds—the bone-deep satisfaction of continuance.

Gradually the crickets ceased their song. The moon hung above the trees, a serene circle it would take both hands to cup. While it was overhead, I could see the wallow clearly, and I held my breath and tried to send out some sort of silent plea for the pigs to come. Once I heard a crashing in the woods behind me, but I didn't dare turn around, and the sound never came closer. Once I was startled to see a dark shape standing at the edge of the stream. An equal mixture of excitement and dread stirred in my veins. I was trying to silently ease the gun to my shoulder when I realized that something was wrong. The creature was too small, its tail too long. While I hesitated, it moved out into a patch of moonlight, and I saw the white stripe.

"We don't want skunk," I whispered.

Hour after hour I dozed and fidgeted. My legs ached, my thighs cramped, my back and hands grew stiff, and nothing happened. The moon inched along the sky and vanished in a maze of branches. After that I sat in darkness, hugging the tree, hugging the gun, dumbly waiting for morning. I felt the dew, gentle and cold, condensing on my cheeks and hair and hands and along the barrel of the gun, and then slowly light began to reappear, slowly shape and color returned to the forest.

Shivering and aching, I watched the dawning and felt a sort of guilty relief—I had tried my best, but the pigs were smarter. *As soon as it gets just a little lighter,* I thought, *I can go home to bed, can sleep all morning, and work in the garden this afternoon. I've done all I could. It wasn't my fault the pigs didn't come.*

Then they came. They were quieter than I had expected. Always before when I had heard them, they were startled and racing away. But now they came in their own time, came to drink after a night of foraging, came down to wallow before their day's rest, and the noise of their coming was little more than a few cracking twigs and gentle grunts.

There were three of them, one slightly larger than the other two. I had been afraid my scent would warn them away, but the wind must have favored me or maybe my smell was familiar to them, because they gave my underpants a cursory sniff and then snorted, walked on. They drank from the pool where the skunk had drunk. The forest grew lighter. I could make out the leaves on the trees across the wallow.

I held my breath, watching them, those monstrous, ancient creatures, blunt and—in this moment—startlingly beautiful. I could see their stiff backs, could see their pointed ears and straight black tails. I heard them muttering together in the mud below me, and I felt honored to see them like that, relaxed and naked and unaware of my presence.

I remembered I was supposed to kill one of them.

Just to see what it would be like, I eased the gun to my shoulder. Without breathing, I twisted around and positioned myself in the oak, one elbow braced against the branch, my stiff knees clinging like barnacles to the trunk. While I tried to find the pigs in the sights of the rifle, they wove around each other in a tender dance, sniffing and snuffling and brushing against each other. *They like each other,* I realized. And then it came to me, more immediate, more visceral than thought—*It's a mother and two sisters.*

That idea sent me reeling, and for an instant I was afraid I would tumble from my tree, would land in the wallow in their midst, where they would trample and tear me as they had trampled and torn my clothes. But I hung on, forced myself to think of Eva and her daughter.

Labor difficulties. Postpartum hemorrhage. Do you want your sister to bleed to death because you can't pull the trigger?

Brain and nerve damage in the neonate. Do you want that baby girl to be born harmed?

Do you want to have to sit in this tree for another night?

I hugged the oak with my knees and thighs. I took three long breaths and tried to remember everything I thought I knew about firing a gun. I waited until the rifle stopped wavering and then aimed down at the center of the old sow's back. It seemed impossible, but I had decided that if only I could sever her spine then maybe she wouldn't run off with my bullet inside her. I took another breath, and held it. I exhaled and squeezed the trigger so slowly I never knew when to flinch.

Everything exploded into noise. The gun roared, though for a stupid second I thought I hadn't fired it because in my excitement I never felt it kick. Birds I hadn't been aware of burst from their roosts in neighboring trees. Leaves and twigs rained down around me. Below me the earth was boiling. The shoats had vanished, and I watched, horrified, shaking, as the old sow thrashed and squealed.

Once I had seen some kids tie a scarf around a cat's middle, and I remember watching with a sick fascination as the cat struggled to walk while its hind legs pitched and staggered drunkenly out of its control. Beneath me the sow was doing a similar thing. Unable to stand, she twisted and kicked, her forelegs scrabbling to pull her body along while her hind legs lurched uselessly.

I did it! I thought, as I tried to run another bullet into the chamber, but my hands shook so hard the first one dropped like an acorn into the mud. Finally I fumbled another from my pocket, rammed it into the gun, and shot again. I missed. I tried again, and hit her shoulder. Clinging to my tree, thrilled and horrified by what I had caused, I watched as the sow battled the bullets, snorting and growling and tossing mud, all the energy of her self unleashed, flung wild into the world.

"Die, die. Please die," I begged out loud. In the midst of her throes, she heard the foreign sound of my voice. She looked up, and her near-sighted eyes seemed to meet mine.

"Please die," I pleaded. "My sister is going to have a baby."

She grunted, tried to heave herself out of the wallow one more time, but her front legs collapsed under her. She stumbled into the mud and lay there, panting, suddenly enormously patient. I shot again and this time hit her where I aimed—in the back of the head. She stiffened with the impact of that final bullet and then slumped through herself, into the earth, out of her life.

Weeping, elated, horrified, I tumbled out of the tree, skinning my hands, twisting my legs. When I got to the ground, my muscles screamed and trembled from adrenaline and lack of circulation, and I almost fainted. I rocked against the tree where I had passed the night, unable to take my eyes from the heap of muddy flesh I'd created. I felt a surge, a roar of power, felt enormous, awed, and proud, convinced—for a moment at least—that my kill had been something more than a novice's dumb luck.

When I could finally stand, I walked over to her, bent to meet the creature whose life I had taken. I saw the torn flesh, the blood on the earth and, sure and hard as the backfire of his rifle, the image of my father lying in the mud his blood had made came back to me. I gagged and retched. Bits of dried apple rehydrated in bile tore their way up from my gut, left their burning trail in my throat.

I threw up until there was nothing left, and then I slumped in the mud and wept. I wept for my father and for my mother and for Eva and her unborn daughter and myself. I wept for Sally Bell and the Lone Woman— those women who had long since lost the sister and daughter I was trying to save. I wept for this sow and her shoats. I wept from exhaustion and elation, and I wept because I knew that when I stopped crying, somehow I had to turn that heap of muscle and gristle into meat.

Dressing, the encyclopedia calls it, though it's much more like undressing, and, as usual, the encyclopedia says almost nothing about how it is actually done. But I knew that somehow I had to stick a knife in her, open her up, drain out her blood, rake out her insides, tear off her hide, hack off her head and legs, cut her flesh from her bones. And I knew I couldn't wait too long or the meat would be rancid and rigor mortis would set in.

You shot her. You owe her a home in your belly. She deserves to live again in you, and Eva, and Eva's daughter.

I rose, stood over her for a moment, and gingerly picked up a hind leg in my fingertips, gritting my teeth against the feel of stiff hair, cold mud, the residual life-warmth. I tugged tentatively at the leg, but her body wouldn't budge. I grabbed it, cringing, and then grabbed the other leg with my other hand and yanked. Her haunches shifted a few inches.

It took a long time, but slowly, grunting and straining, first tugging at one end and then the other, I dragged her up out of the mud and tried to prop her so her throat and belly were facing downhill. It was hard work, but by the time I was through wrestling with her I was almost used to the feel and smell of her. Slowly she was becoming an object.

I grabbed her snout and forced her head back. Gingerly I pushed the knife blade against her throat, but as usual my resolve to do a thing didn't mean it could easily be done. I jabbed and stabbed and hacked, until finally the knife tore into her jugular and thick red blood drained down the slope I had dragged her up, back into the wallow, into that mush of mud and vomit.

I began to work the knife down her belly. I smashed her breastbone apart with the hatchet, and as I drew the knife between the still-swollen teats, her entrails pushed through the hole I was making, flopped out onto the forest floor, heavy and reeking. I hacked a circle around her anus, reached into that sticky, stinking, intimate warmth, grabbed the large intestine, and lifted the long rope of it out.

There's nothing I can't do now, I thought as I sorted through the warm and iridescent entrails for her heart and liver—my first gifts to Eva and her daughter.

All day I labored, separating skin from flesh, flesh from bone, dividing the sow into meat—a few chunks for boiling and frying, a mountain of strips for drying and smoking. I stopped my work only to drink water, to sharpen the knife, or to take off my jacket when the sun warmed the forest.

One shoulder and most of her back and loin were ruined by bullets, but even so we have kept busy for days preserving her flesh. Already the hunter's moon she died under has waned to a crescent—and the color has returned to Eva's cheeks.

———————

I nap at the stump in a patch of pale sunlight, dream I am buried in the earth up to my neck, my arms and legs like taproots tapering to a web of finer roots until at last there is no clear demarcation between those root hairs and the soil itself. As I look out over the earth, my skull expands as though I were absorbing the above-ground world and the sky itself through my eye sockets. My head grows until it is a shell encompassing the whole of the earth. I wake softly, with a sense of infinite calm.

———————

The maple leaves have all fallen, and the days are still clear. We're still eating sow jerky, and I have managed to make a kind of runny soap from lard and ashes and a sort of smokey light from a bowlful of sow fat with a silk wick.

Sometimes I feel as though I were bearing her feral old soul along with my own. Sometimes at dusk, when Eva and I come down off the hill and reenter the house to sleep, I find myself looking around these rooms with a sort of sideways terror. I have to remind myself, *That's just a door. Those are only walls. They can't hurt you.* And sometimes when I wake in the morning, my first thought is panic—*I've got to get outside.*

———————

Last night I woke to the sound of the winter's first rain. I lay in the moonless darkness, listening to the soft wash of water against the window. I remembered how, when the rains began last year, Eva and I were putting together puzzles and eating canned soup and waiting for someone to save us, and I felt a flood of compassion for those scared girls. Now it seems only a distant irony that this was the autumn Eva was to join a ballet company, the autumn I should have entered Harvard, that one of these uncharted autumn days was the day I turned eighteen.

This morning I went into the pantry—just to stand there, surrounded on all sides by our half-year's collaboration with soil and water and sunshine. I stood in that close, windowless room, looked at the food we had canned, at the pumpkins and potatoes piled on the floor, the strings of dried herbs and fruit and beans hanging from the ceiling, the bundles and jars of roots and leaves and barks and flowers, all labeled with notes about where I found them, about what they might ease or cause or cure. I thought of the bags of seeds out in the workshop, all dried and labeled and waiting for spring, and of the barrels in the stump, heavy with acorns and berries and sow jerky, and I felt as though I had passed the Achievement Tests, after all.

———

In the meadow the fresh green of winter is just beginning to appear through the mat of golden grass. In the woods, tiny green shoots rise like sparks up through the wet, black leaves, and the patient spores of mushrooms are suddenly fruiting. In the clearing, the redwood fence post Eva and I set up at the far end of the garden is sprouting new fronds.

Each day brings new gifts. Yesterday we found a fresh patch of sheep's sorrel to add to our dried sow soup. Today I noticed what looked like bright beads spilled on the path to the stump—madrone berries. I gathered a few in my hand, and a sort of thanksgiving passed through my mind. I nibbled a berry. It was bland and faintly sweet—dry yellow flesh around a core of dark seeds.

———

Yesterday it was so wet we stayed indoors, left the forest to its own damp self, and sat close to the warm stove, drowsing and listening to the winter rain, the wind-dashed drops broadcast like seeds against the walls and windows. I had made Eva a cup of raspberry leaf tea as a pregnancy tonic, and between sips she amused herself by balancing the mug on her gigantic belly and watching as the baby's kicking threatened to knock the tea to the floor.

I was pounding a batch of acorn meal by the stove when all of a sudden the whole house shook. From the blocked-off utility room there came a creaking and snapping and crashing that seemed to go on forever. Eva's tea mug crashed to the floor and I leapt to my feet. There was a moment of silence, followed by another loud creaking, another series of crashes, and then everything was quiet.

Eva gave me a look of terror and pleading. "What should we do?" she begged.

"Hide," I whispered.

"Where?" she asked, and I didn't know what to tell her, for in that moment I understood that whatever room or corner or closet she hid in, it would only end up being her trap when he finally broke through the back door.

"Wait by the front door," I whispered to Eva. "I'll see what's out back, and if I yell, you run off into the woods."

She nodded and begged, "Be careful," as I grabbed the gun and snuck towards the kitchen.

As soon as I entered it, I could see something was wrong. Daylight was filtering through the window in the door leading to the utility room, the door I had nailed shut and barricaded with the washing machine. Slowly I eased towards it, the rifle aimed at the spot in the window where I expected a leering face to appear. It seemed to take me forever to creep along the counter, to edge past the dusty refrigerator and stove. When I finally reached the door, I crouched below the window, waiting.

I started to feel dizzy and my legs began to ache, but nothing happened. Flinching beneath the weight of the silence, I raised myself up to peek out the window. What I saw was such a shock that for a moment I could make no sense of it—I looked out on rubble. The washing machine had fallen away from the door and was lying on its side next to the toppled freezer, the floor tilted sharply towards the ground, and the roof sagged above the twisted room. Rain was falling in the gap between the wreckage and the kitchen door.

How could he have done that? I thought stupidly. *Someone must be with him.*

But still no one appeared, and when I went outside to look for tracks, I could find nothing but raccoon and possum prints. The utility room had simply collapsed, the rotting timbers finally pulled down by the weight of the cast iron sink, the empty freezer, the useless washing machine, the dead dryer.

Our parents' house is falling down around us.

———————

Again the moon grows full. There has been a break in the rain, but the weather is so cold and Eva so enormously big that we stay close to home, close to the stove and the pantry and our warm mattresses. Eva dozes and drinks the teas I steep for her. She knits odd little gowns from the silks our mother left, while I scan the encyclopedia for the dreams it contains, and write by the light of the round moon and the open stove, my pen scratching its tiny markings onto these last sheets of paper.

This afternoon I read: *The oldest use of the word "virgin" meant not the physiological condition of chastity, but the psychological state of belonging to no man, of belonging to oneself. To be virginal did not mean to be inviolate, but rather to be true to nature and instinct, just as the virgin forest is not barren or unfertilized, but instead is unexploited by man.*

Children born out of wedlock were at one time referred to as "virgin-born."

––––––––––

Tonight we've eaten well—acorn cakes, stewed dried blackberries, baked pumpkin, a bit of cress from the spot I've been cultivating by the creek. Eva dozes over her cup of mullein flower tea, the steam rising into her face like the rising of a dream.

I wonder what it's like at the stump tonight. I wonder if the roof is tight, if the plywood door still holds. I wonder if anything has taken shelter there, nestled snug among our barrels of acorns and berries. I wonder what it would be like to be there now, listening to the rain and wind, smelling the night, the wet leaves and the earth, and the ancient char of the tree. I wonder what sorts of creatures would watch us from the forest, what spirits would hover above us, circle around us in the rain.

Why does that place seem safer, more alive, than this?

––––––––––

It has begun. I dread to think how it will end, though writing those words scares me—for what if they prove prophetic?

Last night Eva only nibbled at her acorn mush, and a little later she leapt from her chair, ran to the bathroom faster than I've seen her move in months. When she came out, her hands were pressing her womb.

"Feel this," she said. I touched her stomach and it was hard as an oak trunk; it was a thing with a will of its own.

"A contraction?" I asked, as I felt it start to ease.

She nodded.

"The first?"

"The strongest. They've been coming and going all day. But I wasn't sure what they were."

"When was the last one?"

"Awhile ago. Before dinner."

"How do you feel?"

"Okay. A little shaky." She looked at me and asked, "Are you ready for this?"

No, I thought, and answered, "The question is, are you?"

"Yes. No. Maybe. Anyway, it's coming," she answered almost festively.

"What do you want to do now?"

"Go to bed, I guess. Try to rest."

She settled down on her mattress, while I got out the encyclopedia, and tried to glean any last bits of knowledge, tried to memorize the words or pry them from the page.

She slept, and later so did I, lulled by the rain and warm stove. Just before dawn I woke. Eva was lying on her mattress, rocking back and forth and moaning to herself.

"Eva," I rasped through my sleep-tightened throat. "How's it going?"

"Okay, I think."

"Still having contractions?"

"Yes."

"What are they doing?"

"Growing stronger."

"How far apart?"

She managed a laugh. "Got a stopwatch?"

I simmered some alder bark and pressed her to drink the decoction. I fixed acorn mush, though I was the only one who ate. Every now and then, Eva clutched her stomach, and I quit whatever I was doing to sit on the mattress beside her and rub her shoulders until the contraction was over.

The long day passed. I fed the fire and swept the floor and smoothed the sheets and steeped the teas that were supposed to facilitate Eva's labor and calm my nerves, while she lay on her mattress, enduring the contractions that neither quit nor came closer together. Finally, towards dusk, she raised her head off her pillow to ask the question I had been dreading, "How much longer?"

"It won't be much longer. You're doing fine."

"Isn't there anything else to do?"

"I don't know. I don't think so."

"What does the encyclopedia say?"

"It says you're doing fine."

It says, *The average length of labor for the primapara is sixteen to eighteen hours.*

"Sweet Nellie," Eva said, looking at me as though I were someone new. "It's nice of you to do this."

I shrugged and answered as she always answered me, "What else are sisters for?"

But all I can do is rub her back, give her sips of tea and lie to her, tell her, *You're doing fine.*

The encyclopedia claims the urge to push is instinctual. But Eva says nothing about pushing. She says nothing but, "Here it comes," and nothing comes but another contraction.

After another night and day of labor, the house is hot and tight. It smells of suffering flesh and fills with Eva's moans. Hour after hour she lies on her stale mattress, while I feed the fire and rub her back and wait, frantic and helpless.

Damn the encyclopedia.

Eva is dying, and the encyclopedia talks about instinct. Even now it drones on, measured, pedantic, aloof, flattening the world into facts—but withholding the knowledge I need to save my sister's life. What does it know about instinct?

Instinct is older than paper, wilder than words. Instinct is wiser than any article about the three stages of delivery, any article about obstetrical interventions. But where do instincts come from? And how can I find them now, after living without them for so long?

Sally Bell had instincts. She hid in the bushes with her sister's heart in her hands, and when the murderers left she lived on berries and roots, slept naked in hollow trees, and outlived that horror by eighty years. The Lone Woman had instincts. She left her people to save her child, and when she found her child had died, she lived on alone. The sow had instincts. She came for water with her shoats, and fought the bullets until it was time to die.

Surely I have instincts, too.

And it comes to me: *We must leave this house. If Eva is to survive, we must leave this place where she is stuck. If Eva is to be a mother, we must find some other way for her to give birth.*

There is an urgency to that thought so compelling that I speak before I have a chance to question it, "Listen Eva—do you think you can walk?"

"What?"

"Can you walk?"

"Why?"

"I want us to go for a walk."

"Where?"

"To the stump," I answer before I can think. Instead of the incredulity or outrage or indifference I had braced myself to expect, she looks at me with a tiny flicker of interest.

"To the stump?" she echoes.

"Maybe it will help. Do you think you can walk?"

"I'll try," she says, responding to the certainty in my voice, to the relief of action, as she struggles to rise off her mattress.

I fill a pack with quilts and blankets, food, a bucket of ashes at whose heart glows a handful of coals. Somehow I manage to dress us warmly, to lace our shoes. And off we go, stopping in the opened doorway for Eva to bend over the clench of her belly.

As I rub her back, standing in the doorway, looking out at the green-grey forest, I am clutched by a contraction of my own—a contraction of fear. Why am I making my sister hike through the wet woods after having been in labor for almost two days? Am I doing this just to speed up the inevitable, just to get her dying done with?

One step at a time, we cross the clearing. We pass through the ring of rotten tulips and then we're in the forest, walking upstream beside the creek. Eva leans against me, waddling unlike the ballerina she once was, and yet using all her dancer's stamina and courage to take each next step. Sometimes she stops, clutches at me while a contraction sweeps over her.

We reach the hillside we must climb, pause for another contraction, and then head up. And up.

And up. And stop. And on. And up, counting progress a step at a time.

My arm turns numb in her grip. My back aches beneath the pack. Our faces are wet with tears or sweat or mist, and still we climb. At least it's something. At least we're doing something.

But halfway up the slope, she says, "I can't." She looks around wildly, desperately, then fastens her gaze on me, speaks as intently as though she were explaining the world's greatest truth. "I can't."

"It's not much further," I answer.

"I can't," she says. "It's not the hill. It's this. I can't get it out. I can't get out of it. I can't do this."

She sobs and then begins to scream, her head thrown back to the grey sky. Her face looks like a mask, a bit of anonymous flesh wrapped around eternal pain. She is a creature no longer my sister, screaming while we cling to the hill. All around us the forest waits, listens, absorbs our little struggle.

"I can't. I can't," she cries. "I can't."

I grab her heaving shoulders, force her to face me, and say, in a voice horrible with desperation, "What else are you going to do?"

For a moment, Eva returns, looks at me from those anonymous eyes, while I growl again, "What else are you going to do?" Then I soften, plead, "Just climb the hill. You don't have to have the baby. But just please, please climb this hill."

She shuffles forward. Halts. Clings to me, rocking with the effort, then shuffles another step, her feet plowing up furrows in the steep compost of needles, leaves, and last year's acorns.

And so we travel, step by awful step—up and up. When we get to the steepest part, I go behind her, push her up, first with my hands against her shoulder blades, and then at the very steepest, with my hands pressing up on her buttocks so that I can feel the bones of her pelvis through the flesh beneath her skirts, pushing her up, up, an inch, a centimeter at a time.

When she gasps, "Here it comes," we stop, brace ourselves, let her contraction wash over us, until I realize that I, too, am shuddering with its force. I, too, am breathing deep as an ocean. I, too, am moaning, growling, rolling the pain out into the indifferent forest.

Somehow we reach the flat. Eva sinks to the ground, and I fall beside her, holding her, rocking her in my arms, muttering praise and thanks and blessings to all the things beyond and within us that allowed us to reach this place. When I finally raise my head to look around, I see the dank forest, the rain-dark sky, the roofed stump filled with barrels, and for a clear moment I know I am crazy.

But we can't go back. I claw down panic, raise Eva to her feet, edge her on—step by baby step—towards the stump. I remember that old game we used to play. *Nellie, you may take two steps forward.*

Mother, may I?

Yes, you may.

Yes, you must. What else are you going to do?

The light has all but gone by the time Eva reaches the stump. She leans against it, panting and moaning, while I wrestle the barrels outside to make room for us. She crawls in, her belly almost dragging the ground. She slumps against the charred wall. I spread out quilts for her to lie on, and, because she is shivering uncontrollably, I cover her with all the blankets I have brought. Then I rush to find dry wood in the failing light.

I pour the coals from the pan into the fire pit, try to start a fire. Eva watches dully. Finally a spark ignites, licks up the precious tidbits of paper, and I settle back on my haunches to add bulk to the flames.

"It's good here," says Eva through chattering teeth, the first words she has spoken about anything beyond herself for days. I look, and she is right. The fire sparks starward, and shadows the folds and twists of the stump at whose heart we rest. We can smell the clean scents of oak and bay smoke, of humus and charred redwood and the damp night. The moon is just past full, and it seems there is nothing in these woods that would want to harm us. Instead, I think I feel a new benevolence abroad, as if the forest had finally grown sympathetic, as if—huddled here in the darkness—we finally mattered.

Eva doubles with the blow of another contraction, her hand reaches blindly for mine, grasps it until I'm sure the bones will crack.

"I thought I was used to them by now," she gasps. She whimpers, "They can't get worse."

But they do.

Thick and hard and fast, they buffet her like storm gales, leaving her only seconds to gather herself before the next blast. She doesn't scream, but she groans and the sounds she makes are beyond the pain and work of labor, beyond human—or even animal—life. They are the sounds that move the earth, the sounds that give voice to the deep, violent fissures in the bark of the redwoods. They are the sounds of splitting cells, of bonding atoms, the sounds of the waxing moon and the forming stars.

"Drink," I tell her, holding a cup of water to her mouth. She takes a trembling sip, and then says, "I have to pee."

I help her outside, help her to lift her skirts. I support her as she squats, but nothing comes except a contraction. Then I hear another sound, a grunt deep in her throat that makes her eyes narrow with internal effort.

When it's over, she gasps, "I pushed."

It is amazing how closely hope hovers above despair. I thought I had given up hours ago, but a fresh elation charges through me and I think, *Maybe my sister will not die.*

I have no idea how long she pushed. Several times the fire burnt low, and I had to leave her to tend to it. At some point, I helped her to lean against the inner wall of the stump, and finally, when I looked between her legs, I could see, by the dancing light of the fire, her vulva bulging. When she pushed again, I saw her swollen labia part and a slick bit of head peek out.

When the contraction receded, the head disappeared, but with the next one, I lifted one of her hands, guided it down between her legs so she could feel that other flesh, and an ecstasy passed over her face whose traces endured even through the next contractions. I gave her sips of water, held her hands, and added my own growls of encouragement to her grunts, and slowly her vulva stretched thinner and thinner, and slowly that head inched out.

Suddenly her eyes widened in surprise. She pushed again, and the head crowned—its body still inside her, its dark flattened face like a deity from another time. She pushed again, and it slithered towards me. I caught it awkwardly, more to keep myself from being hit than to protect what I was catching. It was hot and wet and slippery and still as death. For a stunned moment, I stared at its naked face. It seemed complete exactly as it was, and I felt an odd reluctance at the thought of coaxing it into life.

But just as I was beginning to try to recall the pages in the encyclopedia about reviving a stillbirth, it drew a breath. And then another. It opened its eyes and looked at the fire, the stump, the predawn sky. Eva sank back, tears falling down her cheeks. I laid the little thing on her chest, bundling all the covers around them.

We wept and laughed, then—far, far beyond words. Eva's contractions returned, and for a horrifying moment I thought, *twins,* but then I remembered the placenta. She pushed again, and it slithered out, liver-purple and blood-red, like an enormous slug.

I remembered I was supposed to examine it, but in my daze of joy and exhaustion I couldn't remember what I was supposed to be looking for. Of course the encyclopedia hadn't said anything about how to cut the cord, so I made my own way, beginning with a tentative little slice, and then, when neither Eva nor the baby winced, doubling it over the knifeblade and yanking it in two.

I built up the fire while Eva murmured to her baby, coaxed it to her breast, giggled as it groped and sputtered around her nipple. A thin smoke drifted through the clearing, filling the dawning air with its tang.

The sun rose.

I looked at the heap of blankets on Eva's chest, and said, "Well, it's bright enough to see now. Let's just take a peek at her."

Eva stroked the top of its skull languidly with her fingertips. "It's a boy."

"What?"

"It's a boy."

I felt myself stiffen. "How do you know?"

She shrugged. "I've known for months."

"But it has to be a girl."

She laughed, bent her neck so she could gaze down at the bundle on top of her. "Nope. It's a boy. A sweet, smart, strong, beautiful boy."

"You never told me."

"You never asked."

"Are you sure it's a boy?"

"I'll bet you."

"You'll bet me?"

"I'll bet you," she answered joyously, "the gas. I'll bet you the gas it's a boy."

She eased the blankets back, and we peeked, and there, between its tiny, red, wrinkled thighs were a startlingly large set of testicles and the fat little worm of a penis.

"A boy," I said, the disappointment so sharp in my voice that Eva looked up to ask, "What's wrong with a boy?"

"Nothing, I guess. I was just hoping we could name it Gloria."

"Well, Gloria would be a pretty silly name for you, wouldn't it, little one?" she crooned to the baby on her chest.

All that work for a boy, I thought. Suddenly the penis stiffened and a quick shower of clear water sprayed from it.

"He's peeing," said Eva in delight and amazement. "He baptized me." She began giggling like an eight-year-old, giggling as if she were drunk on Grand Marnier, giggling so contagiously that I had to join her, to laugh with a relief that left me drained and cleaned.

We laughed and the light grew stronger. We giggled until our grins ached and our stomachs felt weak and giddy, until tears blurred our eyes and ran in unchecked trails down our aching cheeks, and it seemed that if the baby were born and breathing and my sister had once more taken up residence behind her face, then nothing could ever go wrong again.

We rested in the stump till noon, dozing and smiling and watching that rubbery-faced creature stare out at the world through its new eyes. But it was a chilly day, the fire took a lot of tending to keep the stump warm enough for a newborn, and I found myself wanting to hurry Eva and the baby back down to the house. I longed to build a dependable fire in the stove, fix hot food and chamomile tea, and sleep for days.

I buried the placenta and umbilical cord in our new clearing, buried it so deep the pigs will never root it up. I tucked the blankets in a barrel, broke up the coals of the fire, took the baby in my arms, and then—step by step—I helped my sister back down the hill.

———

I woke last night to the sound of the window opening. The dark room spun while I tried to orient myself. For a frantic moment, I thought we had survived the past nine months only for the rapist to return. Then I heard Eva shuffling back to her bed.

"What's wrong?" I whispered.

"Nothing. It's just a little hot in here."

"Are you okay?"

"I think so."

I went to her and she was burning. Her face was slick, her body shook. I lit the lard lamp, got water for her to drink and a wet cloth to wipe her face and arms. Then I went into the pantry, stood among my collection of forest herbs, trying desperately to calculate or intuit which ones might help make her well.

For a long time I sat beside her on her mattress, tendering her sips of strawberry leaf tea, and watching a cold light seep into the room so slowly it seemed I was only imagining the sun that it preceded. Fears and questions crystallized in the half-light like water freezing into blades and spikes of ice. *Eva must have an infection,* I thought—*nothing else could make a fever come so fast, less than two days after she gave birth.*

But I had no idea how she got it.

And I had no idea how to cure it.

Meanwhile, the baby cried—a shrill, impersonal sound that went on so long it seemed eternal. I could find nothing to make it stop. Holding it didn't help. Rocking it didn't help. Walking with it and singing to it didn't help. I swaddled it and set it in the drawer I had fixed for it, but still it screamed. I maneuvered it to Eva's hot nipple, where it struggled to nurse and then pulled away to cry. Finally it dropped off—mid-scream—into a jumpy sleep, only to wake a few minutes later, crying.

Eva stirred, and I wiped her face and held a mug of dogwood root tea to her cracked lips. As she sucked an uneven sip, she suddenly looked around wildly. "Where's my baby?" she asked—although it was lying right beside me, screaming.

"It's here," I soothed. "It's doing fine," I lied.

She sank back down into her fever, muttering, "Lift that leg. Higher. Ankle straight. Head up. That's right. Lift, lift, lift." And then, wistfully, "*Plié to arabesque, temps levé, sauté,* three, four, and *pirouette.*"

I rocked her baby, walked with it up and back the length of the sour room, changed the towel that was its diaper, and all the while it screamed. Wondering how I knew to do those things, I gave it wet rags to suck, offered it my finger. I tried to get it to swallow a little acorn mush, a drop of wood rose tea. I cooed to it, sang to it, finally bit my tongue to keep from screaming back at it.

The house burned with Eva's fever. It burned with the baby's screams, and with my fear. The baby wouldn't stop crying, and its wails were accusation, condemnation, a shrill reminder of my impotence, my ignorance. Its wails sent me spiraling down through helplessness to anger, and through that, to despair, and still it cried, its face hard and red, its eyes—from which no tears fell—squeezed shut.

I tucked it back in its drawer, went outside for wood. When I returned it was still screaming, and the tears it did not cry were coursing silently down Eva's face.

"Why is he crying?" she asked when she saw me.

"I think it's hungry," I answered. "You don't have any milk yet."

"When will it come?" she begged.

"Soon. It's just supposed to take a little longer the first time." *As if there'll be a second,* I thought.

She sighed and rolled fretfully across the bed.

"How do you feel?" I asked.

She answered, "Cold," and I thought, *I'm finally truly losing her.*

Still the baby screamed, and the sound drilled a hole in my skull, needling out all thought but *make it stop.* Suddenly, made wild by helplessness, I swooped on it, snatched it up, my fingers tensed like claws, my arms aching to rip it from its screams, to do any desperate thing to stop that voice and its awful demands.

But instead of shaking it or slapping it or dashing its head down against the corner of the stove, I sank onto my mattress. I was weeping myself and clutching the wailing thing against me. It began to nuzzle and root against my chest and in a daze I give it what it wanted, lifted my shirt to expose my own breast as though it had never crossed my mind to kill it. For a moment its heavy head wobbled frantically on the stem of its neck, and then it latched on to my nipple.

It took my breath away. It was a shock as sudden and hard as sex, the way he sucked—*like a little vacuum cleaner,* I thought, giddy with relief that I hadn't hurt him, with delight at the sudden silence. He sucked intently, his dark eyes open and unblinking, his mouth chomping away at my nipple as matter-of-factly as a turtle eating leaves. He seemed to know exactly what he was doing, and my next feeling was one of remorse for having tricked him with a milkless nipple. I braced myself for the dreadful moment when he would discover my breasts were even more useless than Eva's.

But whether he had given up hoping for food or he was too exhausted to care, he suckled for a long time at my empty breast, nursed as though comfort were more sustenance than milk. I bent over him, cradling his head in my palm, and watched as his eyes oozed slowly closed and his sucking diminished to an occasional chomp and then stopped altogether. Finally my nipple dribbled from his lax mouth, and he slept.

He slept in my arms while the fire burned to coals in the stove and the winter light faded from the house. He slept in my arms until they ached as though they had been clinging to an oak tree all night. He slept for hours while I looked down at him—that tiny human, whole, complete, brimming with promise and intelligence and needs, while I vowed he would not die.

Not even if I had to feed him on my blood.

Elderberry flowers, dogwood root, peppermint and strawberry leaves, mountain balm, blue-eyed grass, and yarrow to bring down fever; horsetail stems, wormwood and bay leaves to ease cramping; redwood sap, yerba buena and mugwort leaves for tonics; rose hips, coyote mint and chamomile for colic; fennel seeds, nettle, raspberry, and rosemary leaves, chamomile and red clover flowers to induce lactation.

I forage the pages of Native Plants of Northern California, gleaning what lore and hope I can. The plants I don't already have in the pantry I search for in the forest, scouring the streambeds, the meadows, the ridgetops, gathering what I find there in midwinter. Back in the stuffy house, I peel roots, crush leaves, boil water and steep herbs, and try not to remember my vast ignorance, try not to think of the experiment I am conducting.

"Drink this," I say, lifting my sister from her mattress, holding the steaming cup for her while she takes docile sips, shudders and grimaces at the astringency, the harshness, the wildness. And sips again.

"This is for your fever, this is for your nipples, this will make your milk come in, this will make you strong," I say, urging salves and poultices and infusions and decoctions, while I boil more water, steep more herbs, and pray to the forest to make her well.

When the baby wakes and snuffles for a nipple, I hold him to Eva's hot breasts. But if she moans and pushes him away, or if he stiffens and wails his frustration, I scoop him back into my arms, lift my shirt, and fit my own nipple into his mouth. Then, sitting by the window where I once memorized the stages of mitosis, I watch him as he drinks from me, wondering at the strange alchemy of love and need and chemistry that fills my breasts with milk, wondering at the fierceness of his tiny brow, at the perfect curves of his ears.

I gave my sister elderberry tea, blue-eyed grass, yarrow, and peppermint, and whether it was those herbs that cured her I suppose I will never know, but finally her fever broke. I gave her stewed fruit and acorn mush and sow jerky broth, and slowly she grew stronger, until finally, when the moon came full again, she could sit up by herself, clasp the hot cup in her own hands. I gave her raspberry leaf and nettle and fennel tea, and her milk came in until now her breasts are swollen to twice their normal size and when the baby cries, dark circles spread across the fronts of both our shirts.

———

Eva has named him Robert after our father, but I have taken to calling him Burl, and he is my constant companion. Hour after hour I cook and clean and care for him and for my sister, and slowly Eva grows stronger, and slowly my Burl grows fatter and more awake.

———

This morning, for a break from the house that has seemed to come to own me, I took Burl for a hike. Using two of his grandfather's shirts to make a kind of pack, I tied him against my chest. Eva was sleeping when I left, and though I thought of waking her to tell her where we were going, in the end I decided she needed her sleep. I stoked the fire, took up my gathering basket, slipped out the door and across the clearing, and headed to my father's grave.

It was a soft, damp day, a day of low grey skies. The forest was lush, moist—rotting back to bloom. Chanterelles appeared like lost balls among the scatter of wet leaves. The tender curls of bracken shoots unfurled from the dank ground, and I filled my basket as I walked.

Burl was good company. Most of the way he slept, neat and quiet as a cat, his body pressed soft and warm against my chest. But even when he was asleep, I was aware of his presence, and the forest seemed keener, fresher, more alive because he was in it with me.

When he woke, he was silent, one soft cheek pressed just below my collar bone, his head turned so he could look out at the world I carried him through. I began to murmur to him then, to tell him about the forest, about mushrooms and ferns, bears and boars, redwoods and oaks and madrone trees. I told him about his family, about his grandfather and grandmother, about Eva and Eli and me—a web of stories spinning round him, catching him already in their weave.

When we reached the grave, it was blanketed with damp leaves and smelled both fresh and old. I hunkered down next to that mound of earth and untied Burl and nursed him. I whispered to the sky, "You have a grandson," while Burl watched the forest.

When we got home, Eva was sitting at the window, and she rose to meet us with a tight face.

"Where have you been?" she asked, reaching for Burl even before I could untie him from my chest.

"For a walk."

"I woke up and no one was here."

"I took Burl up to his grandfather's grave," I explained.

"Why didn't you tell me?"

"You were asleep."

"Wouldn't you think that would be important to me, too—to take my son to my father's grave?"

"We'll go again when you're stronger," I promised.

"But it won't be the first time," she said, pressing Burl to her as though they had both endured an ordeal.

"I'm sorry," I said. "Did you have a good rest?"

"No." She sat down and opened her blouse, and Burl began nursing obediently.

"Didn't he cry for me?" she asked, stroking his flailing arm.

"No," I said. "He didn't. Burl didn't cry at all."

"His name isn't Burl," she said, pressing his head closer to her breast. "It's Robert."

———

The roof is leaking like a foundering boat. Every hour I have to climb the stairs to empty out the collection of tubs and pans that fill what used to be our bedrooms. In the meantime, I try to read the encyclopedia, but it's empty, flavorless—a meaningless habit. I write a little, but I'm running out of paper, and my thoughts keep trailing off the page.

Life should be good, after all our trouble. But once again something has gone wrong, and though I can't say exactly what it is, tonight I keep remembering the lumps of clay on my mother's potter's wheel. They seemed almost alive as they spun between her wet hands, and I remember watching raptly as she centered them and opened them and pulled them into mugs and bowls and vases, formed them to the shape of her desires.

But every living thing has desires of its own. She used to say that a good potter had to listen to the clay, and tonight I remember how the smallest bubble or bit of gravel, the tiniest slip of my mother's hands, and the whole perfect pot could start to wobble. If even the slightest wobble went unnoticed or uncorrected, it would grow larger and larger, taking on its own violent life, out of control and so strong it would finally tear the pot apart— flinging wet shards of clay across the room.

———

Now if Eva is singing to Burl when I enter the room, her song trails off to silence. If I pick him up, she says, *Not now—he needs to sleep.* If I change his diaper, Eva readjusts it. If I put a blanket on him, Eva takes it off.

Now when I try to nurse him, she takes him from my arms.

———

I'm writing this from the stump, writing by the little fire I'm trying to keep burning by myself. It chokes and flares. Smoke rises wildly, now pouring out into the rain, now filling the stump with its bitter plumes. Close and grey, the rain endures. Everything drips or recedes into itself. I've been here five nights, living on the acorns and berries and dried food we stockpiled up here last autumn, living on rainwater and rancor.

We fought.

I left, moved out here, taking only a bucket of coals, more blankets and a packful of clothes, some herbs, my pestle, and this stained and faded notebook. "Keep the rest," I yelled at that witch who was once my sister. "You've already taken everything else that ever mattered."

So this is how the story ends, and who knows how far back we would have to go to find the beginning. When Eva cried, "Leave my baby alone," it was as though we had been fighting for years.

"He was hungry," I said, looking from the Burl at my breast to my sister rising off her mattress, her waking face already hard with rage.

"I can feed him," she snapped.

"You were sleeping."

"So wake me up."

"You need your rest."

"*He* doesn't need two mothers."

"He did when you were sick."

"I'm better now."

"Why can't we both—"

"Nell, he's my baby."

"Your baby," I echoed, looking down at him as he drank from my breast, his milk-fat cheeks ballooning with his sucking, his tender fingers stroking my chest. "Your baby?"

"I carried him for nine months, I gave birth to him. He needs me to nurse him."

She crossed the space from her mattress to mine, lifted Burl away from me. His toothless gums scraped my nipple as she pulled him from my breast.

He began to scream and suddenly I was mean and blind with anguish. "Who kept you alive all these months so you could give birth to *your* baby?

Who helped you with your labor? Who saved *your* baby's life after you got sick? Who saved your life, too—if it comes to that?"

"So now you own me, too?"

Only this stump is mine—though I share it with the forest. I spend my days sitting by my fire, trying not to think, not to remember. Instead I listen to the rain, watch the rain, smell the rain, feel its mists cling to my face. My breasts are huge and tight as fists. They bulge and strain with milk that no one needs. Veins thick as worms twist across them, and my nipples weep— a grief that stains and stiffens my shirt.

Burl was the one thing we had left—and Burl was the one thing my sister and I could not learn to share.

Pomo women used California poppy to stop lactation, so I, too, steep dried pods in boiled streamwater, sip that acrid infusion. I squeeze sips of thin, sweet milk onto the damp earth, and then bind my breasts against my chest—anything to ease the ache and throb of them, anything to help my body forget his suck.

This is hibernation time, a slow, chill time of grey rain and green light. By day I walk, dream, notice where the plants grow that can feed or heal me. With my pestle I pound acorn meal, wrap it in fern fronds, set it in the spring to leach. I chew a few dried berries, gnaw a strip of sow, sip poppy tea to stanch my milk. I gather wood, tend the fire, shake out my blankets, fix the roof. Sometimes it seems I hear voices speaking, neither harshly nor lovingly, but with the forest's own tongue.

Other creatures come to the clearing. The deer browsing towards the stump lifts its head for the breeze, stops at my scent, turns its elegant head to study me, and my heart opens and grows still. Last night a raccoon came to the rim of the fire's light, met my eyes above the flames. It made a noise in its throat—a low, long chuckle halfway between a purr and a growl—and then it turned back to its business beneath the waning moon. This morning I heard a blundering and an old black sow entered my glade. For a moment she, too, met my gaze, and then she grunted, trotted off.

I spend hours watching my little fire, and sometimes a thought comes to me. Sometimes I remember those other sisters of mine, the Lone Woman and Sally Bell, each of us longing for the kin we have lost, each of us learning to inhabit the forest alone.

Sometimes I think of my mother and father, of the web that even now shapes who I am, how I endure.

You are your own person, my mother said.

Finally I think she may be right.

Sometimes I remember Eli, think of him inside me and the leaves of this place plastered to our naked skins. I remember his mocking laugh, the trembling tenderness of his hands, and I wonder who he was, wonder what he might become. I try to think of him in Boston—though it seems harder and harder to believe such a place exists. I try to imagine cars and streetlights and ringing phones, but those images are vague and muddled, and my longing for them lacks the ache and twist and sting of real desire.

Sometimes I think I would like to see Eli again. But if he comes back now, he'll have to find me here—by my own fire.

The wood burns its economical flame. I nibble a dried apricot, sip mugwort tea for dreaming, more poppy to stop my milk. I watch the fire, listen to the fog, muse more than I write. This writing is an old habit. I wonder if I won't outgrow it even before I run out of paper. I wonder if it is still English that I am writing here.

I'm just a core, a kernel, a coal—tucked in a bit of breathing flesh, listening to the rain. My life fills this place, no longer meager, no longer lost or stolen or waiting to begin.

I drink rain and it quenches an ancient thirst.

This is no interlude, no fugue state.

The moon wanes to the barest crescent. I grow content.

I fixed a stew of acorn mush and dried blackberries for breakfast yesterday morning. As I stirred the pot I remembered the berries drying in the late summer heat, the drone of flies and bees, the beads of blood on my arms from the brambles, the indelible juices on my fingers. I remembered the long days of gathering acorns, hour after hour of bending and crawling, until my back felt permanently stooped, my hands had been pricked by a million brittle oak leaves, and when I closed my eyes, I saw a sea of acorns.

The steam was warm and fragrant in the chill air. I was hungry and I could feel my stomach clenching like another strong muscle. But just as I was lifting the first spoonful to my mouth, I heard a voice say *Wait.*

For a wild moment I thought, *Mother.* I even stood to meet her, but outside the stump I saw only the familiar forest, heard only the incessant drip of rain. I breathed the moist, green-tinged air, and then, on an impulse I never tried to understand, I took the mush-pot and walked around the stump, pausing four times to spoon a pile of steaming food onto the wet earth.

I returned to my fire, sat cross-legged just inside the stump, watching the rain drip through the forest. My stomach felt tight and small, my lungs big and loose, my hands were quiet in my lap. I felt as if I were waiting, though I had no idea why, or for what. At times thoughts came to me—*I should gather more wood, I should check the roof to see how it's holding out, I should move the water bucket out into the rain,* but they lacked force or impulse, remained ideas as passive—and passing—as, *the sky is grey, the rain is falling, I can feel the weight of my shirt on my back.*

I was still sitting like that when darkness took the forest. The air thickened, the sky deepened, the woods closed in around me, until at last I could see only the final coals of my untended fire glowing like a heart's secrets. I had to fight an impulse, the first real impulse I had had since I spooned my breakfast on the earth, to pluck one of those red jewels from its bed of ashes and pop it in my mouth.

Even more gradual than the fade of the sun's light was the fade of that handful of coals, but finally they, too, were gone, so slowly that even though they had my whole attention I could never say when they were extinguished, leaving me in the absolute darkness of a moonless rainy night, until the coal inside me was the only fire left.

In the blackness just beyond me, the rain kept falling, masking whatever other noises those woods might contain. I sat emptied before the dead fire, watching the darkness. My eyes felt as though they were wrapped in velvet, and it seemed my cheeks and forehead had grown a thousand new eyes, though they, too, saw only blackness. After a time, I drowsed, still sitting crosslegged, my hands still lax in my lap.

I awoke to blackness, though the rain had ceased. A dozen different dreams rose off me like skittish angels. I woke hungry, thirsty, cold, stiff, and yet unwilling to break the spell of my sitting by rising to find food or water, or even to shift my aching legs.

She came.

I sensed her approach long before I heard her lumbering steps, long before I smelled her rankness. She sniffed the circumference of the stump, stopping to lap the four cold lumps of food. She paused again at the doorway, waiting while I pressed my body against the back wall. She entered, circled like a weary dog, and lay down. I could feel her damp, rough fur, smell the decay that hung on her hot breath. I thought, *This is no dream.*

I sat in a dark my eyes could not learn to adjust to, trapped by the bulk and will of a bear. I listened to the drip of the forest, to my breathing and hers. I curled beside that she-bear and slept.

I dreamed she bore me from the hot mystery of her womb, squeezing me down the tunnel of herself, until I dropped, helpless and unresisting, to the earth. Blind and mewling, I scaled her huge body, rooting until the nipple filled my throat. Later, her tongue sought me out. Lick by insistent lick she shaped the naked lump of me, molded my body and senses to fit the rough tug of her intention. Lick by lick, she birthed me yet again, and when she was finished, she lumbered on, left me—alone and Nell-shaped—in Her forest.

I woke at dawn and she was gone. I crawled to the door of the stump, saw her prints in the soft dead ashes of my fire. I stood, and my muscles cramped, my joints cracked. It felt as though I were rising out of my broken body into a new flesh, and I remembered the way a butterfly fresh from its chrysalis shivers and trembles as the blood fills its haggard wings. Stiff and cold and empty, I hobbled across the clearing.

And entered the forest.

———

Eva was waiting at the stump when I returned, sitting beside a freshly kindled fire with Burl swaddled and sleeping in her lap. Next to her was an enormous pack, a bedsheet bulging like a hobo's bundle.

"Hi," I said.

"Hi," she answered.

I circled her fire, dropped an armload of sticks on my woodpile, and, because of the fluky smoke, sat down beside her, reached my hands towards the flames to warm them.

"How's Burl?" I asked.

"He's fine."

"How are you?"

"Fine," she said. "I'm fine. How are you?"

"Fine, too."

We were silent, and I watched Eva's fire. The pile of blankets that was Burl twisted and stirred. Eva lifted him from her lap and handed him to me. I took him in my arms, felt his hot, slight weight, inhaled his smell. I pressed him against the bone between my breasts, and every cell of myself drank in his feel and scent. He began snuffling and rooting against my chest, and I shot a furtive glance at Eva.

"It's okay," she said. "You can nurse him if you want."

"There's nothing left for him. I dried up my milk. Besides, you were right—he's your baby."

"No," she answered, "I was wrong. He is his own."

We sat for a minute, and then Eva spoke again. "It's good to be here," she said. "This is a good place."

"Yes," I said.

"I've missed you."

All my missing of her came welling up, strangling my answer. Our eyes met. I nodded and she smiled. I rose, handed her son back to my sister. I put the kettle over the fire, and we waited while the water boiled and the rosehips steeped. She handed me some dried fruit, a baked potato still warm from home. I drank and ate, and the fire seeped back into my cold and wild bones.

When the food was gone and our cups were empty, Eva spoke. "Nell. There's something we've got to do. Something I want you to help me with."

"Okay," I said. "What?"

"All this time we've been living in the past, waiting to go back to the past. But the past is gone. It's dead, it's rotten. And it was wrong, anyway."

"Wrong?"

"Look, even if we could go back, even if the electricity does return some-day, where will we be?"

She swept her arm in a circle to include the forest and the stump. "Can you imagine living in a dorm room at Harvard? Or me dancing *Coppelia* now?" She tilted her head and rested her chin on her cocked wrists in a poise so ridiculously coy and doll-like I had to laugh.

"This is our life," she went on with a new urgency. "Like it or not, our life is here—together. And we've got to fix it so we won't forget it again, so we can't make any more mistakes."

"What are you talking about?"

"I want us to live up here."

"Here? In the stump?"

"Remember the gas?" she asked, abruptly changing the subject.

"Yes."

"I won it, right? When I bet Robert was a boy."

"Yes."

"I want us to use it. Now. Tonight."

"Tonight?"

"I'll show you. We'll say it's Christmas. Tonight we'll celebrate Christmas. Okay?"

"Okay," I promised, imagining *Water Music* flooding the darkness, or Eva dancing *Tzigane* again, imagining electric lights and hot showers, imagining the celebration we had been planning for what seemed like centuries.

"Okay," I said again, "we'll do it. We'll have a party. Let's say it's Burl's birthday party, too."

"And I can use the gas however I want?"

"It's your gas," I said. "However you want."

Her mood changed. She lost her intensity and became gleeful, playful. She thrust Burl into my arms, and, running ahead, led me back down the steep hill to the house, teasing me, promising me the best Christmas ever, while I lumbered along behind, clinging to the sleeping infant in my arms.

When we got to the house, it startled me. It was a lair, reeking of chemicals and stale flesh, harsh and cramped, leaking and crumbling. For a moment I saw it with the eyes of a forest creature, with a distrust and distaste that made me reluctant to enter. But when I crossed the threshold, it was once more the only house I had ever known. It still smelled of my childhood, still held the ghosts of both my parents, the ghosts of all my former selves.

"So," said Eva, with an animation that made me think of Father, "I'm going for the gas." She hurried outside while I stood on the floor I had learned to walk on, in the rooms that had cupped most of my life, holding Burl against me and thinking how good it felt to be home.

Eva returned, breathless and pink-cheeked, lugging the gas can. She took the lid off, and its vapors were released in the room. On them I traveled back once more to the gas stations of my childhood. I breathed greedily, closed my eyes, felt as though I could touch my hurried mother and the warm, purring car.

When I opened my eyes, Eva was pouring gasoline on the sofa.

"Hey!" I yelled. "What's going on?"

Fiercely she turned on me. "You said I could use it any way I want."

"But what the hell are you doing?"

"Burning down the house."

She left the room, trailing a stream of gasoline which soaked into the floor like a splash of oily tears. I raced after her, watched in shock as she doused the curtains of her studio, and then headed to the kitchen.

"Stop," I cried. "At least talk to me."

"Okay," she said, turning the can upright and hugging it against her, her eyes already glowing with the promised fire. "What do you want to talk about?"

"What are you doing?"

"I told you."

"But why?"

"I told you that, too."

"But can't we just leave?"

"It'd be too easy to come back. I want us to have no choice. Robert needs you, and I need you. And you need us. We can't afford to get confused about that again."

"We won't. We've learned our lesson."

"This house wouldn't last much longer anyway."

"We can fix it."

"With what? There's nothing in Father's shop to repair the roof or rebuild the utility room."

"We'll improvise something."

"We need to spend our time on other things. Besides—"

"Besides what?"

"Come here."

She led me out of the house into the cold twilight, led me to where the road entered the forest.

"Look," she said, pointing to the ground. There beside a puddle I saw the print of a boot-clad foot. It was a large track, a third again as large as my own, and whoever left it had stood watching the clearing from that spot for long enough to press his bootprint deep into the mud.

"He's come back," I said, scanning the darkening woods with a fear I hadn't known in months.

"Yes," she answered, "or someone like him."

"Did you see him?" I asked.

"No."

"Then why—"

"Look," she said again, pointing up the road.

In the gloaming I made out three more tracks from the same pair of boots, but slurred and far apart and leading out of the clearing.

"I don't understand," I said. "What made him run?"

Silently Eva guided me back past the puddle, and pointed to a final print. It was broad and naked and just slightly shorter than my foot. When I bent to study it, I could see in the mud beyond each wide toe the pock-mark of a claw.

Eva shifted Burl in her arms and watched me as those patterns made their story in my skull.

"He got chased off by a bear," I said slowly, telling it to myself.

"But that was pure luck. We can't count on that happening again." She looked at me intently for another moment and then spoke again, "See what I mean?"

"Okay," I answered. "Okay. Maybe we do need to leave here for a while. But why do we have to burn the house?"

"Don't you see? Sooner or later someone will come looking for us again. If we leave the house here, they could move in. But if the house is burnt, and we're not here, there won't be much reason for anyone to stick around."

"What if Eli comes back?" I asked before I could think.

"He knows where the stump is, doesn't he?"

I nodded. Then I asked, "What if there are things we need?"

"Like what?"

"Well, food. Clothes and things. Dishes. Tools."

"We've got a winter's worth of food in the stump already."

She started walking to the house. "I packed some things this afternoon— knives and blankets and the magnifying glass. Some jugs and pots and pans. The seeds. And if the shop doesn't catch fire, we can still sneak down and get things from it if we need to. But none of that stuff will last forever any- way. It's already wearing out. If we really need something, we'll get it from the forest."

"We don't know enough about the forest yet," I argued, following her back into the reeking house.

She shrugged again. "We'll learn. We need an adventure."

"That's what Eli said."

"This is a real adventure. His was only an escape."

"Let's wait awhile, at least till spring."

"Spring isn't far off. I know we can make it till spring. Besides, I've got a feeling that man will be back soon. If we wait, it'll be too late."

"But this," I swept my glance through the room, "this is all we have. All we'll ever have."

"All we have is each other. And the forest. And maybe a little time. This," and she flung her arm around the room, "this almost killed us. We can't stay here."

"Oh, Eva—"

"Nell," she said, "you know all this stuff."

"All what stuff?"

"How long have people been around?"

"What?"

"I mean, when did they evolve?"

"The late middle of the Pleistocene," I answered.

"So, what's that mean?"

"Man has been around for at least 100,000 years," I said, quoting the encyclopedia. "Maybe even two or three times that long."

"*People* have been around for at least 100,000 years. And how long have we had electricity?"

"Well, Edison invented the incandescent lamp in 1879."

"See? All this," and she swept her arm around the rooms of the only house I'd ever known, "was only a—what did you call it? A fugue state."

She pointed to the blackness framed by the opened door. "Our real lives are out there."

"But what if we run out of food, or get sick? We could die."

"We could run out of food or get sick right here." She laughed. "Nellie, *people* have been dying for at least 100,000 years. Dying doesn't matter. Of course we'll die.

"Look," she added fervently, "you're the one who's already living out there. You've been hating this house for months."

She watched as I considered what she had said, and then she smiled, reached out to touch my face. "Oh, sister," she said, "it will be okay. Whatever happens, this is the right thing to do.

"Think of Burl," she urged, using the name for the first time. "Even if you can't do it for yourself, do it for him."

"Okay," I said. "Okay. We'll do it," and I exhaled so deeply it felt as if I had been holding my breath for years. "But I need a minute. A little time. To say good-bye."

"Of course," she answered. "There's hours till dawn."

Burl woke then, and snuffled at my milkless chest. I kissed him and handed him to Eva. "I'll be outside," she said. "I've already said good-bye."

Then she left me in the house our parents made for us, the place where we both had been conceived. Tears streaming down my face, I climbed the stairs and entered my parents' bedroom. I buried my face in my mother's dresses, inhaling her fading scent for a final time. I closed the closet, laid the photographs of the children we had once been face down on the dresser, and left.

Downstairs, the gas fumes almost made me stagger, so I tried to make my last tour brief—through the kitchen, the front room, Eva's studio, Mother's workroom with its unfinished tapestry and shelves of books.

At the sight of the crowded bookshelves I stopped short. In the half-light of the workroom, I remembered all that books had taught me, how they had comforted me, amused and challenged me, and I was stricken at the thought of leaving them behind. Frantically I began piling on the floor every book I thought we could not live without. *The Dialogues of Plato. Pride and Prejudice. Elements of Trigonometry. The Adventures of Huckleberry Finn. A Field Guide to North American Birds. Antigone. Beloved. The Complete Works of Shakespeare. On Civil Disobedience. The Four-Gated City. The World Atlas. Ethan Frome. Quantum Physics. Howl. Wuthering Heights.*

But even before I had worked through the first shelf, I knew the heap was too heavy to lug to the stump. I saw the absurdity of trying to keep a library in the woods, exposed to the mildew of winter, the spine-cracking heat of summer, taking up room we would need for other things.

Desperately I tried to pare the number down, to keep only those books that were absolutely necessary. But spread across the floor, each volume was its own best defense. Every book seemed precious beyond compare. How could I argue that *The Collected Poems of Emily Dickinson* was worth more than *Grimm's Fairy Tales*, or that *On the Origin of Species* should be left behind to make room for *The Rise and Fall of the Third Reich*?

For a moment it seemed more equitable, perhaps even more merciful, to burn them all. I told myself that the life we were entering was one in which books could not much matter. I thought of Eva waiting for me in the front yard, and it struck me that the encyclopedia had abandoned me during her labor, that no book had prepared me to save my father's life.

Then I remembered how my father had loved books, how much faith he had in them, and it seemed that to leave empty-handed would be as much a desecration as leaving his unburied body for the pigs.

I'll just take three, I bargained with myself—*a book apiece for Eva, Burl, and me.*

They won't last, I argued. *They'll get wet or torn or sacrificed to some more urgent need.*

That's okay, I told myself. *Someday we may get more. Or if we don't, at least I can wean myself from them more slowly.*

Eva's book was easy to choose. I took *Native Plants of Northern California* for her, since it may have already saved her life, because it is the only grandmother she will ever have.

Burl was harder. *Mother Goose Rhymes? Peter Rabbit? Treasure Island? War and Peace?* How could I imagine what he would yearn to know, what one book he would most love to read? *The Odyssey? Don Quixote? Dune?* Finally I decided to take for Burl the book of songs and stories of those humans who had peopled the forest before us, the book that contained Sally Bell's story, the stories of Coyote and Bear, and songs of mourning and thanksgiving, songs for luck.

Then it was my turn, and I felt like Mother Courage, forced to choose between her children. Sorting through the heap of books on the floor, I loved them all. I loved the smell and heft of each of them, loved the colors of their covers and the feel of their pages. I loved all they meant to me, all they had taught me, all I had been in their presence, and I realized the tragedy of choice, because taking one meant leaving all the others.

I had almost decided to save nothing for myself, when a book still standing on the half-emptied shelf caught my eye. I had never read it, had never done more than glance through its thousand pages, but suddenly I knew it was the third book I would take. I lifted it down, traced its title with my finger: *Index: A-Z*.

I could not save all the stories, could not hope to preserve all the information—that was too vast, too disparate, perhaps even too dangerous. But I could take the encyclopedia's index, could try to keep that master list of all that had once been made or told or understood. Perhaps we could create new stories; perhaps we could discover a new knowledge that would sustain us. In the meantime, I would take the *Index* for memory's sake, so I could remember—and could show Burl—the map of all we'd had to leave behind.

Books in hand, I closed the door on Mother's workroom. In the front room I lifted the rifle from its post, took the box of bullets from the closet. Everything else I left. I left my computer and my calculator and my letter from Harvard, left Eva's toe shoes and CD player, left a whole house of things we once thought we needed to survive, and walked outside.

The slenderest possible crescent of a waxing moon had just risen above the trees, and out in the dark yard Eva had built a fire beside the chicken coop and was waiting with Burl in her arms.

"Ready?" she asked.

"What'll we do about the hens?"

"Bring them with us. We can make a coop easily enough. Besides, they're half-wild already."

"All right," I said.

"You want to be the one to do it?" she asked.

"Okay."

We stood for a moment, watching the little bonfire, and then Eva held a redwood branch over the flames until it crackled with fire.

"There you go," she said, and handed it to me. "Be careful."

I climbed the steps, crossed the deck, hesitated a moment, and then tossed the brand in through the open door.

I barely made it off the deck before the explosion came. Behind me as I ran I heard a sound like a quick intake of breath, and immediately afterwards a blast so awful that it rocked the earth. Windows shattered and I stumbled. But in another moment I was beside Eva. Trembling, I turned to face the rising flames, to watch as fire took the house, roaring outward and upward into every room. Silently Eva took my hand, and together we listened to the shattering of glass, the crashing and shrieking of collapsing walls, the wild hiss and roar of that much fire.

Finally I said, "I really did want you to use the gas for dancing. I always wanted to see you dance again."

Eva laughed and turned to me and said, "You can see me dance right now."

She handed me our Burl, and, lifting her arms high above her head, she began to dance. There, beside the burning house, she danced a dance that sloughed off ballet like an outgrown skin and left the dancer fresh and joyous and courageous. She danced with a body that had sown seeds, gathered acorns, given birth. With new and unnamed movements, she danced the dance of herself, now wild, now tender, now lumbering, now leaping. Over the rough earth she danced to the music of our burning house.

Finally, exhausted and exulted, my sister flung herself to the ground.

"Merry Christmas, Nell," she gasped.

"Merry Christmas, Eva," I answered.

We were silent for a moment, contemplating the burning house. Then Burl stirred. "'That's the story,'" I said, quoting my father. "'Could be better, could be worse. But at least there's a baby at the center of it.'"

"I wonder," said Eva, rising to dance again, "why anyone would want to walk on water—when they could dance on the earth."

So my sister dances and the dead house burns, and I scrawl these few last words by the light of its burning. I know I should toss this story, too, on those flames. But I am still too much a storyteller—or at least a storykeeper— still too much my father's daughter to burn these pages.

Now the wind rises and the baby wakes. Soon we three will cross the dark clearing and enter the forest for good.

ABOUT THE AUTHOR

Jean Hegland is the author of *The Life Within: Celebration of a Pregnancy* (The Humana Press, 1991). Her essays and poetry have been published in several journals and anthologies. She lives with her husband and three children in Northern California on fifty-five acres of second-growth forest.

SELECTED TITLES FROM AWARD-WINNING CALYX BOOKS

NONFICTION

Natalie on the Street by Ann Nietzke. A day-by-day account of the author's relationship with an elderly homeless woman who lived on the streets of Nietzke's central Los Angeles neighborhood. *PEN West Finalist.*
ISBN 0-934971-41-2, $14.95, paper; ISBN 0-934971-42-0, $24.95, cloth.

The Violet Shyness of Their Eyes: Notes from Nepal by Barbara J. Scot. A moving account of a western woman's transformative sojourn in Nepal as she reaches mid-life. *PNBA Book Award.*
ISBN 0-934971-35-8, $14.95, paper; ISBN 0-934971-36-6, $24.95, cloth.

In China with Harpo and Karl by Sibyl James. Essays revealing a feminist poet's experiences while teaching in Shanghai, China.
ISBN 0-934971-15-3, $9.95, paper; ISBN 0-934971-16-1, $17.95, cloth.

FICTION

Four Figures in Time by Patricia Grossman. This novel tracks the lives of four characters in a New York City art school. It's full of astute observations on modern life as the rarefied world of making art meets the mundane world of making ends meet.
ISBN 0-934971-47-1, $13.95, paper; ISBN 0-934971-48-X, $25.95, cloth.

The Adventures of Mona Pinsky by Harriet Ziskin. In this fantastical novel, a 65-year-old Jewish woman, facing alienation and ridicule, comes of age and ultimately is reborn on a heroine's journey.
ISBN 0-934971-43-9, $12.95, paper; ISBN 0-934971-44-7, $24.95, cloth.

Killing Color by Charlotte Watson Sherman. These compelling, mythical short stories by a gifted storyteller delicately explore the African-American experience. *Washington State Governor's Award.*
ISBN 0-934971-17-X, $9.95, paper; ISBN 0-934971-18-8, $19.95, cloth.

Mrs. Vargas and the Dead Naturalist by Kathleen Alcalá. Fourteen stories set in Mexico and the Southwestern U.S., written in the tradition of magical realism.
ISBN 0-934971-25-0, $9.95, paper; ISBN 0-934971-26-9, $19.95, cloth.

Ginseng and Other Tales from Manila by Marianne Villanueva. Poignant short stories set in the Philippines. *Manila Critic's Circle National Literary Award Nominee.*
ISBN 0-934971-19-6, $9.95, paper; ISBN 0-934971-20-X, $19.95, cloth.

POETRY

Another Spring, Darkness: Selected Poems by Anuradha Mahapatra, translated by Carolyne Wright, et al. The first English translation of poetry by this working-class woman from West Bengal.
"These are burning poems, giving off a spell of Light...." —Linda Hogan
ISBN 0-934971-51-X, $12.95, paper; ISBN 0-934971-52-8, $23.95, cloth.

The Country of Women by Sandra Kohler. A collection of poetry that explores woman's experience as sexual being, as mother, as artist. Kohler finds art in the mundane, the sacred, and the profane.
ISBN 0-934971-45-5, $11.95, paper; ISBN 0-934971-46-3, $21.95, cloth.

Light in the Crevice Never Seen by Haunani-Kay Trask. The first book of poetry by an indigenous Hawaiian to be published in North America. It is a revelation about a Native woman's love for her land, and the inconsolable grief and rage that come from its destruction.
ISBN 0-934971-37-4, $11.95, paper; ISBN 0-934971-38-2, $21.95, cloth.

Open Heart by Judith Mickel Sornberger. An elegant collection of poetry rooted in a woman's relationships with family, ancestors, and the world.
ISBN 0-934971-31-5, $9.95, paper; ISBN 0-934971-32-3, $19.95, cloth.

Raising the Tents by Frances Payne Adler. A personal and political volume of poetry, documenting a woman's discovery of her voice. *WESTAF Book Awards Finalist*.
ISBN 0-934971-33-1, $9.95, paper; ISBN 0-934971-34-x, $19.95, cloth.

Black Candle: Poems about Women from India, Pakistan, and Bangladesh by Chitra Divakaruni. Lyrical and honest poems that chronicle significant moments in the lives of South Asian women. *Gerbode Award*.
ISBN 0-934971-23-4, $9.95, paper; ISBN 0-934971-24-2, $19.95 cloth.

Indian Singing in 20th Century America by Gail Tremblay. A brilliant work of hope by a Native American poet.
ISBN 0-934971-13-7, $9.95, paper; ISBN 0-934971-14-5, $19.95, cloth.

Idleness Is the Root of All Love by Christa Reinig, translated by Ilze Mueller. These poems by the prize-winning German poet accompany two older lesbians through a year together in love and struggle.
ISBN 0-934971-21-8, $10, paper; ISBN 0-934971-22-6, $18.95, cloth.

ANTHOLOGIES

Present Tense: Writing and Art by Young Women edited by Micki Reaman, et al. CALYX celebrates its 20th anniversary with this groundbreaking anthology, which features writing and art by women who have come of age during CALYX's lifetime. Their voices are at turns bold, contemplative, sexy, energetic, political, intellectual, and angry. Available August 1996.
ISBN 0-934971-53-6, $13.95 (pending), paper; ISBN 0-934971-54-4, $25.95 (pending), cloth.

The Forbidden Stitch: An Asian American Women's Anthology edited by Shirley Geok-lin Lim, et al. The first Asian American women's anthology. *American Book Award*.
ISBN 0-934971-04-8, $16.95, paper; ISBN 0-934971-10-2, $32, cloth.

Women and Aging, An Anthology by Women edited by Jo Alexander, et al. The only anthology that addresses ageism from a feminist perspective. A rich collection of older women's voices.
ISBN 0-934971-00-5, $15.95, paper; ISBN 0-934971-07-2, $28.95, cloth.

CALYX Books are available to the trade from Consortium and other major distributors and jobbers.

Individuals may order direct from CALYX Books, P.O. Box B, Corvallis, OR 97339. Send check or money order in U.S. currency; add $1.50 postage for first book, $.75 each additional book.

CALYX, A JOURNAL OF ART AND LITERATURE BY WOMEN

CALYX, A Journal of Art and Literature by Women, has showcased the work of over two thousand women artists and writers since 1976. Committed to providing a forum for *all* women's voices, *CALYX* presents diverse styles, images, issues, and themes which women writers and artists are exploring.

"The work you do brings dignity, intelligence,
and a sense of wholeness to the world.
I am only one of many who bows respectfully—
to all of you and to your work."
—Barry Lopez

"It is heartening to find a women's publication
such as CALYX *which is devoted to the very best*
art and literature of the contemporary woman.
The editors have chosen works which create images
of forces that control women; others extol
the essence of every woman's existence."
—Vicki Behem, *Literary Magazine Review*

"Thank you for all your good and beautiful work."
—Gloria Steinem

Published in June and November; three issues per volume.

CALYX Journal is available to the trade from Ingram Periodicals and other major distributors.

CALYX Journal is available at your local bookstore or direct from:

CALYX, Inc., P.O. Box B, Corvallis, OR 97339

CALYX Books and CALYX Journal

CALYX is committed to producing books of literary, social, and feminist integrity.

CALYX, Inc., is a nonprofit organization with a 501(C)(3) status.
All donations are tax deductible.